W9-BVU-764

This Large Print Book carries the
Seal of Approval of N.A.V.H.

THE LUSTER OF
LOST THINGS

SOPHIE CHEN KELLER

THORNDIKE PRESS

A part of Gale, a Cengage Company

GALE
A Cengage Company

Farmington Hills, Mich • San Francisco • New York • Waterville, Maine
Meriden, Conn • Mason, Ohio • Chicago

GALE
A Cengage Company

Thorndike Press® Large Print Basic.
The text of this Large Print edition is unabridged.
Other aspects of the book may vary from the original edition.
Set in 16 pt. Plantin.

LIBRARY OF CONGRESS CIP DATA ON FILE.
CATALOGUING IN PUBLICATION FOR THIS BOOK
IS AVAILABLE FROM THE LIBRARY OF CONGRESS

ISBN-13: 978-1-4328-4574-2 (hardcover)
ISBN-10: 1-4328-4574-8 (hardcover)

Published in 2017 by arrangement with G. P. Putnam's Sons, an imprint of Penguin Publishing, a division of Penguin Random House LLC

Printed in Mexico
2 3 4 5 6 7 21 20 19 18 17

To my mom, Lihua Yao,
my first reader and last believer,
who taught me all I know of
strength and goodness

1

Somewhere in the Fourteenth Street subway station there is a statue of a little bronze man who waits for a train that never comes. I looked forward to stopping by his bench, so that I could take the seat next to him and inspect my reflection in his shiny bald head. My mom, Lucy Lavender, always said that I was just like my dad, Walter Lavender Sr. — the same eyes and patience for listening, and that gentle way of curiosity and kindness. But no matter what surface I looked in and how hard I studied my features, I saw only my own face, bland and uncomplicated, and it was that, along with my silence, that others attributed to the dumbness of a slow, amiable boy.

I did not mind, mostly, because then I was free to observe. Without the distractions of speaking and being noticed, I could listen more closely to what people said to each other and to themselves. I could watch more carefully as the skin of the world glided and stretched, and when I was open and attentive enough, I caught glimmers of the underlying bones and gears and my understanding of the secret workings of life sharpened.

In kindergarten, the teacher read aloud the story of Helen Keller and had us sit in the dark until our ears tingled, our fingers too, and we smelled and heard things we had overlooked. I wondered if that was what happened to me — the silence embedding itself into the crevices of my brain, forming a singular sense that reached into the borderland between the real and the imagined to discern the echoes of the imperceptible.

My whole life, my mouth had been shut and my eyes wide open, and the deeper and darker my silence became, the more I began to sense outside of it — traces of light, shifts in matter, changing undercurrents. As I grew older and it became clear to me that Lucy didn't perceive what I perceived, it was already just another part of me, and there was nothing so incredible about that.

The things I noticed were small and fleeting, easy to miss — scratches or flourishes in reality, clues that pointed the way to the larger truths buried beneath the surface, like the molten ripple along the base of a vase of lilies in danger of tipping over or, when it came to people, the disappointed hiss of something doused before it could be said. Later, at Lucy's suggestion, I began recording these truths in my notebook, so that my mind did not turn into a prison for my thoughts.

"Write down the things you pick up that the rest of us miss," she said. "That way, you won't forget a single one, and one day, you can tell me everything."

My notebook was my companion before I found Milton. It became a part of who I was — an observer, a witness. When I noticed a small detail about a person and jotted it down, I had a feeling that I was speaking and an ear was listening.

Sometimes, though, I looked down at my handwriting — unreadable to anyone who wasn't me, the letters distorted and toppling over like towers of blocks — and a bolt of rage ripped through me because these thoughts did not matter; I could not communicate them to anyone. I was trapped in my role as an observer, separated from everyone else and unable to be a part of the story.

That changed a few weeks before I turned seven. I learned that I could do *something*

— that my ability to see around corners to flashes of the truth made me better at finding things. It first happened when a customer finished paying for her strawberry cheesecake profiteroles, and while Lucy printed the receipt, the woman touched her ear and discovered that her diamond earring was missing.

I hadn't yet devised my rules for finding but that time the telltale sign was an easy one to spot. As Lucy hurried around the counter and the woman crouched to sweep the floor, I noticed a delicate strand of silver trickling down her arm — a sign that she seemed to look right through. I tracked the silvery strand to where it stopped and reached forward to pluck the diamond earring caught in her sweater, and that was the beginning.

The next time I passed a flyer for a pair of missing sunglasses, I found myself lingering, copying down the information in my notebook. Soon, it wasn't just the cases that came to me by accident; I scoured the city for flyers and posted flyers of my own — LOST SOMETHING? COME TO THE LAVENDERS — and I jumped in when I saw someone searching on the subway or in the streets or in the shop.

I felt compelled to help, because I knew

what it was like to lose something too. Walter Lavender Sr. had been lost my entire life; he disappeared while co-piloting a flight en route to Bombay, and searchers toiled through the winter and into the spring, looking for the missing aircraft. They couldn't find any signs of it, or him — not by any rules of seeking and finding. Eventually that flight was pronounced his last, and he dissolved into the gray mists of the Arabian Sea.

Three days after Lucy said farewell to him she said hello to me, her heart full to bursting and the taste of tears in her mouth. I cried rarely and slept often and before Lucy knew it, I was five months old and the shop sign — wooden, smallish — went up, and it said, THE LAVENDERS, each letter gleaming a slow, rich chocolate brown. At the bottom, gold script winked in the sun like polished pennies, and it said, *little things desserterie.*

That first afternoon, Lucy propped the door open and planted her feet in the doorway, smiling bravely as she waited. This was the shop she'd dreamed up with Walter Lavender Sr., the shop she'd opened with every last cent from their savings and the settlement, and as she hiked me higher on her hip, she must have thought, with a hope

11

that felt as crushing as desperation, that this might be a new beginning.

For me, that was the start of everything: the two of us in the door frame, the empty shop beyond. My eyes were gray pools, searching even then, my toes curled into tiny question marks. Perhaps I was still keeping an eye out for the namesake I never met, long after everyone else had given up.

Over the years, Lucy told me stories of Walter Lavender Sr. and I gulped them down whole like grapes, one by one, but there was one I savored most because it felt more like a memory than a story, like it had been carried with me from one world to the next — a vivid split-second impression of the heavens churning and constellations turning and I am swirling, kicking, and a deep voice rumbles across my sky and my swirling slows so that I can listen. It was the last story he told to Lucy, to me, before leaving on that flight, and I asked Lucy to recount it over and over.

Once upon a time, there was a boy who never imagined he could fly very far. He lived close to here, across the East River, in a tenement over the subway tracks next to a pawnshop and a liquor store. Every day after dinner he went down to a spot

12

on the beach, and one day someone else happened to be there first.

The woman reminded the boy of a wild mermaid, lounging there with crystals of salt and seaweed tangled in her hair, and although she wasn't, that's what she became in his recollections in the years to come. He minded his own business at first, walking until the Atlantic touched his toes and he couldn't go any farther.

The mermaid watched him looking out over the waves and sketched a picture of him, not as he was but as she saw that he could be. She called him over and he said he had no money. She framed the picture and gave it to him as a gift, that little picture of a plane winging over the water, and in the little window of the little plane was a boy with chipmunk cheeks from smiling.

Before, he'd felt trapped in a life that was not meant for him. But in those wings, he saw a way to escape. Ever after, when he walked from his home to the beach and stopped at the water's edge, instead of seeing an end, he saw how there could be a beginning.

The boy grew older and when he left home to follow his dream of flying, it felt like he was arriving instead, into a place that was all his own. He went on to journey across many lands and oceans and mountains, and he wanted to thank the mermaid but couldn't find her again, and later he lost the portrait she drew to inspire him. But he never forgot about the power of an act of kindness to change someone's life.

"So, little guy, that's it for now," he had told me in Lucy's belly. "I have to go, but don't you forget it's only for a little while. Do you know that airports have beacons, and you can see them from incredible distances? I'll look for the light to find my way back, and before you know it, I'll be here to meet you. Cross my heart, so don't be sad."

I hadn't yet found traces of him in my reflection or anywhere else out there, but I had read that the world was full of strange and miraculous things — seas that burned and healed your sores, and springs that bubbled and steamed in glaciers, and trees that twisted and walked on water. Since there was no evidence and no one knew for certain what had happened to Walter Lavender Sr., I made a light of my own, a beacon for him to follow home. I used a mason jar, and I put it in the window and refilled the oil and replaced the wick and tended to the flame, even as the days became years.

But I also prepared myself for the other way his story could end, where he could no longer return and knock on the door. I monitored the paper and the mailbox for new developments, and I also reread old reports and gathered stories about him from Lucy, collecting as much information as I could and poring over it for clues on where to look and what to look for. That way, I would be able to recognize the sign when I saw it — the one that would mean he was not returning.

Lost things could be found; Walter Lavender Sr. did not just disappear, and until I knew for certain what had happened to him, he was at once searching for the way back and already gone.

Over the years, when he did not return and I did not find any clues that pointed to him, I began to wonder whether he did not want to be found. Maybe he was embarrassed of me, because I was not like him and also not like most people who talked without thinking, just opening their mouths to release a volley of words like arrows. All I could do was hope that wasn't it — that he knew I was learning the one lesson he left me, about kindness and changing lives.

15

■ ■ ■

For Lucy, the months after opening the shop were even worse than the months after Walter Lavender Sr.'s disappearance. The emptiness around her seemed to grow large and larger still — the floor echoing, the ceiling cavernous — and a slow fall turned into a winter that saw few holiday sales, just record-breaking low temperatures and relentless snowfall. The doors froze over and ice crystals formed on Lucy's scarf like a bitter beard as she shoveled the sidewalk and scraped the shop windows, and in our apartment upstairs she swaddled me in blankets and put on both of her coats and lowered the heat to get by, and we waited for the storm to pass.

Then, one very late night in January, a stranger stumbled upon our doorstep.

That was where Lucy always started the story of the shop's new beginning, when she led new customers through the tour of the shop. In the winter dark, some way from midnight and morning, she woke and saw that it was snowing.

She approached the window and hovered over the hushed street, hardly daring to make a sound for fear of shattering something important. Her breath fogged the glass. She cleared it with a swipe of her hand and noticed a shadow moving under the shop awning.

She pressed her forehead against the window and felt the cold bite as she realized that the shadow was a woman, trying to build a trash-bag shelter around a footstool piled with canvases. A gust of wind rattled the windowpane, tipping over the canvases below, and the woman lumbered after them as they slid across the black ice, her braid swaying with the movement. She knelt to pick up the last canvas and a taxi turned onto the street, its headlights sweeping low across her so that Lucy caught a glimpse of the drawing.

A plane, coasting over the waves.

Lucy's breath seemed to freeze and expand in her chest. She had never seen the portrait from Walter Lavender Sr.'s story; it had been lost a long time ago, but she thought it would probably look just like that. The water rippled with reflected light, casting a glare across the plane's windshield — or it could've been the pilot's smile, shining bright as the sun.

The headlights faded and the window fogged over again and Lucy's exhaustion returned, clouding her mind, and she decided to let it be. I stirred and she hummed "Auld Lang Syne" until I quieted. I went back to sleep but she could not. She was thinking about Walter Lavender Sr. and the story that meant so much to him, about how he found his wings and the mermaid he didn't get a chance to thank.

His mermaid was an artist too, and Brighton Beach was just forty minutes away on the B train. Lucy kept returning to the lost portrait and thinking, What if that's her?, and thinking again, That's not possible, and then she reconsidered that too, and thought, Why not? — and what did it matter, really, if it was or was not, now that she had seen?

When she returned to the window, she noticed how the woman's braid, long and heavy, swung as she worked. To Lucy, it looked just like a fish tail.

She took me down to the shop and turned on the lights and opened the door, and a honeyed light poured out onto the sidewalk.

"There's room for three," Lucy said in invitation, but the woman hesitated, not quite ready to trust her good fortune.

So Lucy left the door open and carried me into the kitchen. With her one free hand she melted dark chocolate in a saucepan and whisked in milk and cornstarch, and over the slow simmer and the hush of blue

18

flame she heard a door shutting, a chair scraping, and she let out a breath. When the hot chocolate was thick enough to coat the back of a spoon, she added a pinch of salt and a dash of vanilla, and then she joined the woman at the front of the shop.

They sat at a table together and drank from bowl-cups and watched the blizzard blow through the emptied streets. The hot chocolate seemed to course through Lucy's arms and surely the woman's too, until their veins grew strong and thick as vines and it was good to be there and alive, to see the ruthless beauty of the night freezing over into a stark dawn.

That day there were no customers, and Lucy was glad for the company even though the woman didn't speak as she sketched and smudged in a leather book. At closing time, she gave Lucy the book, and at the sight of the first page, Lucy's heart stirred and the hairs on the back of her neck stood straight up. She closed the book and said, "This is too much," but the woman told Lucy to take it. It was a gift. It was a story — the woman's own, that she did not want to go untold.

Lucy turned the pages, moved, and by the time she looked up to thank the woman, she had slipped out without a word. That moment would stay with Lucy: the woman looking up to reveal her face, her eyes incandescent in the haze of twilight, and the book in her outstretched hand.

Lucy put the book on a shelf and locked up the shop, and the next day she rose before dawn to mix and flavor her batters in the usual way, unaware that the shop had changed. It didn't take long, though; she checked the first batches and all thoughts of testing the centers and trimming the edges fled because what she saw was unbelievable — unmistakable.

The shop came alive that very morning. The desserts yawned awake after they baked or rested, as if the ovens and refrigerators had sighed hot and cold and breathed life into them except it was the Book driving the magic, assuming its place at the heart of the shop, at the center of my world.

"Then," Lucy liked to tell her enraptured audiences, "like flicking on a switch, people started coming in. The ones who could look past the surface and see a little magic."

Customers talked and word spread, but people also had their routines and their lists and the Herculean weight of a hundred worries and fears bearing down on their shoulders, so not everyone came looking, and not everyone who looked found the shop, and not everyone who found the shop had been looking.

The initial finding was a mystifying thing. Neither of us could decipher what sort of logic the shop followed; all I knew for sure was that sometimes, when a particular person came by and they were looking and discovering and probably a little hungry, the shop decided that it wanted to be found. Before signing the lease, Lucy learned from the landlord — an energetic man with ink-stained hands and a hairy face — that the building had been around since the nineteenth century, protecting the secrets of smugglers and lovers and underground protesters, and it made sense to me that the shop would understand that in order to survive, it would need to know how to hide and how to be found.

The shopfront was small and plain, a solid gray-blue that your eyes wanted to skip past. But on the right day, when you finally saw it, you'd step through the door and take in the brass trimmings and the saucer chandeliers, the black-and-white checkered tiles and the gleaming glass cases, and you would be transported.

Inside the shop, it smelled like whipped butter and light and sugar, and a happy breeze seemed always to be dancing through. Dazzling mirrored displays encased little desserts like gems, and dark polished surfaces were offset by battered accents collected by Lucy on her early travels with Walter Lavender Sr., here a dappled giraffe carved from a jacaranda tree in South Africa, there an embroidered scroll arrayed with the colors of Tibetan folklore.

But the most extraordinary thing was that something happened in the slice of time when the vols-au-vent baked in the oven or waited to be dressed, because when they appeared finally in the displays, stuffed with fig mascarpone cheese and outfitted with chocolate whiskers and ears and tails — before they were chosen and eaten, the undersized treats sniffed endearingly at each other and squeaked and sometimes stood on their hind legs and bounced.

It wasn't just the mice, either, that awoke with distinct personalities. There were lime custard tartlets topped with sour cream that struck poses in the mirror behind the display, admiring their pleated key lime skirts, and there were amaretti biscuits that hovered over whirlpool coffee cups and every so often dipped themselves enticingly into the ever-steaming liquid, and pear and ginger upside-down cakes that flipped forward and back into layouts and tucks, and crispy rice squares that snapped and popped when they stretched lazily like cats.

There were rum-infused black-and-white penguin cookies that waddled and tipped over each other and competitive chestnut tortes that galloped across the display and trampled the molasses pecan cinnamon rolls, which glided sedately along, and there were desserts with other unique qualities, too: pumpkin five-spice ice-cream bombes that didn't melt until you ate them and wedges of salted-butter country apple galette that trickled into your knotted muscles to relax them and towering squares of fizzy angel food cake that rendered you just a bit lighter and monogrammed petits fours that reminded you of the places you came from and lemon verbena chiffon cupcakes that freshened you up and chilled lychee puddings that slowed time and made you breathe deeper.

Naturally, our customers crowded around the desserts, drawn in by the lively displays, but they also gathered over the display near the window, which contained only an inconspicuous leather book — slim, with seven pages that were heavy and yellowing and loosening from the spine like old teeth.

It was *the* Book, the gift left for Lucy because of her kindness. Returning customers knew how important it was and that was why they gathered to look at it, displayed in its case, open to the first page: "It was a dark and stormy night," against a wintry hand-painted sky alive with wild stars and tumbling ribbons of light and whorls of wind and whimsy, and spread below it was the city, darkly alluring and diamond-sharp, made of steel and water and concrete, a labyrinth of streets and reflections and shadows that dared you, with each shifting, multiplying line, to look for an end.

Before I turned two, it was easy to believe that everything had worked out. Walter Lavender Sr. was not there, but when I opened my eyes they were just like his, tracking closely the sounds of life — heeled footsteps approaching or the kettle whistling or the hinges squeaking. Yet something about me was different anyway. It was just emerging, barely noticeable.

There was no way for Lucy to peer into my brain, into the neon-bright streams winding through its passages, and pick out the sets of signals that twisted down deviating or truncated pathways, becoming lost and arriving at different times in my jaw and lips and tongue or never arriving at all.

The first pediatrician patted Lucy's hand

and said, "Not to worry, dear. Even Einstein didn't talk until he was three."

The second pediatrician shrugged and said, "He's a late bloomer. Boys are like that, you know."

Months passed and I did not speak or even babble. The neurologist suggested autism and the preschool teacher said, "Give it time," and the developmental pediatrician said, "Intellectual disability." There were blood tests and brain scans and evaluations and checklists, and finally there was the speech pathologist saying, "Speech disorder — some standard speech therapy will do the trick."

So I started attending therapy sessions three times a week with ten other kids and a therapist who looked terrified and resigned at the same time.

"Fish," she would say, holding up a flash card.

Fish, I told myself, and the group chorused, "Fish," and I heard myself say, "Shh."

"Again," said the speech therapist.

Fish, I reminded myself, and the voice in my mind said, Fish, but in the same moment I heard, "Fih."

This was accompanied by the disembodied feeling of being torn in two, my mind humming underwater with a voice that was loud and close and *mine,* while hearing at the same instant the sounds that were flattened and shapeless — distant, *other.* My brain shouted, Fish, *FISH,* and the outside voice that was and was not mine honked, "Fuhhh."

Progress was slow, laborious, but at least it was there. One afternoon, after three years of silence and an ocean of lost words, I woke from a nap and somewhere in my brain, as signals flared and flew, one stream of signals banked and connected and I opened my mouth and gurgled, suddenly, "Dada?"

Lucy dropped the sugar corkscrew she was holding and let out a breath that lasted a long time.

Even with the apparent progress, the sporadic words, connections failed to come easily and saying nothing remained the easiest of all. The right diagnosis came eventually but by then I was eight, and comfortable in my silence. Dr. Winkleberker looked young and distinguished, and I called her Doc because her full name was a series of jumbled vowels and consonants, impossible for me to say. She only had to interact with me for five minutes before she put her pen down and looked Lucy square in the eye and said, "He knows exactly what he wants to say, but his muscles aren't listening."

She explained that our brains formed pathways to transmit signals for everything we did, but for signals to be successfully sent and received, all the pathways involved had to be fully intact. When they were, talking happened seamlessly, unconsciously. But my pathways were deviant — missed connections, short circuits — and so my muscles did not hear my brain, and they did not know how to produce the sounds I wanted.

She called it a motor speech disorder, and we learned that my group therapy sessions were good for children with stutters or lisps but not for me. Those were years that I could not get back, Doc said, but new pathways were constantly being formed and old ones rerouted as new connections were forged and strengthened through the right kind of repetition, so we should try, of course, and expect what was realistic and hope for the best.

Lucy tried to wait until we were home but halfway through the subway ride she found herself sinking in a slick of guilt, and she started to cry.

There was no wailing or sobbing, just tears the size of quarters and half-dollars pattering onto the floor. For two days she cried and made meringues, and on the third day she put away the mixer and dried her eyes. She told me that I was more than she could ever want and she loved me more than I could ever imagine, and then she recounted my favorite story, about the boy who met a mermaid and escaped his ocean-side prison.

As the years passed, it was no longer just the two of us standing in the door frame. Flora puttered across the shop, wiping the tiled floor smooth, and our golden retriever, Milton, plunged into the crowds, whipping his tail joyfully, punishingly, against everyone's legs, and José biked past the window, heading out for a delivery.

He made all the deliveries except the special Sunday ones because those belonged to me. They were for our most devoted customers who had been with us from the start, like Mrs. Ida Bonnet, who had not forgotten any of her three children and six grandchildren even though they had begun to forget her. On one particular Sunday ten months ago, I was headed out on a delivery to her and it could have been any other Sunday, but it was not exactly the same. It was the twelfth anniversary of the shop's opening and it was also when my story — *this* story — began.

Up until last year, my stories always belonged to someone else. Walter Lavender

28

Sr. had his story and so did Lucy and so did everyone who lost things, and they were a million points of light in my solitary darkness: these stories like stars, illuminating the silent nights.

But for the first time in my thirteen years, I have a story of my own to tell and I am the one who will tell it, and it began on that particular Sunday ten months ago.

So there I am: waiting at West Fourth Street for the A train to arrive and carry me to Fourteenth, and I'm scuffing my red canvas high-tops against the platform with Mrs. Ida Bonnet's delivery box balanced in one hand. The box is layered with sweet vanilla wafers with sea-salted caramel filling, a new product Lucy developed to commemorate the anniversary, and I am careful not to jostle the wafers because they are delicate and because a whiff will fill my nose and chest with a pleasant nostalgic ache and there is no time for that when I have a job to complete.

The platform is empty, which means that I have just missed the previous train, and I pull out my notebook and lay it open on top of the delivery box and pass the time by watching other people trickle in. I see a woman in yoga pants drinking a bottle of green mud, and a fair family of four speak-

29

ing rapid French, and two young men carrying portfolios, wearing suits, sharp and fresh-faced. There is no sun to cast shadows here but I see bruised smudges following them, mimicking their confident movements.

PROUD BROADCAST OF EXHAUSTION AND IMPORTANCE, I add in my notebook.

Someone pushes past me and I slip my notebook back into my pocket and look up. The boy's shirt is rumpled and the buttons are in the wrong buttonholes, which means that an extra button flaps against his Adam's apple, and a plume of distress rises over him as he rips off hunks of tape and slaps flyers onto every other green column.

MISSING!

That is my cue. I tear off a flyer and hurry after the frantic boy, bracing my arms in front of me so the delivery box does not bounce. When I catch up to the boy he is picking up some flyers he dropped. His black hair sticks to his forehead in stringy waves; in the pictures on the flyers fanned out on the platform, he is wearing a short-sleeved button-down shirt again but his hair is slicked back from his forehead with gel.

30

MISSING! BEAUTIFUL BASSOON, MAPLE.

In the picture, he is holding a bassoon that is almost as big as he is although he is taller and older than I am. In the picture, he looks whole. I pick up a few flyers and we stand up together, and I take a focused breath and steel my thoughts.

"I find lost things," I say. The words sound straight enough, almost perfect and paced normally, because it is the phrase I am most familiar with and the first phrase I practiced with Doc.

Since then, I have used it countless times, and it is how I always introduce myself in a new case and the only way I can introduce myself at all. The musician doesn't say anything in response but I can tell by the recognition in his eyes that he has understood.

I give him a card for The Lavenders and again with great care I gesture at the delivery box and say, "Not now. Tomorrow after school?" and hold up four fingers. His eyebrows pinch skeptically but two or three rumples on his shirt relax as he nods, and the train announces itself in a screech of wind and juddering metal.

During five years of finding, I have learned

that everyone loses things, musicians and non-musicians alike — the elderly when they forget and the young when they don't pay attention and the middle-aged when there are too many things to do. In the things they look for, parts of people turn clear as glass and you can see into them and what they are made of and how they live, without needing to exchange so many words. There was the long-ago transplant who lost a piece of Maine driftwood, and there was also the man with lupus who lost an unused barber kit and the tattooed biker who lost a picture of his grandmother and the teenager with scarred wrists who lost *George and Martha.*

I keep finding because it is a way for me to be part of something bigger, even if it is only for a while. Whether it is for a Lost camera in Nikon bag, sentimental family photos, or a Runaway cat, tough sweetie with a spot under her right eye, or a Missing heirloom, buttons and badges from the Civil War, people are willing to share pieces of their lives with me, and when I patch these scraps of information together I catch a glimpse of who they are.

Usually when I speak, people have trouble understanding and before I can finish one sentence they are already turning their toes away, shuttering their ears, assuming that whatever I have to say will not be worth listening to. But finding is different, because of the meaning that drives it — the lost thing. It makes people want to hear me and knowing this makes it possible for me to speak. With just a few phrases, two or three questions, I will know enough to understand someone, because people only bother looking for the things that matter. There is also something that forms when a lost thing is returned, a feeling of belonging like coming home to the shop except with finding it is something I have created. In those moments, I do not miss my voice so much.

Beyond that, I have discovered some rules in the course of my finding, and this is the one that keeps the rest in motion: the more you persist in searching, the more likely you are to stumble across something unexpected. In looking for someone else's lost thing, I am also looking for mine — some sign that will lead me to Walter Lavender Sr., and tell me what happened to him.

At Fourteenth Street I take an extra moment to join the little bronze man at his bench, leaning over his round head and picking off some bubblegum stuck to his cartoon bag of money. Outside, the city is cool and shiny-bright as a coin. Mrs. Ida

33

Bonnet is accustomed to my silence and my steady gaze; she does not say much, and I hear the ticking of the clock and the wafer snapping dry and crisp between her teeth like a small bone. The room fills with the gentle ache of vanilla and the sound of the sea, and she closes her eyes and lays a wrinkled hand over her heart and smiles at the memory of things I cannot see.

2

The next morning before the shop opens, I lug the olive oil out of the supply closet and pick my way to the front window, sidling around tables and chairs to avoid stepping on Milton, who is so occupied with watching my face and peppering me with questions — *Where are you going? What are you doing? What are you holding?* — that he does not realize when he gets in the way.

I top off the oil in the mason jar and Milton pushes his nose under one cuff and sniffs my ankle and sneezes. I touch the lighter to the wick and nudge him away so Lucy will not notice that I am wearing mismatched socks I pulled out of the hamper.

I met Milton three years ago in a LOST DOG flyer. In the picture, he was gripping the leg of a wooden coffee table and adding fresh chew marks on top of the old ones, heedless of the camera's reproachful eye.

The woman who posted the flyer had recently moved in with her boyfriend in a doorman building on Fifty-seventh and Third. We sat in the lobby on hard acid-green chairs. She had a pinched face with a narrow nose and hazel eyes that sat close together, and she wore a neat dress with flowers printed on it. I started as always by asking her about the thing she lost and her mouth pinched even more when she spoke about Milton.

"John had always wanted a dog but his mother had these allergies, and when his coworker mentioned that his golden had puppies, John jumped at the chance — of course, he didn't even check with *me*," she said, breathless and aghast. "He went off to Westchester and came back with it! Like some surprise handbag — right, like he would ever!" She made a snorting noise and rearranged her neat dress.

"What was the dog like?" I asked carefully, a smoky ache gathering under my temples from the effort.

"John picked out the worst one. It ate underwear and dripped toilet water in my lap and destroyed the furniture," she said. "And John is away for work and now it's lost." She shrugged with her palms up and sat back in her chair.

36

"Since when?"

"Two days ago. I came home from happy hour and one of my pumps was sitting in a puddle in the middle of the room, with that dog nowhere to be found."

I asked her where she had looked.

"Oh, the usual places," she said airily, gesturing at the front door. "Walked around a bit outside, too."

I asked about the daily routine, which took her ten whole minutes to discuss, and then I asked her if she was sure that she had looked in the obvious place.

"Checked his pen," she confirmed, but she had only glanced into the other rooms of the apartment. I thought it was worth a closer look, so up we went to the fourteenth floor, which was actually floor thirteen but the landlord was superstitious.

The apartment was pristine and lemony, with all signs of dog scrubbed away. I checked the closets and cabinets and behind the doors and did not find a single dog hair. I returned to the living room, where the woman looked on.

"No hair," I said grimly, and the woman beamed at her spotless apartment while I looked around one last time — and *there,* the coffee table was wavering at me, shimmering like a mirage. It was modern, made

37

of glass and steel. I consulted the picture in the flyer and the table the dog was chewing on was wooden.

"Where is this?" I pointed at the picture. The woman peered over my shoulder and said, "That old thing. The favorite chew toy. I had it taken to the corner for garbage."

She saw me to the lobby and shook my hand, pressing something into it. I looked down and it was Benjamin Franklin, grimacing wry and wise.

"Sadly the dog is lost, but John and I must go on. Your reward, if you find it, for keeping it," she said, flashing her eyebrows.

On the corner of Fifty-seventh and Third, I saw a black trash-bag heap and a chipped bookcase and a wooden coffee table. Underneath the coffee table, working on the leg that was now almost gnawed in half, was the dog, gleaming gold as treasure. When I wrestled him away, he licked my face and lashed his tail against my stomach. Milton, carelessly lost, was delighted to be found.

The journey home was a disaster. Joy coursed through Milton and he hurled it into the world and wherever it landed there was pandemonium. He nearly caused a five-way pileup when he spotted a woman across the street in a leopard cape, and then he swerved, spotting a trim jogger in sporty

38

spandex with sagging ears and a blinking helmet. The jogger dodged this way and that and Milton enthusiastically tackled him, hoping to join the game. The jogger clutched his chest and screamed, "Boy, are you out of your mind?"

Two overturned trash cans and a mouthful of rancid newspaper later, Milton careened into The Lavenders and startled a little girl into dropping one of her marzipan dragons. The dragon shook off its fall and charged at Milton and breathed fire, and Milton scrabbled back. The dragon hissed and Milton whimpered and scrunched himself into the corner, and sprays of pee drizzled onto the shiny floor.

As an irritated Lucy mopped and disinfected, I went to the kitchen to find two more dragons. When I returned, Milton was nowhere to be seen and I found myself on the verge of doing the number one thing I told bereft owners not to do — panicking, and who would keep him out of trouble and defend him and how could I be so careless?

In the end, I discovered him standing outside in self-imposed exile with his tail between his legs. He took one look at the dragons in my palm and backed away. I inched closer; he watched, wary. I picked up a dragon and placed it on my tongue

39

and closed my mouth, and a puff of steam curled out of my nose. I deposited the remaining dragon in front of him and it spat fire his way and he stared at it and glanced at me. I nodded and he snapped it up before he could change his mind.

That was his first taste of Lucy's desserts. No longer afraid, he followed me back inside, and he kept following me for the next few months until he knew for certain that I would always come back. He would not let me out of his sight, and when he couldn't follow he sat and blocked the doorway and ignored customers who offered him treats, thumping his tail against the ground until I reappeared from school or finding.

Regulars grew used to seeing him by my side, a shadow that grew larger every day and sometimes crushed their toes. I snuck him broken rosemary tuiles and bourbon peach pie scraps, and he helped himself to unattended trays when Lucy was looking the other way, and his belly swelled with the sweet fullness of being loved.

This morning, Milton licks my ankle again and twitches his nose at me, earnest and approving — *Nice socks!* — and the wick catches fire. There is a knock at the door and Flora waves at me from the other side, and her face is soft and plump as a peach. I unlock the door and she plods into the shop with a stubby sock and a pair of knitting needles under one arm because it takes her at least half an hour to come in from Astoria.

She dumps the knitting needles and ball of red yarn on a table, and she sets down her bags and pulls out her blue apron. Lucy gave her a new yellow one but Flora insists on wearing the blue one whenever she works and it looks older than her, a starched threadbare gingham that still had its lace trimmings when she started six years ago but doesn't anymore. Besides her thriftiness, she also spends her evenings after work clipping coupons, because her ex-husband gambled away all their money before catching a bus to Florida.

She gathers her bags and I follow her into the kitchen. José is already there, crouched over a white bucket whacking pomegranates with the back of a spoon, and Lucy is swiveling from the refrigerator to a wooden worktable, pulling out sheets of croissant dough.

"Ready to roll?" she says, reaching for the rolling pin next to Flora, who has started topping a tray of genoise sponge mini-cakes with white chocolate feathers and raspber-

41

ries; she has a flair for decoration and the most delicate touch with the piping bag.

I grab a fistful of flour and dash it across the wooden worktable. Beside me, José tosses aside a de-seeded pomegranate and says, "How's it going, man."

He rises for a quick sliding handshake and a close-lipped smile. He is careful about not showing his teeth, embarrassed that two are missing from the top row and two and a half from the bottom. Sometimes he forgets himself and an enormous smile spreads unchecked across his face, like yesterday when his son won the class spelling bee and Lucy made him a saffron cake and I striped it with chocolate cardamom buttercream. He looked more like himself than he ever had, grinning with the little cake buzzing around his head — right before he remembered and his mouth snapped back like a rubber band.

Before he fled El Salvador he lived with his mother and she taught him how to make a mean tres leches. He was the shop's first full-time employee and we get along fine, me and José, from eight years of sitting side by side on Friday nights supreming oranges and chopping chocolates, listening to the salamander sizzling and the people rushing outside the window with the silence between us thick and warm and hearty as a slow stew, and once in a while on summer nights he remembers sunsets from the old home and playing soccer by the beach, aiming the ball into the ocean, between the volcanoes.

Lucy cares about the tres leches and not the missing teeth and that is why she hired him, but he still mashes his lips together when he smiles at me and stays in the back of the kitchen cleaning and doing prep work between deliveries, so that the customers in the front won't accidentally see.

"Junior says —" He pauses, sighs like he is already regretting it. "T-H-A-N-K-S for the bu*zzzz*ing bee," he finishes stonily, prying a pomegranate apart.

Lucy stops rolling out the croissant dough and tucks her hair behind her ear, leaving behind streaks of flour. "S-U-R-E. *Bzzzz*," she teases.

"He made me," José says.

Two years ago he laid out some newspapers and snipped at Junior's hair, a chunk from the front and from either side and he started to slice a chunk from the back and stopped. Gently, he touched the lump with one finger. It was pale and hard, nestled in Junior's soft dark hair like a frozen egg. José had saved enough money for new teeth but it was not enough for the operation Junior needed, and so Junior is six years old now and the lump has gotten bigger and José is still saving with his four and a half missing teeth.

Whap-whap-whap-whap, goes his spoon against the pomegranate, and a ruby rain falls from his fingers and Lucy sweeps a brush across the dough and the flour-dust makes me cough.

"What's on the agenda today, Mr. Walter?" she asks, marking the dough and cutting it longwise into runways. I take the flyer for the musician's bassoon out of my pocket and show it to her.

Lucy nods and positions a large knife over the dough and rocks her wrist left, right, left, right, cutting out precise isosceles triangles with each click and clack of the blade against wood.

"You're becoming quite the master finder," she says, giving me a small smile.

A surge of strength or lightness floods my limbs and I stand a little taller as I reach for a triangle and focus on shaping a croissant.

"By the way, I'll be talking to Doc today about scaling back to once-a-month sessions." Lucy's voice is casual but she cuts faster, clickety-clackety, her wrist flashing with the knife. "She says there's no point in seeing her every week. You've made so much progress you could say what you wanted, if you wanted."

Of course Doc would say that. I roll the croissant, keeping my motions smooth and applying just the right amount of pressure, and I reach for another triangle. In Doc's sessions, we practice words and phrases for any kind of case that might arise, bicycle and snake and passport and lock and skateboard, and Where do you keep it and Tell me more and When did you last see it and What do you think, and when I am finding snakes and locks I can also find the words I want and string them together and push them out, and the pathways of my mind stay open and clear and connected all the way down to my mouth.

Lucy wishes for my words so much I can see it on her breath like stardust, and I have learned to look away. Doc wants me to practice my words in normal settings, not just when I am finding, but when I try to do that a chill spreads through my body, sloshing around my stomach and freezing the stretchy parts of my face. I reach for the words only to find that my mind is frozen too, and I have no idea how and where to start chipping out the words I want and the ringing in my ears is a definitive reminder of exactly who I am and who I am not.

Now, I roll one, two, three more croissants, listening to Lucy and Flora chatting about the temperamental air conditioner and thinking that at least I have figured out how to navigate through this kind of life, and this is just how things are and they are good and comfortable. Lucy and Milton understand me well enough in their own ways and there is the shop, thriving, and on top of that I have my finding, the cases lining up faster than I can solve them because people have heard about what I can do for lost things.

"Already thinking of case number eighty-four?"

My thumb twitches and I squish the croissant I am holding.

Lucy has been watching me, even as she chattered, and now she closes her eyes, counting, and she opens them and says, "The bassoon is case number eighty-four, isn't it?"

I nod at her and by now I should not be surprised but I am, and comforted too, by how much she knows.

She picks up her knife and I fluff the flattened croissant, trying to resuscitate it and giving up. I fall into the rhythm of rolling and pressing the croissants, and then Lucy is beside me and her elbow brushes my shoulder as she reaches for a triangle. Both of us are rolling and pressing now and on my other side José is whacking pomegranates and Flora is arraying the genoise sponge cakes on a platter, and at my feet Milton shakes flour and crumbs from his whiskers and laps at the floor and all around is the heat of croissants baking, and the smell of everything is pure and rich as butter.

Roll, press. Roll, press. I push the thought of school away. Ninety-eight, ninety-nine, one hundred. The most I have rolled is two hundred and eighty. It is a game I play with myself, seeing how many croissants I can shape, because time seems to stretch when it is made of water and flour and butter, just triangles of dough and my hands rolling and pressing.

One hundred and one. One hundred and two.

Inevitably, 8:20 will come around, but I can carry this stolen half hour in the kitchen with me to school like a warmed rock and it is just enough to last the day.

Milton slips out of the kitchen and there is some guilt in that slink; he must have gotten into the port caramel, which is his favorite because he can continue licking his nose and tasting the sticky sweetness plastered there long after the crime.

Lucy does not notice Milton but she does notice the clock. "Time for school," she says, kissing my cheek. "Better get going — you're late."

I loop my lunch box around my neck and start running past restless trees shaking off the summer heat, hurdling over a cat, darting between honking cabs, my right little toe starting to wiggle a hole into my high-top. Cool air lifts the back of my jacket and my lunch box thumps against my chest and I fly up Sixth Avenue toward the corner of West Fourth in time to see the bus nudging its way into the flow of traffic. I put on a burst of speed but the light turns green and the bus emits a feeble roar.

I wave my arms, run faster, and my jacket streams out like a banner and the ends of my breath are ragged. The bus is slowing down — I pull even with the back windows — see a few faces I do not want to see, Beaver, Todd — but then they blur as the bus roars again.

I continue waving my arms as I chase the bus down the block. Beaver appears in the window; he makes Frankenstein arms at me and dissolves into laughter. The zipper on my flapping jacket hits me in the eye and tears well up but I squeeze them aside.

The bus stops at Waverly Place to make way for a man struggling against a cloud of dogs. I dash to the door and pound, startling the driver, and then I am on board.

3

I make my way to the only open seat in the back and it is quiet on the bus until Beaver belches, "Waaall-rus."

"Good run?" Todd says. His neck is stretched forward, skinny and red as a vulture's, and they both lean over to poke me. Beaver pokes harder and I flinch.

"It's alive," he says, shivering his shoulders, and I pick at the dough under my fingernails to keep from getting mad. If I become too angry and try to say something, I will mix up my words and they won't come out right, and it is best to keep my mouth shut.

"Dumbass," Beaver says. He turns his attention to drawing body parts on the window in permanent marker and I prop my knees on the seat back and think about things not related to this bus and Beaver and Todd.

M422 is a gray fortress with windows like

hollow eyes and an incongruous cherry red door for the mouth. The trees are cucumber-green, cooling underneath a sky that looks clean and new like someone has sponged off the sticky brine of August. First period is with Miss Bradshaw and it smells the same as always, lemon wipes and wood-dust. I take my seat and give tiny hello waves that my classmates do not see as they walk past.

At 8:40, the bell rings and Miss Bradshaw is nowhere to be found. Five minutes roll by and some boys start making spitballs. A little later, the girls in the front with pigtails and Popsicle-colored sweaters start squealing.

At 8:55, with no teacher to rescue them, the girls move behind the empty fish tank to mount a defense. The boys dodge a flurry of sharpened pencils and more boys join in the war effort. I stay seated in the middle of the room, a rainbow of pencils and spitballs arcing over my head, thinking that the croissants should be out of the oven by now, the air swirling with golden flakes and Milton gamboling in the flurry.

When a substitute teacher finally lunges into the classroom, everyone except me scrambles like they are playing musical chairs.

"Good morning, class!" she says, shutting the door. She begins taking attendance and when she says my name I raise my hand but say nothing.

"Walter Lavender is here," Becky Darling supplies. She lowers her voice. "He doesn't always — *get* — what's going on. You have to talk slow, make things easy." She turns around to give me an encouraging smile but the sun turns her glasses into mirrors.

When morning classes are over, kids stream into the courtyard on a tide of legs and arms and lunch boxes and voices. I gather my things, taking my time, and head out to my table behind the basketball hoops. I sit on the end of the bench and make myself small and quiet and invisible. A game of dodgeball starts and food spills and wrappers crinkle and a red rubber ball hits my shoulder. I jerk forward and knock over my carton of juice and Beaver laughs.

"Walrus Dodgeball," he shouts.

I move to the other side of the courtyard and sit cross-legged under a tree, lolling my head back to watch the gray clouds spreading across the sky. A leaf drifts into my lap. It is broad and smooth as candle wax or maybe dough, and I roll it like I would roll a croissant and hold it under my nose to breathe in the buttery morning quiet, and I

52

close my eyes and imagine the shop now —
a beehive of activity, Lucy managing the
lunch rush and José sprinkling chili sugar
onto hazelnut chocolate pizzas slated for
delivery and Flora holding her breath and
inverting a tarte tatin and Milton inhaling
the pear slices that slide off.

Some of the kids move to share my tree
and I drop the leaf and it uncurls. They
stand in a circle linked by their upturned
palms to start an old clapping game and I
think about leaving because I do not belong
here, an intruder in their world.

"Down by the banks of the hanky-
panky . . ." Slap, slap, one palm rising and
slapping the next palm. "Where the bull-
frogs jump from bank to banky . . ." Rising
and slap slap slap, faster and faster the
palms go, and the sky is gray and close and
strange and I am peering up and watching
until it all becomes a ripple and a blur.

4

After school, I clatter off the bus and jump-land on the sidewalk and head to the hardware store for wicks, down a street jammed with traffic and people and two policemen on horses and across an intersection with traffic lights arranged in six different directions. I pass a cheese shop that sells wheels the size of hubcaps and a seafood bar with oyster happy hours, and there is Mrs. Witherby's stationery store with its Gutenberg-style press in the back and a tattoo parlor with grinning skulls emblazoned on the window and a staircase that leads to a basement thrift store with five-dollar pants.

I turn onto a street that is leafy and forgotten like a garden maze and the hardware store is sandwiched between a corner apothecary that hosts poetry slams and vegan chili nights and a shoe repair place that is small enough to warrant one half of a street number.

The hardware store has been owned by the Dickson brothers since 1981 and its aisles are cluttered and filled to the tin ceiling with paints and nails and tapes and bulbs, and the fiberglass wicks are on the bottom shelf of the candles section. I buy one pack and Roy Dickson zips it into my backpack so that I do not have to shrug in and out of the straps again.

I am running late for my interview with the musician — case number 84, which means that while I have not found what I am really looking for, I have found a lot of lost things and have spent a lot of time looking, and I am eager to get back to work. I hurry toward the shop, pushing through a line of people waiting outside a pizzeria with patched booths and the same menu they've had since the 1920s.

On the next block a cook pops out of the sidewalk like a groundhog and I steer around his head and the smell of dishwater and fried shallots wafts out as he props open the cellar doors. I walk faster and my backpack bounces and then I am one block away and then I take the turn onto Carmine Street, and I see the oil lamp in the window.

At the sight of it, the bleak fog of the day burns away. I push the door open and step inside and my eyes sweep across the row of round brass chandeliers hanging over the front counter. Lucy is working the register and the tables are full of friends and couples and the kitchen door swings open and I catch a glimpse of Milton pulling his nose out of a mixing bowl and rushing toward the door, and in the moment before he crashes into me I think, Here at last.

I look around and know that I am home, and the numbing chill of being alone fades. I can look into the faces of those I know and even those I don't and figure out if they are in the mood for a plum-butter Berliner, a pillow of homespun comfort, or if they would prefer refinement, a green matcha croissant. When they bite down and smile behind their hands with powdered sugar mustaches, I can smile too, because I was a part of it.

Milton's fur slides between my fingers and he wriggles in my arms and breathes loudly into my ear. He takes a seat facing me and I search for the musician and see him standing near the displays, holding a stack of flyers and looking lost with his sloped shoulders bunched up around his ears.

I wave at Lucy and tap the musician's elbow as I pass. He startles upright and Milton sniffs his flyers and he startles again.

To cheer him up, I step behind the counter and search for the squeaking mice, nudging away a ring of passion fruit marshmallows engaged in a sumo match. I wait, looking into the display case as a jelly frog studded with chopped dates and hazelnuts hops across the second level. My reflection rises up from the glass and I search for traces of Walter Lavender Sr. — those eyes like two moons, that inquisitive turn about the mouth.

I wait a moment longer for the mice but none come sniffing forward to investigate. I select a stack of yogurt pretzels instead and shrug in apology when I give them to the musician. He watches them spin in his palm, throwing off sprinkles like fireworks.

"I say, they're exploding," he says, rubbing the rainbow dust from his eyelashes.

We leave the shop and Milton follows, nipping at the flyers. We find an empty bench in the little park on the next block because more people use it as a shortcut than a place to sit and think and be outside.

Milton trots away to see where everyone else is and what they are eating and I start as I always do by asking the musician about the lost bassoon. Gathering the backstory helps me set up the possibilities, and it usually contains information that directs my search.

"He's my oldest friend," the musician whispers. "For years and years. It's been so long that he's having some problems now, like his whisper key gets sticky all the time. My instructors, my roommate — they all say, time for a replacement. *I* say, so what?" His voice reaches a crescendo, his soul ablaze so that his eyes crackle with passion. "*I* say, he stuck with me through the beginning when I didn't know what I was doing. He warmed my fingers when they froze, opened up doors, led me to my best friends in the reed quintet, so how could I even *think* about abandoning —"

He burns out and sighs. "I've been meaning to get him fixed up at Giuliano's for my first master's recital on Thursday. It'll decide whether or not my scholarship is renewed. This school was my grandmother's dream, too. She took the last of what she'd saved and put it into my plane ticket. We've put everything into this program — I'm doing Jolivet, for God's sake. I can't lose it all, let her down after she believed in me. . . ."

I ask him when he last remembered having the bassoon. If he is able to remember and retrace his steps, we will be able to focus the search early on and cut down the

58

overall search time. If he does not remember, it gets a little trickier and it takes more creativity and time to systematically search the immediate area and then the natural places and the accidental places.

The musician purses his lips and furrows his brows. "I — I was practicing. In my apartment. The whisper key had been stuck in a worse way lately — every time I played in the upper register the notes would *crreeeeak*! *Creeeeeak!*"

Milton races around the fountain and plows into the musician, a rope of spittle draped over his nose, digging wildly for the source of the screeching sound. The musician flings a pretzel and Milton does an arching half-twist and catches it with atypical grace.

The musician relaxes and continues. "The first time it stuck my roommate came running to see what was dying. Now he bangs from the other side of the wall and yells, *Shut up. Shut up!* He even took off last week, road-tripping to California — for the music festivals, he said, but I think he'd had enough of my practicing."

Milton tries to crawl under the bench to help the musician carry his sadness and the musician tries to scoot the bench away except it is screwed into the ground.

59

"So I stopped for the night, cleaned up, put him to rest in his case, and left him by my bed as usual. When I woke up the next morning, he was . . . gone." The musician puts his head in his hands; crouched under the bench, Milton drops his head between his paws.

"Search the case again?" It sounds unnecessary but in many cases people are overwhelmed and they conduct a brief and frantic search and miss the obvious.

"He's not in the case. Or in the department practice rooms. Or in my room — I triple-checked under the laundry and in the drawers and beneath the bed. I cleaned out the apartment and organized my closets."

He hasn't been haphazard at all. It sounds like he has thoroughly checked the ZOLA, the Zone of the Lost Article, which is the surrounding area where many lost things end up being found — a pair of reading glasses knocked behind the desk, a set of keys hiding under the mail catalogs. He has also checked the obvious place and the natural place and even the accidental places, by cleaning the apartment. Which leaves . . .

"Stolen?"

"What would a thief do with a broken bassoon that's falling apart?" the musician says, confused. That is a good point. Not stolen, then, and I scratch a finger across the black cover of my notebook. The musician puts his head between his knees and contracts like a pill bug.

"The concert is on Thursday," he moans through his nose. "There goes my scholarship — *ugh,*" he squawks when Milton licks his face sympathetically.

The musician's future will change because of the lost bassoon. If he does not find it, he will not be able to use it to deliver his performance and as a result his scholarship will not be renewed. His dream will be over and his grandmother will be disappointed and I am the only one who has answered his call for help. The weight and responsibility of it keeps my mind open, gives me purpose — connects me to him.

I draw a diagram of the musician's room in my notebook, starting with four walls and then the door, bed, desk, window, bassoon-in-a-case, and music stand. I write KITCHEN along one side of the bedroom's outer wall, and on the other side, I write ROOMMATE. Underneath the diagram, I make a list.

Frame of the Lost Article (FOLA): Before
Sleep, in Case by Bed. By Morning ⇨ Lost.

1. Not in the obvious place: the case
2. Not in the ZOLA: the bedroom
3. Not in the accidental places: anywhere in the apartment
4. Not in the natural place: the practice
   rooms
5. Other: Too big to fall somewhere
   and hide, or to be carried out the
   window in the arms of a gusty wind.
   Not stolen.
6. Someone must have carried it out.
   Hypothesis: The musician. Does
   the musician sleepwalk? Did he
   carry the bassoon somewhere?

The musician says no and he does not
think so, and we lapse into silence and he
stands and paces clockwise around the
fountain. On his third revolution a business-
man catches him with his square shoulder
and the flyers spray into the air, and passersby in collared shirts scatter like pigeons
as the musician scrambles.

I help him gather the flyers and Milton
helps by sitting on them to keep them from
running away, and when we return to the
bench I pass the flyers back and study the

picture of the bassoon. I think over the story the musician told me, and I return to my list and pause at the fourth point — the natural place. It made sense for an instrument to be in the practice rooms, but this particular bassoon was broken and the natural place for a *broken* bassoon would be a repair shop.

"Giuliano's? I would remember if I had taken it there," he protests.

I shrug; it is a place that makes sense whether he remembers taking it there or not, and I rise and wait for him to follow.

5

We swing by the shop so I can tell Lucy where I am going and that I will do homework later, and I reassure Milton that I will be right back, and then the musician and I are ready to go to Giuliano's. We move like pinballs through the neighborhood, swinging right and swerving left and detouring around construction sites, and I almost walk past Giuliano's because the sign is cracked and faded and hung in the corner of the dusty window.

Inside, a man surrounded by a sea of instruments and cases is tinkering with a saxophone. He adjusts the height of his worktable and glances up at us and says, "Ciao!"

When he comes over I unfold the musician's flyer. "Have you seen this?"

"Bassoon," he booms, and the musician becomes an attentive statue, still and intense. "Ready tomorrow. Am-a still a-fixing." He disappears into the back room and reappears with a bassoon and it is beautiful and maple, exactly as described and pictured.

Giuliano depresses the sticky key a few times to indicate its continued stickiness and the musician throws his head back and bays with joy and relief, and then he laughs and laughs and up and down his arm sparks of happiness swim under his skin like tadpoles.

"You crazy, weird, *genius* kid —" He squeezes me so hard that I creak like his broken bassoon, and then he is skipping, pulling me along, flinging us around the shop and singing, "You found it, you found it — I can't believe you found it," and we are both laughing and dancing in a world bursting with living color now that his heart is whole.

Giuliano clears his throat. "Chop, chop," he says, flicking his eyes at the instruments piled on his worktable. He hands the bassoon over to me and I cradle it gingerly because it is a little prickly to the touch, bristling with irritation. I look more closely at the wood and the musician runs his hands down the keys and says proudly, "Pure maple."

For him the case is closed, the missing

bassoon found, but I have more to think about later. I am not sure what the prickliness means and how the missing bassoon got here in the first place. Maybe the musician did sleepwalk after all?

I hand the bassoon back and Giuliano holds up a hand and says, "Ciao." I mirror his gesture and he sinks back into the watery light of his shop.

The musician shuts the door behind us and says, "You're my favorite person *ever*. Besides my bassoon." He turns to me, his eyes still glossy. "Thank-you-thank-you-thank-you for saving us. Come to my concert on Thursday? In fact, free tickets to any of my concerts."

I accept, pretending I do not know that he will move forward and I will move forward, separately. For now, though, we walk together in the direction of the shop and he chatters away, telling me story after story that make up his life — about feeling heartbeats in the bottom of his feet right before he walks out onto the stage and about his favorite place in the city for looking at lights, which is not at a rooftop bar but through the curtain of water erupting from the fountain in front of Lincoln Center, glittering and liquid gold like dreams; and about waiting for the C train, which shrieks in C-sharp, and the satisfaction of finding a spot in Washington Square Park and unwrapping his Sunday-morning every-thing bagel.

I listen and he talks, eager and easy and free, and it is just like we are long-lost friends until we reach the subway entrance and he hesitates and says, "This is me."

I say good-bye and he says, "See you later." He starts down the stairs and I think that maybe I will, one of these days — we could run into each other in a subway sta-tion, or I could walk past a coffee shop and see him taped to the window in a Carnegie Hall poster and know that his first master's recital went just fine after all.

The neighborhood unfurls as evening falls, people coming and going and on their way, picking up dinner and sipping wine and looking for a friend and buying a bouquet and hailing a taxi and unlocking a bicycle and anything except standing still — look-ing around. So when I stop in front of the Second Chance House, someone trips over me and says, "Fucking tourist," and I am confused by what I am seeing, which is this: a mix of people gathering on the sidewalk, and some of them are waving picket signs and a girl in a stroller has two. The poster in her hands says, Compassion Not Condos,

67

and the poster tied to her stroller says, A Second Chance for Second Chance. Sisters in gray habits stand in a semicircle around one Sister who is gripping a yipping Yorkshire terrier. Their faces are all turned uptown, and I follow their gazes up the street to where a big man with flinty little eyes is barreling toward them with a crowbar in his hands and a crew of men with sledgehammers in his wake.

I stop and reach into my pocket for my notebook as the man slows to a halt and announces, "We gave you the terms, we've sent you numerous notices — you're aware of our tight timeline for construction —" and someone says, "Fuck your timeline," and the crowd cheers and the Sister pleads for silence.

The man raises his chin although he is already tall and bulky as a high-rise building. "If you don't vacate within the hour, you'll be trespassing on private property."

"These people have nowhere to vacate to," the Sister implores, bouncing the Yorkshire terrier in her arms. "We'd like to request an extension so we can transfer our families to other programs."

The man wipes his shiny forehead. He has a hanging belly in a navy pinstripe suit and its sharp lines are somehow out of alignment with his limbs.

WOLF IN COSTLY SHEEPSKIN, I write.

The man says, "I'm sorry, Sister, I really am, but we have people waiting to move in, too. Families who need places to live, just like yours —" and at this the other Sisters darken and murmur and the rumble spreads across the protesters like a storm cloud. The man puffs his cheeks and exhales and the terrier growls at him and the man looks like he wants to growl back.

Someone stops next to me and takes a picture of the crew, and two people move under an awning and light cigarettes, shaking their heads, and they are minor hiccups in the unceasing movement of the street. People part around me, streaming around the big man and his crew, and some are looking at their watches, their papers, and others are looking at the store numbers, the curb. People glance at the sledgehammers; most everyone keeps going. A duffel bag swings and pushes me off the sidewalk and a car slams its brakes and horn and people cut in front of me and I am forced farther away, swept up by the current.

The sunset turns the streets to gold and I am feeling cold again, and anxious to get back to the shop. I pass the Italian bakery, which is a neighborhood landmark, and I turn onto Carmine and the crowds thin enough that I can run the final stretch home.

The next day starts off well. I shape two hundred and sixty croissants and I get to the bus stop before the bus comes and Beaver and Todd are not on it. At lunchtime, I troop outside with everyone else. The game is Wiffle ball instead of dodgeball and I keep an eye on it in case someone sees me and gestures for me to join.

While I wait, I ponder the unresolved case of the bassoon — the smooth wood gone prickly, the musician's potential for sleep-walking — and I turn my thoughts over slowly, letting them break down and mingle so that I do not run out of things to think about before lunch is over. I am used to fill-ing empty tracts of time, and I am used to not being seen when I am right there, although I think it would be a nice surprise if someone invited me and I could nod yes.

If Walter Lavender Sr. was around, he would have taught me how to bat and how to field and that way I could join without being asked, just catch the ball and jump right in. Lucy said he had no particular fire for sports but he spoke often of the summer he spent playing catch on the beach with the sand soft between his toes and the sun peaked in the blue sky, and those were the moments that stayed with him.

It is another reminder of what I am missing, and not only because of my silence. It is there when I pass a barbershop and see a father and a son sitting side by side in front of the mirrors, or when I overhear someone at school talking about a weekend fishing trip, or when a girl at the shop mentions the model rocket she is building with her father.

But I tell myself that I have Walter Lavender Sr.'s stories, and by their light I can almost see him, or at least the outline of him, and I have the swirling almost-memory of the last story he told me and I recount it to myself now — Once upon a time, there was a boy who never imagined he could fly very far — and a gust of wind pushes the Wiffle ball off course and it flies straight at me, bounces toward my feet, and I start again from the beginning, Once upon a time.

The rest of the day scrolls by from a distance and when the afternoon bell rings, the cherry red doors fling open and the kids pour out like spilled birdseed. When I return to the shop, I narrowly miss being flattened by Milton, who is hot on the trail of a panna cotta squirrel. Before doing anything else I check the oil lamp and the flame is steady and I stare into it, drifting, and something sticky bumps against my hand. Milton has abandoned his squirrel. His eyes are bright and open and crimped into smiles at the corners, and he wonders what is wrong.

I shake my head but he can read my thoughts and hear my soul. He tips his face up to mine and waits, listening earnestly, and I tell him that it is harder for me to forget today. Couldn't Walter Lavender Sr. try a little bit harder to come back or send a sign? I am the one doing all the looking even though he is the one who is supposed to be here, to teach me the things I do not know. The squirrel reappears in the window and I move away to make room for Milton to resume the chase but he pushes his head into my hand. *You can play catch with me.*

In that way of his, he has understood the knot of things I cannot say, and he reminds me that I am home. My head clears like standing on a mountain vista and I look up to see that Lucy is waving over the crowd, trying to catch my attention. We slide behind the counter and Milton retreats to the kitchen for scraps, and Lucy presses me into her apron and she smells like gingerbread.

"Fifteen, twenty." A boy in an oversized jersey reaches over the counter and lays down a few coins. The woman next to him ruffles his hair and he flinches and she says to Lucy, "We'll definitely be back — have to make up for all the time it took us to find you!" She laughs and widens her eyes at the same time. "We've lived around the corner for years and we just always — walked right by." She makes a whooshing motion and glances at the boy and he ducks reflexively to keep from being ruffled again.

"Oh, certainly," Lucy says with a wave of her hand. "This place has a way of hiding until it wants to be found."

Lucy whistles and four vols-au-vent mice pile out of the display and line up at the rim of the counter. She holds out a gift box and the mice reverse-dive into the box like squeaky synchronized swimmers.

"See that, kiddo?" The woman reaches out for a surprise attack on the boy's hair and in response, the hair on his arm rises and sways like a field of wheat. I reach for my notebook.

BRISTLES WITH INDIGNATION, I write, stealing another look at the boy's arm, and I have a sudden thought because it reminds me of the prickly bassoon. I flip back to the diagram of the musician's apartment and there is the label I have not considered: Roommate.

Lucy sticks a gold seal on top of the box and I reconsider the roommate's role in the case.

"Voilà," she says, and there it is, the why and the how: the roommate, tired of the high-pitched intrusions on his evening and the musician's empty promises to have the bassoon repaired, had taken action right before rambling away to the other coast. The indignation was the clue; the instrument had not liked the uninvited handling by someone else.

With satisfaction, I close my notebook and case number 84, and I head to the kitchen for a sliding handshake with José and collide with Flora, knocking over the platter she is carrying out, and I hear her gasping and the grasshopper pies splatting against the floor and that is not even the worst of it, because then the big man with little eyes ducks through the shop door.

6

Flora heads back to the kitchen for a mop. "Be careful where you step," she warns.

I nod, watching the big man as he unbuttons his expensive suit jacket with one hand and appraises the customers and the displays, stocked and vibrant and squeaking and crackling and bubbling. His eyes inflate like bloated ticks and I write, FEEDING A GROWING APPETITE.

He bows at four women on their way out the door and grabs a box of double butterscotch pops without looking at them and strides toward the register.

Lucy smiles at him. "Hello there. Did you find what you were looking for today?"

He puts the box down on the counter and extends a hand with fingernails like broad polished plates. "I'm the new landlord," he says, and my thoughts spiral and even as I am checking his other hand for a crowbar I am thinking, He would *never,* and I look around his feet for a sledgehammer and think, He *couldn't*, could he? I take a step back, sliding on the smashed pies.

Lucy's hand shoots out to steady me. She releases my elbow and pleats her forehead. "Did something happen to Albert?"

"Oh — nothing like that. Didn't mean to worry you." He shows his palms like he's surrendering and my lungs are tight and starting to burn. "He was ready to retire, that's all. I figured I would stop by, introduce myself, take a look around. New kid on the block and all."

"Then it's a pleasure to meet you. Welcome to The Lavenders," Lucy says, reaching for the butterscotch pops. "Let me know if you have any questions."

"Actually, I do, if you can spare the time," he says, and I shiver as the words slip down my back like cubes of ice.

Lucy turns to Flora, who is steering a mop and bucket out of the kitchen, and says, "Can you take over the register?"

I reach for the mop and the landlord says, "Wonderful," and wrestles out of his suit jacket. "Place looks great," he adds, his breathing labored, and when he drapes his jacket over one arm there are dark half-moons welling under his armpits where the heavy silk of his shirt pinches too tightly.

"Between you and me, I think I prefer you to my other new place — the Italian bakery? It looks a little . . . dingy. Empty, too. They're underutilizing a prime location — so much more could be done with the space."

"That's the beauty of it," Lucy says, sliding out from behind the counter. "The place is an institution."

And so it is, like the Dickson brothers' hardware store — unchanged as time swirls and eddies around it, for as long as anyone can remember. It is a connecting thread in the fabric of the neighborhood, a place where people go to buy pizzelles and bump into old friends.

"It appears you have an affinity for bakeries," Lucy continues, and the landlord laughs in a voice thick and robust as our house-made jam and says, "Guilty — voracious sweet tooth."

They head away toward the front window and I let out a trapped breath. The big man does not have a crowbar tucked into his belt and there is no sledgehammer crew waiting to barge inside; he did not come here to seize the shop after all, but to consider it, and I think we have passed his test because he is at ease, making small talk with Lucy with his elbow propped on the Book's display case.

I do not like him because of what I saw at the Second Chance House and I do not like him eyeing the shop like he could swallow it whole, but now that he has met Lucy and tried the butterscotch pops and seen how the shop is filled with satisfied people, he has no reason to take it away from us.

I wring the mop and push it across the floor and the misshapen pies hop away from it. This would be a lot easier if Flora had been bringing out the molasses cinnamon rolls instead, and I lean against the mop and wait for the pies to grow complacent. Lucy and the landlord are still standing over the display case, only now they are both looking at the Book and there is a sailor there too, kneeling next to his daughter as she tips her head back, and I know Lucy is telling them the story of the shop's new beginning.

She always starts it with the line from the first page — "It was a dark and stormy night" — and she continues with the stranger at our doorstep and the gift that was given and accepted. Then she removes the Book from the case and flips through each page, recounting how the scenes pulled her in and sang to her, and the first was the breathy croon of a city furious and driving as the elements, and the second was an anthem of adventure as a girl sweeps in on a carpet of wind and her cloak swirls behind her, made of a hundred tangled snowflakes and stars.

On the third page, a young man catches a glimpse of the girl on the other side of the subway platform, framed by the white-blue glitter of her cloak, icy and immaculate and needing no one. He falls in love with the idea of her and the love ballad soared on into the fourth page as the girl sheds her cloak of ice. But that shatters the illusion the young man has of her and Lucy broke out in goose bumps to hear the broken chords of the fifth page as the girl lies abandoned on the floor, and the haunting choir of the sixth as she wanders the streets in search of her lost love, memories lurking between buildings and taking on human forms as they slip behind the girl like shadows, like a city of the lost, and on the last page a gentle lift, an open question, the stormy wilderness retreating to the corners as a banner of light tumbles across the page, from the door that has unexpectedly opened.

The artist had found a way to tell, in her own voice, the story of how she found herself at the shop's doorstep — of how she arrived in the city a young woman in search of excitement, and there she found love and lost it and continued to search in vain for her lost love until she lost herself too. Then, on a lonely winter's night, a door opened, and through that doorway — that gesture of kindness — she saw how there could be more for her, a realm of possibility beyond the seventh and final page.

When Lucy closed the Book that night, she thought back to a simpler time and a voice she missed, telling a different story but with the same ending, of a life changed by one kindness. She lifted her head and blinked and looked around, and it was the shop that seemed like the dream.

After Lucy finishes telling the story, the landlord and the sailor and the daughter take a good hard look at the Book because it looks completely ordinary in the display, the spine soft and the pages ragged on the edges and the cover old and worn like a favorite pair of jeans, whiskered with dark scratches and lighter where the leather is rubbed thin from handling.

Under their scrutiny, the Book remains as plain as the shopfront, and if they are perceptive they will ask next, "So was it her? Was the wandering artist also Walter Lavender Senior's mermaid?"

Lucy will just smile and lift a shoulder. "I like to believe she was. Wouldn't that be something?"

It would be the rarest kind of story, not confined to a static and linear space that begins in the one place and ends in the other. Rather, it is told and retold so it is never really over, growing bigger each time it loops back and starts again. Walter Lavender Sr. never taught me to play catch or ride a bike or fix a blown fuse or grow to be a man. He left only one lesson for me and the Book is the embodiment of it: physical proof of how much a gesture can matter and how it can even expand across time and place — passed on and on again from a mermaid to a father to a mother, a sketch that became an invitation that became a second beginning that became everything, to a son who had already lost so much.

7

I am glad to see the landlord leave after Lucy's story, and José helps me pour out the swamp-colored mop water and then it is time for the mail to arrive. I make a quick trip to the window and sure enough, Mister Philipp is coming up the sidewalk, pushing his mail cart with its swollen blue mailbags. Milton is already sitting under the shop's mailbox, looking around vigorously for him because he always has a jar of dog treats on hand.

Milton waits for the mail cart to come to a full stop, and then he uncurls and approaches and wags his tail in friendly greeting. As he crunches away on a rock-hard biscuit, Mister Philipp reaches back into the blue bags and pulls out stacks of mail, balancing them on his arm like cocktail platters. I don't have to open the door to know that he is whistling while doing this, because he's been on this route for as long as I can remember.

He knows my name and Lucy's name, and his own name is among the first that people moving into the neighboring walk-ups come to know. Every December he grows a beard and puts on the same tattered red hat and drops off letters from the North Pole with our names inscribed in the same gel ink he has us use to sign for packages. The employees at the bodega leave dripping bottles of tamarind soda out for him in the summer and when Lucy makes bird's milk cake she saves a slice for him so that the cake slice and Mister Philipp can whistle in harmony until the raspberry Jell-O top wobbles.

I step out and he looks the same as he always does, round face and round glasses and a blue uniform that has a brass watch chain hanging out the front pocket.

He hands me the mail and before I can rifle through the stack, he says, "Not today, son."

That is the first thing he says whenever I meet him at the mailbox, which is whenever I am not too busy with the shop or with my finding. I can't remember when he started working this route but I do remember when he began to notice me waiting behind the window. He stopped whistling then and

83

said, "I know that look. What are you waiting for — package from Aunt Geraldine, letter from Uncle Gilbert? I'll see if I have it."

I shook my head and did not say anything, and even if I could, what would I say? That all this time nothing had come — a tip, a scrap of news, some unmistakable sign that points to Walter Lavender Sr. — but that I knew I would recognize it when I saw it, even if I did not know what form it would take or where it would come from? It made sense that the mailbox would be a possibility, where messages and news arrived every day from all over the world.

I passed so many hours wondering what the sign might be that I could fill the mailbox a hundred times over. I imagined a cracked bottle containing Walter Lavender Sr.'s hurried final message, or a padded envelope from a fisherman who discovered Walter Lavender Sr.'s wedding band in the belly of a four-hundred-pound tuna. Maybe it would be a charred lotus flower salvaged from the ashes and pressed between leaves of paper, or a short article clipped from the middle of the newspaper by a vigilant stranger — aircraft wreckage washing up on the rocks, a cruise liner in the Arabian Sea picking up a black box.

Mister Philipp probably got to talking with Lucy because the next time he caught me watching behind the window again, he crooked his finger and whistled as he waited for me to come out.

"Tell you what," he said, "I'll keep an eye out for you, save you some time. The second I see anything about your dad, you'll be the first to know," and the next day he said, "Not today, son," in place of Hello, and arched deftly to scratch a spot in the middle of his back.

He does that now, reaching around his back, although with more difficulty. "I reckon that's my last delivery to you. I'm transferring to another route — they say it's gonna have less stairs to climb. Even issued me a truck to get there," he says, struggling to reach the trouble spot. I know about it because he joked once that he had to buy a bamboo back scratcher to relieve the itch since he was losing flexibility and had a hell of a time reaching it, and there was no one around to scratch it for him because he lived alone.

"Chin up, son. Tell Lucy for me, too." He smiles and I wave, and he whistles the ice-cream truck song as he walks away but to me it sounds a little blue because of the parting of ways, and I watch until he disappears into the door of the next walk-up.

I step back inside the shop, where the shadows have lengthened and Lucy is announcing the fifteen-minute closing call. The last customers make their selections and trickle out and Lucy locks the windows and doors after them and flips the sign to Closed so stragglers don't stumble in as we go through the steps of putting the shop to bed.

The closing routine has become a nightly ritual, cemented over the years, and it is as comforting and familiar to me as the lines on my palm. We fill the sinks with soapy water and submerge trays and baking sheets; wipe down the refrigerators and tabletops and chairs; empty the displays and scrub them clean; remove the Book from its case for dusting and replace the Book with care, open to the first page; mop the floors and dim the lights and lower the heat and blow out my oil lamp and the final turns of the lock, one and two.

Over the next two weeks, the leaves start to turn and at lunchtime I watch as they smoke and crisp at the edges and a thin ribbon of ants unspools over the tip of my shoe and between classes I become a leaf too, buffeted by students through the hall, and I watch through the bus window as the city passes by in the brisk light of the afternoon sun.

Each evening, everything is as it should be, the earth balanced on its axis just so, and customers continue coming in to sample chocolate pots de crème with orange whipped cream, their faces lighting up as the little pot pours itself luxuriantly over the waiting ladle.

The first Sunday of October brings with it a whisper of the winter to come, and a delivery for Mrs. Ida Bonnet. I wrap a scarf around my neck and then I am on my way — past the church with its bells tolling for the faithful, and street vendors setting out handmade jewelry and jewel-colored pashminas, and the ice-cream shop announcing its limited edition seasonal flavors, and the bookstore with its cramped nooks and teetering paperback towers like being in an eccentric professor's attic.

The streets teem with a kaleidoscope of locals and visitors united in their determination to drink in the last honeyed drops of sunshine, brunching in sunglasses and peacoats and ordering scoops of pumpkin spice gelato. I skid to a halt in front of the Italian bakery, my shoes squealing like race car tires. The lights are off and the tables and chairs are stacked in the corner and the counter is empty and the displays are empty and the floor is empty and all is still. The walls watch as dust settles on the stools.

For a moment, I think that I have gotten my storefronts mixed up. There is a sign taped to the door and I run over to it, forgetting to hold the delivery box steady. The letters are lopsided and bleeding in spots like the writer was pressing too hard, stringing together a sentence that did not want to end. CLOSED AFTER 40 YEARS OF SERVICE: Lost our lease thank you for your support over the years and allowing us to live the dream every day it has been our privilege to be a part of the community and we will miss you our dear customers our friends.

I walked by just a few days ago and the bakery was right here where it had always been, a feature of the landscape like a gnarled tree stump, marking the fork in the road where things converged — the story of the neighborhood, and of the old friends living in it.

How could such a place vanish without any warning?

I have not seen the landlord since he visited the shop but now he rises out of my mind like a submarine that has been lying in wait. My other new place, he said to

Lucy. Dingy, underutilizing. Maybe it is a warning. It is unsettling to think of what else the landlord could do, if he could erase a place that time itself could not touch.

I imagine what Mrs. Ida Bonnet would do if The Lavenders disappeared without any warning — she would wait for her delivery, believing that I was on my way, and when there was no knock at the door she would ease out of the armchair and look for her shoes and it would be a long journey, her joints creaking with the stairs, people parting and rushing around her on the street, her mouth dropping open when she stood bent in front of the empty shop, seeing that it, too, had passed, and left her behind.

The rest of the journey to Mrs. Ida Bonnet's apartment, I can't stop thinking — what would *I* do?

"The Italian bakery has gone out of business?" Lucy repeats, raising her voice to be heard over the whirring mixers.

She pulls a tray of meringues out of the oven and takes one look at my face and says, "You're worried about the shop." She pushes the kitchen door open with her foot. "Come with me."

She puts the tray on the counter and one by one, as if awakening from a deep slumber, the meringues stretch and pop into the air and hover like cumulus clouds. When she nudges them into their section of the display, three little girls squeal and drag their mother behind them and squash their noses against the glass, and Milton trots up and places his nose against the glass with a sigh too.

"We'll take two dozen," the mother says, squeezing in next to Milton to admire the weightless meringues. His nose, sticky with residual caramel, is glued to the glass, and so he lifts just his eyes to look at her.

Lucy puts both hands on my shoulders. "Look around," she says, and I see the meringues floating, the vols-au-vent mice bouncing on the little girls' shoulders, the desserts fidgeting and showcasing their personalities. The air moves with a million oven-warm breaths, invisible eddies conveying impossible properties.

"You see all of this?" She does a significant sweep with her eyes, encompassing the simple chandeliers and the decorative moldings that frame the ceiling and the working fireplace along the side wall and the hand-painted floor tiles and the brass trim lining the mirrors and banisters and narrow arched doorways, and all of it goes back to Walter

Lavender Sr., who convinced Lucy that she could.

I turn back to Lucy and she lifts a flour-bleached brow. "No one is evicting us," she says, and I am reminded that she has un-canny powers of knowing. She can stir and smell and know if she needs to add a twist of Meyer lemon juice, an extra quarter cup of raw sugar, a dash of chili flake, and she can tell with her back turned if the crêpes in the griddle are taking on too much color or if the batter I am mixing needs more water to thin it out.

When a regular comes in with a creative block or a scratchy throat or a sleepless night, she knows to add a dusting of wasabi powder and black sesame to the dark choc-olate frosting, or a nugget of honeyed Brie in the center of the cupcake, or a quenelle of cucumber sorbet on the side of the plate. Her sense of intuition means that she is usu-ally right, even if she has not yet figured out what to add to a dessert to keep my mind open and confident so that I can speak. She would not let the landlord catch us by surprise and push us out — not before she stumbled across the solution and not before Walter Lavender Sr. could see what he helped create, not when I could still believe that he was looking for the light in the window, and finding his way back home.

8

I am sure Lucy is right but two weeks later I dream about the submarine rising out of night-water and I sink to the sandy bottom and find myself face-to-face with a skeleton wearing a pilot's hat at a jaunty angle.

My head is waterlogged and my limbs float, and in the lonesome darkness before dawn it feels like I have accidentally slipped awake while the world slumbers on, at peace, as one.

I work my way around Milton, who is sleeping at the foot of my bed, and ease onto the floor. His paws are twitching and I wonder what he is running after. I tiptoe down the steps and the stairwell smells warm and sweet and light seeps under the door; Lucy will be behind it, preparing for the morning rush before José and Flora arrive. I crack the door open and Lucy looks up and sets down her sifter. The radio in front of her is dusted in flour and set to low on a golden oldies station.

"Early morning. To both of you," she says as Milton pads half-asleep into the kitchen after me and collapses under the sink. "Wash up and you can help me with this olive oil cake."

She resumes sifting dry ingredients into a large bowl and I tie off my apron and pat my hands dry against the front. I heat a pan and add a stick of butter, and while it melts I pour out the milk and add the olive oil, watching as it separates into beads on top of the milk.

Once the finished cake comes out of the oven, Lucy will set it on a cooling rack and pour a grapefruit glaze over the center. Her olive oil cake with grapefruit glaze is a favorite with the Pilates crowd and, less obviously, with the students. When midterm exams roll around in a few weeks, they will turn up seeking peaceful refreshment in the pale yellow squares, eating with their hands and licking the glaze off their fingers as the angry stress-induced bumps on their faces clear up between bites.

The mixer switches on with a metallic whir and Lucy cracks eggs and zests tangerines into the bowl as I whisk melted butter into my olive oil and milk. When the eggs are pale and thick, Lucy paddles in a quarter of her flour mixture.

"Now you," she says. I tilt my bowl over the mixer and we alternate adding our wet and dry ingredients so the bubbles of air in the batter don't pop and the cake emerges tender and fluffy from the oven. Lucy pours out the batter and it cascades across the first baking pan in a butter-silk curtain.

"Masterful," she pronounces. She slides the pan into an unoccupied oven and I trudge up the stairs to get ready for school.

Throughout the day, I think about Clyde, the lost cockatiel I am searching for. Since finding the flyer last week, I learned that Clyde belongs to a girl my age who is losing her hair in Memorial Sloan Kettering, and that her mother was the one who posted the flyer. At lunch I draw a diagram and make a list in my notebook but the tabletop is lumpy and the straight lines of the birdcage look like they are shivering.

I knock down the walls with my eraser and start again but each time I do Beaver throws a ball and it hits my table or my back or my knee and my pencil jerks and punctures the paper. I pick up my lunch and retreat to the bathroom, locking the stall door and sitting on the toilet seat to start a new list undisturbed.

The FOLA is this: the girl's mother had cleaned out the cage in the morning and when she came to change Clyde's water in the afternoon, the bird was gone. So far, we have searched the cage, looking under the toys and inside the nesting box and behind the mirror and around the play wheel, and after that we looked in the ZOLA, cleaning and organizing the living room where the cage sat, and then we checked the natural places, the eaves and gutters where other birds liked to roost.

At that point I started to feel drained from the extended period of talking; it takes a lot of energy to focus on all the muscles and movements and rhythms involved in keeping my words straight. When we resumed a few days later, I asked the mother to return to her thoughts as she cleaned the cage, hoping to trigger a forgotten memory. It is an effective technique — the shooting guard who lost his lucky socks had been thinking of how hungry he was as he unpacked from his trip, and that made him remember that he had wandered to the pantry, where he saw a pack of sesame buns, and that prompted him to grab the burger patties in the freezer, and that's where he found his socks, frozen solid and unharmed.

The girl's mother said that she had been

worrying about things as she vacuumed seed husks off the cage floor — the lab results, the runny consistency of Clyde's droppings, the strange cautious tone in the nurse's voice, the arugula that would wilt in the crisper if not eaten soon — and when she returned Clyde to the cage she worried also that she might have left the latch loose.

After that, we searched every inch of the apartment, high and low, in case Clyde had accidentally flown into a cabinet or made a nest in the spare linens. He has not turned up yet and it is time to widen the search. Someone clomps into the bathroom and I put my notebook away and flush the toilet.

After school, I set out to search for Clyde, keeping my eyes open for signs and thinking back through the stories the girl's mother told me. She is not sure what to make of me — she was excited at first to have me there to stifle the echoing silences of her home, but I was not what she expected or knew and she floundered uneasily and took a little longer to realize that I could not respond to her chatter in the normal way.

I asked her my usual questions and she answered with upbeat force, slowly and brightly, with her limbs held in tight, controlled lines. I listened to her talk and watched carefully, and this made her more uncomfortable and so she blinked too much and repeated her simplified answers without being asked, her eyes flashing red with alarm. EMERGENCY PLANNING FOR CONTINGENCIES, I wrote as she locked up her disappointment and prepared herself for what she would say later in the hospital.

Still, I teased out the information I needed, and there was a moment as she described Clyde when she forgot about being guarded. She said that he was yellow and white with coral cheeks that fooled you into thinking he was bashful when he was very affectionate, actually, and vocal with his singing. She said it was silly and wouldn't help with the search but she would never forget this one moment — walking back into her daughter's room during chemotherapy and seeing Clyde perched on her daughter's gloved hand, cocking his head at her and whistling "Strawberry Fields Forever," coasting around the lilts and dips.

I wonder if Clyde has gone south for the winter and wander that way, keeping an eye on the sky. A large flock of silver birds rises and falls like a mushroom cloud over Washington Square Park, and I change direction to follow the sign. As I am walking past the

98

place where the Italian bakery used to be, I notice a makeshift banner strung across the front, emblazoned with a name I remember seeing on the food channel, the letters arcing over a smirking man who slices into an onion with knives like lightning: Coming Soon. Jacques Pierre Patisserie. Men in hard hats and boots take weighty steps over paint cans and hammer at the walls and their saws bite into slabs of wood. I feel a twinge of melancholy for the bakery, and I imagine what is to come and tell myself that it will be inventive and fresh and sleek, and it will not be a threat.

In Washington Square Park I sit by the fountain and look at the coins bright with wishes, and something brighter flashes among the pigeons roosting on the arch. I reposition myself under the arch and hum "Strawberry Fields Forever" and wait for Clyde to land.

The girl's mother goes still when she opens the door and sees Clyde with his feather-light claws gripping my wrist. I give her a moment to pack away her shock and then she lurches into motion, inviting me in and making tea, and in her relief she relaxes and slouches into the chair, unguarded and herself, and for the first time since the musician, it feels like someone else finally knows me.

9

Halloween descends in a flurry of first snow and polyester costumes, Little Red Riding Hoods and Spider-Men entering the shop for sour eyeballs that purse their lips and raise the hair on their heads. I watch through the window as pumpkins and princesses and gladiators dash by, their grown-ups hurrying to keep up. The other kids from school must be out there too, but it has been years since I ventured out with them.

One week later while I am out on Sunday deliveries, I am caught in the tentacles of a slow-moving street parade and by the time I return to the shop the sky is a deep blue dome flushing orange along the rim. I open the door and the energizing noise of customers hits me first and I wait for the warmth but there is a foreign chilled bite to the air. Sugar snow glitters as it swirls through the displays, and in one of them the mice are squabbling over the limited number of

101

fondant scarves that Flora must have decorated and distributed among them.

Still, the crowd is as thick as ever and Milton struggles toward me, panting as he swims against the current, a dark substance staining his gums. A harried Lucy chases after him.

"He stole a hot chocolate beignet," she says irritably. She reaches to pry his mouth open but the crispy beignet has already liquefied and rich hot chocolate oozes between his teeth. "No," she says to him, and he huddles against the backs of my legs. "You know you're not authorized to eat chocolate."

She shifts her attention to me and the roots of her hair lighten as her bad mood recedes. "How were the deliveries?"

I draw a check in the air. "Well done," she says. "You are my bright spot in an uncooperative day." She scowls at the air conditioner behind me and to my surprise I see José next to it, bracing himself on a stepladder and unscrewing a panel.

Just seeing him up there makes me nervous that he will fall and sweat pools now on my palms and I stuff my hands in my pockets. Walter Lavender Sr. was fearless when it came to high places; he climbed easily into the sky while the highest place I have been is a beginner ski hill, and even then I could only peer down and cling to trees until Milton, barking in alarm, broke free of the barriers and pumped his way up the slope to rescue me.

José climbs down and we do our handshake. "Broken," he says, to explain his uncharacteristic appearance in the front of the shop.

"José's tinkering with it to see if he can get it unstuck but if he doesn't, the repairman should be here any minute. Can you two look out for him and holler when he gets here?"

Lucy heads back to the register and I check the oil lamp before going upstairs to collect my math homework. When I come back down, I take a seat against the window so that I can see the door from the corner of my eye. Milton crowds under the table with my legs and Flora drops off a plate of sliced apples on her way out of the shop, along with a mug of cider with a cinnamon stick that stirs itself clockwise and then counterclockwise.

"It was an indecisive batch," she says in apology. "You enjoy your night now."

Four graphs later, the door bursts open and the chandeliers tremble and my spine snaps ramrod straight, vibrates with the ominous pluck and thrum of a low bass. The landlord fills the open doorway and my mind darkens and jumps to him raising a crowbar and smashing the tables and I reel it back in. It could be an innocuous visit to pick up another box of double butterscotch pops — except there is a dull roar coming from outside, stomping feet and a muddled chanting that separates into words when he clears the door. I push my seat back and the customers around me stand too, everyone straining to see into the black night, the reflection of the shop like a thin gloss of ice on the window.

Lucy appears next to me with her arms full of fairy lights and pine wreaths. "*What is that racket?*" she says, dropping the decorations and pressing me to her side, and someone blows a whistle and the stamping picks up again, the chanting rattling the windowpanes, and suddenly I am terrified that the landlord has brought a mob to drive us out and I imagine them pumping their picket signs, the bottoms sharpened into glinting stakes. The screech of a loudspeaker pierces the air — *"What do we want?"* — and I screw my eyes shut, slap my hands over my ears, and Lucy leaps forward.

She grabs the landlord's elbow and yanks him inside, shutting the door and snapping the curtains closed, and the noise of the protesters falls back into a formless roar once more. Lucy drags him to my table, where he drops into a seat and spreads his legs and Milton shimmies out from under the table with a chiding bark — *Some space down here?* — and customers hover and look uncertainly at one another and at the landlord as he catches his breath, mops his forehead.

"What the hell?" someone says, and the shop erupts into laughter and chatter and I can't help glancing at the curtains and wondering if a Sister is out there, or an Italian woman flinging her hands, releasing a curse.

The landlord leans into the back of the seat and crosses his legs, and then he uncrosses them and leans forward, and the rich fabric of his suit bunches in a few places and bags everywhere else like it does not want to lie flat and touch too much of his skin. I ease my books away from him and perch on the edge of my seat, trying not to make any sudden movements.

"Can you believe it? Totally uncalled for," the landlord says.

"Sure I can," Lucy says, smoothing her apron and standing. "You do realize that your closures affect a lot of people — real people. Those places were their *lives*."

The landlord crosses his arms and chews his lip, brooding. "Why am I the bad guy here? I don't control the market — I follow it, and if people weren't so up in arms they'd see that I'm also *improving* lives. When the street's more valuable, everyone wins."

Lucy shakes her head and turns to go. "I'm sorry, but you'll have to excuse me. I have customers waiting, seasonal accents to put up, a kitchen to close, and a repairman to hunt down since you weren't getting back to me."

"I've had a lot on my hands, as you can see, but I'm sorry that you feel —"

"You're welcome to hide out here until they leave. We close in half an hour." Lucy crouches next to me and when I convince her that I am fine and have homework to finish, she gathers up the string of fairy lights and takes a second to compliment a regular and sweeps away.

The landlord shifts, his chair creaking. His presence clashes with the shop and the discord grinds at my teeth, sharp and shrill as a dentist's drill.

"These people," he says, making an explosion with his hands. "They blow my mind. What do they expect when I've got someone

106

lined up who can pay market value? Am I supposed to say, No thanks, bud, I'll stick to this health code violation paying below market? Tell you what, I wish I could, I really do —" He shakes his head, presses the pads of his fingers into his chest to indicate his sincerity, and I look around for an empty table I can move to and from the corner of my eye I see José glancing at me as he returns to fixing the air conditioner.

"— but I can't afford to run a charity. I have a job to do. I tune in to the market, and do you know what it's saying?" His jowl twitches and his eyes quiver with intensity. "It's saying, you should be getting two, three times the current rate. And that's not counting the unicorns — a bank or chain comes knocking, offering six times as much. What operation can compete with that? So you get your space ready, you wait. You create opportunities. It's good business." He slaps the table like throwing down a winning poker hand and Milton picks up his head, instantly alert, and José climbs down the stepladder.

"Sure, change can be tough. People are stuck in their ways, progress doesn't come easy. But you have to keep your eye on the bigger picture — you'll see, everyone wins. You're going to love the new patisserie. I have kids, too — two girls, a little younger than you, rambunctious — they can't wait for it." The landlord studies my face and narrows his eyes and seems to see me for the first time. "Why aren't you saying anything? Are you deaf or something?"

"Is everything good here?" José says as he comes up to our table, his eyes dark as they move between me and the landlord.

I shake my head and the landlord says, "What's wrong with you then? Is it me?" His voice cracks like he has been wounded. "You don't like me?" and I do not say anything but José raises his palm at the landlord and says, "Let it go, man."

The landlord snorts. "What, you think I'm the big bad wolf, too?" He looks down at my books. "Write it down, if you're shy. I want to know what you have to say about me." He swipes at my pencil and José grabs his arm and Milton latches onto a chair leg and tries to drag the landlord away. The landlord looks down at the trunk of his arm, at José's fingers digging into it, blackened with grease and slender as twigs.

"I *said,* let it go." José flashes a smile that glitters cold as the snow in the displays and the landlord yanks his arm back as if scalded, staring at José and his four-and-a-half missing teeth.

The landlord brushes at the stains on his jacket. "All I'm saying is, I clear out the dumps, make the neighborhood beautiful, and they get upset. How's that for thanks?" He glances at the door as it opens and the sounds of the protest filter in.

"You want to go tell Lucy the repair guy is here?" José says quietly, nodding at the person stepping through the door, a bald man with a bushy beard and a toolbox tucked under one arm. I snatch up my homework and leave the landlord alone to get Lucy from behind the counter.

"Huzzah," Lucy says when I point out the repairman. José is already shaking his hand, and the landlord is on his feet now, peering behind the curtain with one hand braced against the Book's display case.

Ten minutes later, Lucy locks the doors and windows to begin the closing routine. I turn on the taps and adjust the water temperature and empty the displays while the sinks fill. I wait for the hypnotic rhythms of the routine to set in but the calm does not come because the landlord is still here.

"We're closed," Lucy says through the glass door, pointing at the sign.

"Not for sale!" one of the protesters cries with renewed vigor when the landlord appears in the glass next to Lucy.

She raps the door and says, "It's late. Let him go home."

They circle like weary flies and Lucy sighs and steps outside, and with that the routine is disrupted. She talks to the protesters under the awning and Milton dances on fours and twos trying to eat their signs while the landlord lurks behind the curtain, and finally Lucy comes back in and says, "They're leaving. Thanks, Milton."

He barks sharply — *All in a day's work* — and pokes around hopefully for his reward.

The landlord does not leave the safety of the shop until the protesters disband, and even then he slinks out first, checking for stragglers, before making a strutting double-time retreat into the night.

Lucy locks the door behind him, and from there the rest of the closing ritual goes without a hitch even though the silence is, to my ears, less comforting than usual. We wash and dry and scrub and wipe and polish. I blow out the oil lamp and we mop ourselves to the kitchen door and survey our gleaming handiwork and call it a good night.

10

The next morning, on Monday, I hear Lucy rise before the sun as she always does. I put on my red high-tops and clatter down the stairs and burst into the shop, ready to shape croissants.

It looks the same. I hear a timer *ping!* and the hum of the refrigerators and the floor rumbles faintly like a hungry stomach as a train thunders past in the tunnels far below my feet. I move toward a table in the front, slow and quiet and holding my breath, and I sit and observe and try to put my finger on what it is — the thing that is wrong with the shop.

Lucy emerges from the kitchen with Milton and a tray of warm vols-au-vent mice. They look golden-brown and delicately puffed and layered. She sets the tray on my table and sits across from me, stunned, and Milton sits and the mice sit too, perfectly still, delicious and dead.

I turn in my seat and see that, of course, the Book is missing.

There is a moment of incredulity, when a treasured thing becomes a lost thing. The world stills and sound fades and you are suspended in a fuzzy, foggy place, before your surroundings resolve and you splinter into sharp little pieces of panic.

I float to the case but the Book is not on the floor next to the base. It is not on the window ledge. Not on the surrounding shelves. No. No. Nonono — and with that my stomach plummets and clenches, cold with fear, and my chest burns hot and I am shaking and my teeth are chattering.

I want to run to everywhere at once, upend every drawer and rifle through cabinets and stack the furniture and turn out every nook and cranny like the Book will become more lost with each second that passes.

With great effort, I sit down and I stop and I breathe, so that I can organize and think.

"Don't you worry. It'll turn up — or you'll find it." Lucy kneels and tries to catch my eye, peering up at me until I can't help but smile a tiny bit.

She stocks the displays and they look like glass coffins and I wait for the feeling of panic to subside, and the minutes linger like oblivious houseguests and a feeling like emptiness displaces the panic.

José arrives and then Flora, and the smell of croissants wafts out of the kitchen and Lucy comes out and turns the sign to Open. There is a rhythm to the shop; things get busier as the week goes on, with purchases peaking on Friday after work and crowds peaking on Saturday and Sunday. The cycle starts again on Monday but quieter does not mean empty, and too soon a man comes in with two boys dangling from his arms, one willowy and towheaded and the other sturdy and dark-haired, and a stroller rolls through the door like a tank, pushed by the mother. I grip the counter and wait for them to approach.

The boys hop and skip and kick their way to the displays, their chubby cheeks bouncing with anticipation and their eyes fixed on the displays, tilted toward glee, wholly unaware that the shop has changed.

I stand behind the glass and the towheaded boy draws back from the desserts arranged in unmoving rows. "What's wrong?" he whispers shyly.

The dark-haired boy pounds on the glass. "Wake up, dragons."

The rest of the family catches up, breathless and eager, and Lucy comes out of the kitchen and wipes her crumb-flecked hands on her apron and breaks the news that the Book is gone.

The boys look at their parents.

"Totally fixable, boys," the mother says, and she says to Lucy, "We can fix this, right? You're working on finding the Book? What can I do?"

"What do you mean, the Book is gone?" the father says, confused. "Are we too early?"

The towheaded boy presses himself into his mother's legs, looking forlorn, and the dark-haired boy peers around the counter. "Is this a prank?" he says suspiciously. "It's not funny."

"I'm afraid not," Lucy sighs. "We'll do what we can to find the Book and restore your favorite desserts, but this is the best we can do right now."

"I'll ask around. We'll find it and fix this," the mother vows, energized, and she wheels the stroller around to leave.

"Fix?" the father explodes as the truth dawns on him. "This should never have happened! What kind of business are you running?" He narrows his eyes at the stiff desserts, incensed, and Lucy waits for him to finish and her disappointed judgment is

a cool, unnerving thing. He shakes it off and stalks to the door.

"That was a bad joke. Can we come back in the afternoon?" the dark-haired boy says, grabbing his father's arm.

The towheaded boy is the last to go, running for the door after the rest of his family has left, and a woman with a severe bob holds it open for him before entering the shop. The ruffled, padded shoulders of her blouse make her waist look absurdly small.

"The angel food cake," she says without looking at the display, and I reach for a square and Lucy takes the plate from me.

"I'll take care of this," she says, sending me away gently. "You should get to school."

Lunch box, I think halfheartedly. Backpack — notebook — pen — making sure that everything else is in its place, and on my way out I catch a glimpse of the woman pushing the plate of cake back across the counter, and she surprises me by reaching for Lucy's face.

"There, there," she soothes, resting her palm against Lucy's cheek. "Everything will be all right."

Over lunchtime I make a list to think through the case and the possibilities, and I return to the shop that night with a plan of action, itching to search for the Book. I greet Milton and we join Lucy behind the register and I ask if she was the one who dusted the display case and replaced the Book.

"I don't think so," she says, but she does not sound confident. "It's a little bit of a jumble, but . . . I don't remember myself doing that."

A woman orders a peanut butter silk pie and shuffles to the side. Lucy beams at the next customer in line and I watch the woman dig in with her fork.

"This is heavenly," she says to me, rolling her eyes back, and I am about to smile when she adds sheepishly, "I suppose it's an awful lot to live up to, though, isn't it?" She shrugs and scoops up another heaping forkful and says around the cream cheese and fudge, "Did you hear, the new Jacques Pierre is opening soon?"

I dodge the comment and march into the kitchen to continue the search. Flora is piping yogurt whipped cream frosting onto a poppy seed cake and José is spraying dishes in the sink, and when he sees me he brings up his hand for a soapy handshake and everything about the scene is so familiar, so ordinary, that it slides between my ribs, a cruel knife.

"This is rough, you know, about the Book," José says.

"When did you see it? Last."

José does not remember and Flora scratches under the elastic of her hairnet and says she remembers dusting the case last week, but they do not remember removing the Book and dusting the case last night and neither do I. That leaves Milton, and he stops wagging his tail and backs away when I look at him thoughtfully. Would he chew up the Book, drop it into the toilet?

I inspect his mouth, peel back his lips, and he tweaks his whiskers and twists his head away, miffed — *Really? Who do you think I am?* I hug him around the neck, knowing that I should not have doubted him, and he puts his wet nose into my ear and farts, and I suppose that is forgiveness.

I reason out the scenarios, starting with the FOLA. The Book could have become lost after we locked up, but I think it is more likely that it happened before. Perhaps it was misplaced in the chaos of the protesters and the interrupted routine, and that means it is hiding somewhere in the shop, in an accidental place where it doesn't belong. Tuning out the sounds of the kitchen, I clean and organize the cabinets and closets, searching.

As I sort through cartons of milk and cream in the refrigerator, I hope that the Book is indeed hiding in the shop, because if it isn't, then someone carried it out and the case becomes more difficult. Perhaps it was taken out with the trash, or the display was jostled and a customer unwittingly carried it home in a shopping bag — or it could have been stolen, too.

Milton pads behind me as I move from cabinet to cabinet, sniffing at the things I discard and disagreeing occasionally — *Not the good sponge!* — and I tug the molding sponge out of his mouth and start to wonder about the landlord. He was a new variable in last night's equation, but then again, so were the protesters and the repairman. I run the hypothesis by Milton anyway, and he spits up a chewed teaspoon and walks away without a second thought.

I toss out the sponge and the teaspoon. He is right; the landlord does not like old things. I will need to keep my eyes open and continue searching, and there are a lot of places in the shop I have yet to scour and I remind myself that something — some clue — is bound to turn up.

On Tuesday after school, I repeat my meticulous sweep of the shop, hoping that I have overlooked a clue. I go through bins of all-purpose flour and cake flour and pastry flour and almond flour, shaking them one by one and listening intently and keeping an eye on Lucy as she unloads the week's supplies herself, because she gave José the day off.

She shuttles back and forth, faint creases etched in parentheses around her mouth, and she does not stumble or falter, just waves me away, saying, "I'm fine — I'm fine," and keeps going.

It is not the first time she has had to carry a load bigger than herself. The first restaurant her parents owned and operated was a modest bistro in Ohio known for its juicy pork chops au poivre. She doesn't remember that one; she was a few weeks old when the tornado ripped down the block on Palm Sunday, looking like it might miss but veering at the last second into the main room of the restaurant.

Uprooted by the disaster, the family moved westward to Iowa, where they reopened the restaurant and Lucy learned how to tenderize meat with red wine and thicken soups with roux. One Good Friday, an unattended kitchen fire grew out of control and in the very next instant, the family lost its second restaurant and Lucy's mother nearly lost her leg.

They moved west once more and opened their third restaurant in Santa Cruz, California. Lucy studied business management and helped run the restaurant and carried her mother around on her back when her leg buckled with the old pain, and they barely had time to forget before an earthquake struck and swallowed restaurant number three.

It had to be a sign. They would not try again. But one month later when they sat around the TV and watched looping footage of the fall of the Berlin Wall — East Berliners storming the Bornholmer Strasse bridge and thrusting champagne bottles into the sky — Lucy's parents turned and saw Lucy's chin give a defiant hitch, and they were filled with the same sickening mix of fear and happiness they saw beamed through the screen.

They gathered their money and courage and sent Lucy as far away as they could, to culinary school in New York, so that she would have a chance to escape the family curse. She was twenty-five, and she vowed to see them soon and threw her arms around both of them even as her mother pushed her away with a guttural cry.

"Don't come back," she said, afraid that

the misfortune that plagued them would also spread to their daughter like a disease. Lucy could not — would not — make that promise until she saw the importance of it glistening in her mother's eyes. She shouldered the burden and turned away, and that was the last time she saw them.

She forgot what the instructors taught on the first day, but the important part was that she stood in the kitchen among her white-capped classmates, smoothing out the chef's coat she had ironed the night before, cheeks flushed pink, and she breathed in the smell of sugar cookies baking.

She became captivated by the pastry arts first and, later, by a calm, soft-spoken pilot with gray eyes like moons, simmering under the surface with delicious exotic dreams. When his plane became lost, it was my cry, raw with the desire to live, that made it possible for her to carry yet another impossible load, even as her parents stayed away for fear that they would tempt fate into bringing down a new calamity.

Lucy has found her way. She built this shop, our home, and defended me when I could not find a voice of my own, and when things got lonely, I knew I was never really alone. Remembering Lucy's strength makes me feel stronger too, and gives me perspective. She bore those burdens and moved forward, and a lost Book can hardly compare to all of that, coaxing the shop to life and creating a world for me out of hard-fought victories and losses, days full of a certain kind of moment — small and sweet and distinct as a fluttering petal-bright macaron, a most ordinary and extraordinary magic.

On Wednesday, I search the last walk-in and alphabetize flavor compounds, and Milton dreams in the corner and the shop feels like a ghost town. Flora finishes knitting the body of a sweater, which normally takes her two weeks, and José drifts around the shop with a bottle of disinfectant and a towel, wiping down polished surfaces and untouched tables, no longer confined to the kitchen by throngs of customers. Lucy stays in the kitchen, though, whipping and folding and baking, springing out to the register when the front door opens. The sporadic tinkling of the bell becomes almost a mockery, a jaunty reminder of the dwindling crowds.

I have found a lot of things over the past few days — a rusted serving ladle and a box of leftover New Year's sparklers and an amethyst brooch of Lucy's — but no clues that point to the Book. I rack my mind and open my eyes as wide as they will go, and I see the sweat beading at Lucy's temple as she works and the worried crease of José's face when she tells him that he can head out early.

The street outside is buzzing with more energy than a wet November evening can typically muster. Mere blocks away, Jacques Pierre is celebrating his grand opening, and it is hard to concentrate. I finish my homework and enlist Lucy to help prepare Lost flyers to hang around the neighborhood. Maybe then the Book will turn up before Thanksgiving, so that we can be thankful for its return along with our family and turkey and good health and good fortune.

Lost Leather Book, she writes at the top of a blank sheet of paper. With my guidance, she makes a large sketch of the Book, the way it looks when it's closed, shading the cover with patches of light and dark brown to represent the leather.

I lean back to study the page. The rendering feels incomplete although there are no other details to add. The Book is nondescript but you would know if you were holding it. I gesture at the fleece I am wearing and Lucy draws an arrow and labels the center of the Book sketch: Warm to the touch. Comfortable.

We move on to the bottom half of the flyer and she sketches the Book when it is open to the first page. We decide not to re-create the drawing with all its intricacies, and after a moment of thinking Lucy draws another arrow and labels it: A winter's tale of lost love. I nod; that captures exactly the right image, and at the bottom of the flyer, we add, Seven pages, hand-drawn, and one-of-a-kind, and then we squeeze in, Priceless — no $$$ value! Please return if found!

The door opens and a man steps in and wipes the bottoms of his shoes on the mat. His friends crowd behind him and he looks around the empty shop and asks dubiously, "Is this Jacques Pierre?"

I shake my head and point to the left and they leave. Splaying my hand across the flyer, I count to five, and that is more than the number of times the door opened tonight. Lucy did not bake as much today and despite that, I know there will be even more untouched trays left to wrap when we close.

On Thursday, I wake early to post the Lost Leather Book flyers around the neighborhood, and throughout the day I shovel through time by thinking of the people who will have seen the flyer and the people who might come forward. When the bus drops me off after school, I barrel toward the shop and fall through the door and the space is completely empty, the crowds faded with the memory of the summer sun. Nothing moves; nothing stirs. I feel like I am in the wrong place until Milton rockets out of the kitchen, into my legs, and the sound of his excited breathing fills the room and warms the air and reminds me — *You're home!*

We take up our post behind the window next to the oil lamp, my chin propped in my hands and his tongue lolling out, watching and waiting as shriveled leaves pile on the outside ledge and blow away and pile again.

Lucy is behind the register, doing some bookkeeping and shaking her head, and Flora is finishing up her sweater's sleeves at a table, and I hear the sound of the mailbox closing and step out to retrieve the mail and walk straight into a customer on his way in.

I back away from the hanging belly, the elaborate stitching. The landlord flicks the corner of a letter and winks a beady eye and says, "Never trust a mailman. Personal delivery for your mother."

"Anything interesting?" Lucy calls, coming to the door, and her voice pitches higher with surprised recognition. "Hello."

"Take a seat," he says, and we sit and Milton sniffs his ankles and José eyes him distrustfully.

The landlord hands Lucy the letter. She scans it and he blows his nose and the legs of his chair creak and then the letter is traveling through the air with graceful swoops, landing on my high-tops. I pick it up and when I straighten, Lucy is bloodless and fragile as the last leaves clinging to the skeletal trees outside.

"You've made a mistake," she says.

"Hmm? No mistake," he says, and I try to read the letter but Flora clinks her knitting needles and José pumps his spray bottle and the landlord's armpit stains are growing bigger and I am embarrassed for him.

"It's a mistake," Lucy insists. "It says here that the rent's going to be doubled next month. That's in two weeks."

The knitting needles slip; a fine mist settles over the two-top. I force my gaze away from the armpit stains, struggling to catch up with the conversation.

"Yes. I understand that you and Albert were operating on a month-to-month basis?" The landlord checks his watch, looking exceedingly pained to see the seconds slipping away.

"We've been good tenants here for over a decade. There was no need — he must have told you we had a mutual understanding —"

"I have no doubt, but surely you can look around and see that times are changing. We have to keep up to survive, and I have to ask for what the space is worth. Actually, if a luxury label comes along, they'd offer many times that number there, so don't let it be said that I'm not a fair man."

Lucy stares at the letter and the landlord places his hands on the table and pushes his chair back. "I'll expect you to clear out by the end of the month," he says, and Lucy's head snaps around.

The landlord regards the unoccupied tables and his voice turns soft as the ointment Lucy smooths over my cuts when I am careless with the knife. "It's obvious that you can't afford to accept these terms," he says, almost kindly, like putting down a lame horse.

Lucy opens her mouth and closes it and I hear a fragile crack like an egg dropping onto the floor, the sound of her heart breaking. The landlord eases back in his seat to button his jacket and gives her a courteous little nod. I silently urge Lucy's hair to darken and crackle, unnerved by this limp, disheartened version I have not seen before.

In my uneasiness, a voice tells me to stand. Now it is my turn to become her voice, after all the other times she stood up for me; I will stare down the landlord and tell him that we will accept the new rent and we can pay and the shop is not for sale.

The landlord stands instead and his shoulders fill the room and he could reach up and touch the ceiling and bring it all crashing down. He starts to walk away. I look down at the table and pick at a patch of chipped paint and then I hear a chair toppling over — Flora rushing forward with her flimsy apron askew, racing him to the door.

"Where are your manners? Lucy has something to say." She puts her hands on her rounded hips.

Lucy glances at Flora and José, looks at me, and locks her shoulders. "Yes," she says, her voice gathering strength. "Give us more time. We've had an . . . unexpected setback."

The landlord lifts his arms and crosses them behind his head and I stare at the ripe orbs of sweat, tempted to pull his arms down over them.

Lucy takes a step forward. "If you can give us a few more months, we can meet your terms."

128

The landlord is firm. "Property taxes are through the roof. I can't keep absorbing the losses."

"We're talking about *losing our shop,*" Lucy argues. "Give us time."

He taps a finger to his chin and José reaches for my shoulder and none of us breathe.

"Tell you what — since you've been a longtime tenant in good standing, I'll give you one day to think about it. Tomorrow, go through your books. Assess the alternatives. Do what you need to do to let reality sink in. I'll need your decision by Saturday."

He reaches for the doorknob and smiles graciously. "People are always blowing things out of proportion, protesting and pointing fingers, but let it be known — I'm not unsympathetic to your situation."

He leaves us with the letter. Lucy covers her face and says into the silence, "We're going to lose the shop."

At that, I am steamrolled by the enormity of what is happening and it cannot happen, not for any of us, and this is what I know: without a home, things get lost. I grasp at Milton's fur and gasp for breath, and I know that this is the last chance to save my world.

I have one day to find the Book.

On Friday morning, I freshen my oil lamp and put on my black fleece and lace up my high-tops. I fold the one remaining Lost Book flyer into my notebook and slide the notebook into my pocket next to my Metro-Card and an old packet of cashew brittle I unearthed in the back of a drawer. I leave my backpack behind because wearing it will remind people that I am supposed to be in school, and I say good-bye to Milton and he licks me on the nose because everything else is bundled up, and he trots me to the door.

I head toward the bus stop but do not stop there. From a distance, I watch the city bus come and leave, and then I am alone on the sidewalk with people flowing around me from all directions and the day stretches ahead of me like an empty highway, racing into the horizon.

11

I flash the flyer at several passersby but the morning rush hour is not a good time to ask for their attention; they push my arm out of the way or regard the picture with unfocused eyes or try to take it, mistaking it for a handout. I persist anyway because there is no time to waste and no room to fail. I realize that I am not alone when a heavy breathing begins to follow me at knee-level. A soft body bumps against my leg and Milton's brown eyes meet mine and his eyebrows squirm, excited and pleased — *You forgot me. It's a good thing I remembered.*

Actually, I had wanted to leave him behind for Lucy, but when I hold his swinging tail I feel my limbs solidify like bravery. At the end of the day, he'll lead us back; his compass points to home.

I find a spot on the corner by a trash can and Milton settles back onto his haunches and lifts his face toward the thin colorless expanse above. I open my eyes wide, scanning the bustling intersection for signs of the trail a lost thing might leave — a chunky silver-blue thread like an unraveling sweater, or a slick sheen like a passing snail, or the distinct rush of a smell like home.

I don't know where the trail will start or what it will look like until I spot it, and so it helps to have an idea of where to focus. That is why I like to ask questions and gather information, and that is why I made these flyers. But I have yet to find anyone who has seen the Book, who can give me a clue, and so I am faced with the staggering task of having to look everywhere and notice everything at once, the banks and eateries and smoke shops, the rush-hour faces, the fenced triangle of park.

Over there is the coffeehouse where Walter Lavender Sr. had noticed a man crying in the street. You couldn't miss it, Lucy said, and that's what made it horrible, not the grown man sobbing but everyone too uncomfortable to do anything.

Walter Lavender Sr. held out his handkerchief, which had embroidered planes rolling like sea otters across the top. "Can I help?"

The man clutched the handkerchief to his nose and sniffled and shook his head.

"At the least, you look like you could use a hot coffee."

They went into the coffeehouse and as they nursed their drinks, Walter Lavender Sr. learned that the man's mother had died last week, and then the lights in his apartment blew out and he had been sitting in the dark for the past two days. Today he had been going to pick up the death certificate, and when the door of a deli opened and exhaled warm cinnamon onto the sidewalk, it smelled just like the monkey bread his mother was forever pulling out of the oven when he was a kid and now on visits with his own kids — and that was finally what did it.

"One of those things I can help with. I almost became an electrician," said Walter Lavender Sr., and he went to the man's house later that day and fixed the lights.

That night, Lucy had kissed her husband and was grateful her own mother was still alive even if they could not see each other. She told me kindness was like a code Walter Lavender Sr. lived by, ever since his father died and hardly anyone came to the funeral because somehow, as he'd turned, turned, turned through the wheel of his life, the only person who had gotten to know him at all was his son. Standing in the cemetery, Wal-

133

ter Lavender Sr. had seen how his own life would go — just like that, one day here running an electrical shop and the next day gone, like he was never there, never mattered.

When he packed up the few things worth taking from his father's house, he picked up the portrait the mermaid had given to him on the beach, and he wondered who and where she was and if she knew how she had changed his life with that gesture. He was going to college, after all, and after that he would be a pilot, and in that instant he realized that by showing a little kindness to the people he came across, he could make his life a little brighter and it would matter that he was there, everywhere he found himself.

After that, he was never content with looking away and letting it be. He had a fear of living without meaning, Lucy said, and he knew he didn't have forever to make his mark.

Now, as I turn away from the coffeehouse, the street becomes busier and my flyer passes under more eyes. A man wearing a suit coasts by on his skateboard and says, "Nah, dude," and a woman with damp hair and serious eyes asks thoughtful questions and purses her mouth as she tries to remember, and two women jog in place and fawn over Milton and a man puts his head down like walking into a hurricane and a woman trips over the curb and mutters, "I'm fine, I'm fine, no, no," in her haste to escape.

After a while I sit on the curb and watch the traffic light change colors. My eyes ache from searching and not finding any pulse of light or flash of radiance. Classes will have started and Lucy will be pouring coffee and replenishing the croissants and I am out here, wasting the one day that we have left before Lucy has to sign the new lease or make the closure official.

I look at Milton. What if I end up standing here all day with no plan and no leads, failing? I need to be doing something, getting closer, but the more I tell myself this, the more helpless I feel.

In reply, Milton bumps me with his nose and I stand again and hold up the flyer. I try not to think of what will happen if I fail and that becomes all I can think about, and the fear is paralyzing.

I hear the rattle of an approaching shopping cart. Mechanically, I raise my flyer and turn to see a swaying mountain of white and blue trash bags stuffed full of cans, piled two and three bags deep on all sides, and the mountain keeps veering to the right as it comes closer.

I crouch to scrutinize the bottom of the cart, wondering if a wheel is stuck, and that is how I spot the sparking underneath the back right wheel, which is indeed broken, blue-white light zinging every which way like shooting stars. At the sight of it a spray of light ignites in me too, and my chest swells with pictures of the shop filled with customers and the Book in its case and I could cry out because the shop could be safe and there, there — a sign, at last, to go by!

The cart stops in front of the trash can and an elderly Chinese woman inches out, not noticing how her pant leg glows briefly where sparks land. She cuts a diminutive figure next to the towering piles and I bound toward her with my flyer outstretched, feeling like I am flying now that I have picked up the trail.

She leans into the trash can and I throw myself at it, folding my torso over the edge, silently trying to catch her attention. Her hands close around a half-full bottle of water and her nails are clipped short except on her pinkie, where the nail has grown into a talon, and when she straightens, she looks surprised to see me flapping around on the other side of the trash can.

She wiggles the bottle and breaks into a smile that settles deep into the lines connecting her eyes and nose and mouth. She is wearing what looks like a little girl's pink shirt with flowers stitched along the scoop neck and a few of the flowers have gone missing, and her shoes — they are high-tops like mine but in blue, and laced tight so that the sides touch.

"One more, one more," she chuckles, and I take a deep breath and prepare to ask her about the Book and then, without warning, she buckles and my questions vanish and her legs twist under her like they have turned to pipe cleaners, and she squeezes her eyes shut and her gapped grin is gone.

"My leg," she wails with a yelping edge of pain, and the bottle rolls away and into the path of a rushing taxi.

I duck under her arm and help her hobble into the empty doorway of what used to be a hole-in-the-wall pizza joint. She puts a hand on the wall and slides down with her leg stretched in front of her, and she leans her head back and closes her eyes again with a grimace. I nudge Milton to her side and shove the cart next to her and dash across the street to the pharmacy.

When I return, her eyes are open and she is rubbing her leg with one hand and

137

scratching Milton with the other. I twist the cap on the bottle of water until it cracks, and then I hand the bottle to her. She cackles with appreciation, nodding her head and sipping. She pats her leg and lets it rest, and she heaves a sigh.

"Leg not so good now. Sometime, work too hard and stop working, feet bleed. Collect all night, before sun up, go to bar at closing time and they put out bin filled with bottle." She makes a face and says wryly, "A lot exercise."

We grin at each other and I ask her where she lives by pretending to sleep on a pillow of my hands.

"My home in Chinatown near bottle machine, can walk there, not too far. But you are right, that is only place I sleep. Home very far, very far. Home in China, where daughter is. But I stay here, make bottle money, send bottle money home to help her. Or home with husband, but he die. So I go now, bye-bye."

I offer a hand to pull her up and her hand is tough and compact in mine and she tests her leg and limps toward the cart and I follow her, eyeing the piles of bags and longing to sift through the cans to find the Book.

I hold out the flyer as she faces forward and grips the cart handle, and I ask her if she has seen the Book but she only grunts in response, preoccupied with the task of restarting the cart, and she continues leaning her weight into the handle and the cart is not budging.

She grunts again and applies more force to the handle, and the imposing bulk of the stack rises above her, swaying to the right, and despite the toughness of her hands she looks so small and insignificant and I focus on repeating the question but my throat clogs with worry.

I clear it, reminding myself that she knows where she is going and it's not too far away — but at the same time China is on another continent and her husband is gone, and she can't travel into the future or the past so she will never make it home, especially when her legs are starting to fail her.

That makes me afraid, how easily she can become lost, and I see her throwing her slight weight forward and the cart pitching over onto its side and taking her down with it, and her ankle trapped underneath and cans rolling haphazardly into the gutter and the blue of her high-tops fading to gray like the street, and it is impossible for me to blink that image away and forget.

So I place one hand on the handle and she bows her head and says, "Unh," and shuffles to the side, and I will go with her, then, to make sure she reaches the place where she sleeps, and when we are there I can ask her my questions and find the Book, because the sign is pointing to her and as long as I go with her I will find my answers.

Together we heave and the broken wheel screeches against the sidewalk and the cart slides forward, and with me on the right and Milton trailing, we travel east into the sun.

Once the cart is rattling merrily along, blue-white sparks flaring as they touch down on my shoelaces, I let go, pull out my notebook, and scribble, MANY MILES, FORGOTTEN ROAD; BUT HOMEWARD-BOUND, WITH SPIRIT.

The cart slows and lists toward me and I put my notebook away and restore my grip on the handle. Up close, I see other items hidden between the bags of cans — a flashlight, a glove with a hole in the tip of the second finger, a plastic watch, a doll made out of rags with a red yarn mouth — but no Book, not yet.

"I make for my daughter many year ago," she says, squeezing the doll's protruding foot. "Carry with me when look for bottle, can look for bottle longer."

We walk under a scaffolding that smells

140

like urine and the clatter of the cart and Milton's panting fills the tunnel. A mother and her daughter are entering on the other side and as we pass the mother quickens her step and draws her daughter in and whispers, "Not too close," and her whisper echoes. I give her a look that she does not see and they are gone by the time I have marshaled a series of words and they wither away on the back of my tongue, a stinging reminder.

"You quiet, like me when I first come with husband," the can collector muses. "Not know English, embarrass to talk. Make life very hard. First day go out and do chore, get lost. Walk for hour but not find way back, still too embarrass to talk in bad English. Make you alone, because have no friend here, miss family and friend too far away, over many ocean."

That strikes me as a sad life indeed; I have Lucy and Milton and when I am not in school I have the shop and the people who work in it and visit it, and I have my finding and the people who have lost something, and that is enough for me.

"Not only no friend — if I don't talk, I don't make living. Earn money that time is hard to do. When husband and I come here, we come with nothing, we hold hand and

141

have each other. Then we start business — wash clothes. One day, customer take dry clean and will not pay. Ohh, I am so angry. He leave, I follow. I am so angry I begin to talk, and when I start, no stop! Practice more, English better. Some good person see you try, they try hard, too. Who care if one or two person laugh, no big deal. Who can tell you what matter, you keep try and do for yourself, that is what matter. Maybe you laugh with them and share joke."

Speaking is hard for her like it is for me, although in a different way because for her it is a different language. I think about how when I used to try, the confusion or disinterest or casual cruelty reminded me that my island was even farther away than I imagined. My attempts yielded nothing except fatigue from the effort, and no one cared about effort after all; it was just proof to me that I did not belong and was not there.

But the can collector is also transparent, invisible behind a cart, and yet she is still trying and pressing forward with small brisk steps and speaking the words she can. This time, today, I am listening, but there are other times and days when no one is listening and she practices and speaks anyway. Is there a purpose simply because these words and small triumphs belong to her? Maybe her small battles and unheard words did not become meaningless when they were batted aside by everyone else, because now when she speaks, imperfectly and on any day, she can test the strength of her edges and remember the many miles she has journeyed, the vast distance she has come.

My jaw aches to think about it, and I wonder how far I could have gone had I not fallen silent and stood still.

Two other people are in line at the recycling machine, which is behind a grocery store in Chinatown where they keep the Dumpsters.

"My place is right there. You go-go," she says, and I decline and stay because I need to ask her about the Book.

We maneuver the cart to the back of the line and the can collector peruses the items on offer in the vending machines as we pass.

"Sometime my husband surprise me with Caravelle bar at dinner. Even though not much money, he know I like the taste. Taste good, very sweet. After husband pass, shop close — cannot run it just me. Candy bar disappear from machine. I cannot find in store, either. You look — not here, right?"

I shake my head to say that I can't find a Caravelle bar in the machine, either, and I hand her my flyer and ask her if she can do the same and take a look. She leans in, blinking rapidly as if clearing her vision, and we look down at the rendering of the Book and the anticipation takes on a metallic tang in my mouth.

"This your book?" she asks, stepping up to the bottle machine and pushing a button, and I nod vigorously like shaking a soda, the contents of my head fizzing. "I find at beginning of week, in trash can when look for bottle. The one from before, where you and I meet."

The sounds and movements around me fade out and the world slows to white. I clap both hands over my mouth, fumbling for words that are big enough to contain this moment of finding, and my mind runs in circles and plows through all of them. How did the Book end up in that trash can on the corner of a street? If someone had taken the trouble to steal it they wouldn't throw it away, so perhaps it was an accident after all and it does not matter anymore now that the Book is found.

"I pick up to give to old lady next door. As gift," she continues, untying a trash bag and feeding bottles into the mouth of the machine. "But have no more, no more. Bad man, he steal my bottle, my cart, he run

144

away. I see him again but no good, bottle gone, only cart left, he bang into tree and wheel break."

I realize that the clue meant the Book was here on its journey to becoming lost, not that it is here now, and it is not the end of the trail as I thought, but just the start.

The can collector closes and opens her eyes and says, "I see this book very important book to you. I am sorry. There is one thing. Something that fall out of book, stick to cart, so maybe you want."

She finishes depositing and in exchange the payment machine churns and ejects a single twenty-dollar bill. She takes it and lines up the ends, folds it carefully in half.

"I am Lan. You come with me?"

Lan lives near the grocery store in a housing block with a few narrow windows striped with iron bars like a prison.

"Watch, light here no working."

We climb up the dark stairwell and the stairs creak under our feet, and by the third flight of stairs Lan's breath sounds raspy and I wonder about her leg and offer her my arm. She waves me ahead and pauses to rest against the rail. Milton looks back at her with his ears perked and when she does not continue climbing, he waddles down the steps and stands next to her and barks like cheering her on.

"Yes, yes, one more," she tells him, and hauls herself up the last flight of stairs. She reaches the hallway and points to the right.

"First thing, say good morning to old lady next door," she says, bobbing her head and grinning. "She come from Russia. Not speak much English but I can see, must have many story to tell, when young, must be beautiful. Now she have many beautiful hat. She has good hat, I like her hat, but she very thin. I think she need protein. I save sunflower seed and give to her in morning. Do for close to twenty year now. Protein! Crack the seed, also give you something to do in day."

She knocks and the door opens immediately with a wheeze, and it is a woman in a wheelchair with toothpick legs. She sees me and Milton and then she sees Lan and she breaks into a toothless grin. Almost self-consciously, she touches the wide brim of her hat, which is velvet and purple and tilted to one side, with a spray of purple flowers over her ear.

"That is *splendid* hat," Lan says.

The woman gives her hat a final pat and cups her hands together and lays them on her lap, and Lan puts her hand in her pocket and opens the bottom of her fist so that the handful of sunflower seeds trickles out into the woman's hands. The woman closes her hands over the sunflower seeds and Lan squeezes her shoulder. They don't exchange words and I'm not sure how it happened but however they managed it, that single thread has worked to keep them together all this time.

Lan unlocks the next door over and steps inside and sighs like letting the air out of a tire. She waits for me to follow and turns on a lamp. Her apartment is shaped like an I. At one end is a two-burner stove with a stool next to it, and a discolored refrigerator and a television with bent antennae sitting on an upturned cardboard box. She has arranged a strand of artificial flowers on top of the television. At the other end is her bedroom, a mattress on the floor and a tall vase in the corner, and the vase could be out of place but it is made all the more beautiful by the lived-in simplicity around it.

Milton is not sure where to put himself and after banging around the kitchen for a while he squeezes ahead and curls up by the bed. I concentrate on making out the details of the vase, clay painted with blue dragons and blue flowers, and the dragon eyes are incandescent with mother-of-pearl inlays. Lan sits on the stool and unlaces her high-tops and slips into sandals with buckles that are stretched out of shape, and I raise my hand as if to touch the vase even though I am too far away.

"You want come look," she says, walking over to the vase, and I follow. It reaches my waist and the top is sealed, and I bring my face closer to look into a dragon eye.

"Use jug to make *jiang.* Paste made of soybean. I eat all day when I am young girl. Now I make one time per year in spring, take one year to make. That way, taste better." Lan sits on the bed and kicks her feet out of her sandals and rubs her leg.

"My mama teach me right way to make. Need patience." She closes her eyes and says in a placid voice for reciting, "Take soybean and boil. Cook in slow pot of water for whole day. Sit on floor and pound bean until bean turn to mushy paste."

With her eyes still closed, she mashes the air with an imaginary pestle. "Shape paste into square. Dry in sun like brick. Wrap in paper and tie with string. Hang on wall for eight week. Unwrap and put in jug. Mix with liquid, put in salt and season. Open lid and stir every day for many more month." She stirs and snores and taps her foot.

"When finish, can eat with lettuce leaf, with rice, with onion." She pretends to crunch on an onion or a lettuce wrap. "Stinky for you, but for me, give me some taste like home. Important to me like I see book to you. Wait here."

She leans over the bed and rifles through a stack of papers and bills. It's making my jaw ache again, thinking of her year of unknowing, leaves crisping as winter crept closer and spread its slow burn, and rain and snow and gasping cold until spring sprouted up again.

I look to Milton imploringly and he looks back at me, and his eyebrows move as he reads my thoughts. If something goes wrong with Lan's *jiang*-making, too much oxygen or not enough sun or stirring and the pungent flavor takes on a few sour notes, then it will all be wasted, that year and that mother-of-pearl vase and the effort and hope fermenting inside it. But her hands are tough as leather, and she would pick up the pestle and try again.

I had not been able to do the same. There was no point in trying or thinking that my efforts to communicate could produce something meaningful, when I know by now what would happen every time — I would find nothing but a stinking mess in the end, and it wouldn't taste anything like home.

Suddenly, all I want is to go back to the shop and shape croissants with Lucy and forget. If this was any other case, I could go back to the shop right now and know that I could keep searching later, for as long as it took to find the lost thing, because I do not close a case without seeing it through to the end. There is no giving up on a lost thing, even if it has been twelve going on thirteen years, and even in the cases where I find that the lost thing is gone, the owner is able to move on after getting the closure.

But with this case I cannot go back yet and even worse, I could search all day and all night and still not find the Book. I have never searched for that long at once before, and the more I speak without resting the more exhausted I become and the harder it is to talk. The shop has never seemed farther away. I wish the Book was safely in its case. There was no wondering then; the Book in its case meant a world suffused in magic and certainty and a place to belong.

How long will I have to be away from the shop and how far will I have to go, and what if I tire out and can't concentrate enough to say the words I need to, and what if I fail and it is all for nothing?

I do not have much time. Perhaps I should

rush back to school before they realize I am missing. The situation will snowball once that happens, the school notifying Lucy and Lucy notifying the police and the police launching a net for their own search. I do not know if I am brave enough for all of that.

Milton yawns wide and bored as a lion. I touch my nose to his and search the brown pools of his eyes. They are warm and un-complicated, and they see to the heart of the matter and remind me, *See? Easy.*

He looks away to see why Lan is still rum-maging through her papers. With the Book gone, I have to be brave enough; there is no other choice. If I go back empty-handed everyone will be disappointed — Lucy and Flora and José and Mrs. Ida Bonnet and anyone else who relies on the shop in one way or another, who has woven it into their life. Unlike my other cases, there will be no comfort in the knowing this time, just Flora with her empty cupboards, clipping coupons against the faded rose wallpaper of her home, and Junior's tumor ripening like a tomato on the vine and José not bothering to hide his teeth because there will be no need for smiling anymore, and I will know that I could have changed everything.

I think of Lan, and her courage reminds

me to find my own. I have to see this through to the end, and when the day has spun away we will see where things have landed and go from there.

She sits up now, holding a yellowed piece of paper with ragged edges. She turns it around so that I can see the illustration — grasping walls like a forest of weeping woody trees, twisting toward a girl lying limp on the floor, her dress and her hair fanned out around her, stark haloes of light in a grieving room.

It is a page of the Book.

Stunned, I take the page and it adheres to my hand with a faint static electricity like it has tumbled through the dryer, the soft persistent cling of warmth and comfort, and I peel it away from my palm.

"I think now is bedtime for this old lady." She wraps one of my hands in both of hers and then she wraps a blanket around her shoulders and yawns. Milton licks her face and she pushes him away lightly and says, "Yes, I rest a bit, get up later." He comes back and licks her again for encouragement and she cackles. "Yes, yes, nag dog. Soon, soon."

I stop on my way out and take a moment to concentrate. "Where did you see the man last?"

"See him every day. I look for bottle, he camp outside. Essex near subway."

Milton barks and she echoes him with a faint, "Wong wong," and turns to me. "You look for thief? For book?"

I nod and she says, "When on journey, you remember. You start, you keep going, you make sunflower seed friend."

That is what matters. I still don't know what lies ahead and maybe I will fail, but my mind is lucid and my movements too, and my fear is no longer so paralyzing. My newfound courage is frail, still taking root, but I have started, and now I set off for the F train to see what I can find next.

12

We get off the train at Essex-Delancey and emerge from the station and the bottle thief is camped out right there, shoving a box of crackers under one of his bags. He has sharp cheekbones and skinny legs folded into a pretzel, and a wooden shark's tooth spikes one earlobe and a helmet of sticky curls hugs his head. His sleeping bag is balled up next to him and his sign says: Free!! Hit me with a quarter.

I fish out a quarter and fling it at him for stealing bottles and books that are not his, and I am rewarded with a sharp plink off his forehead.

"Heyyy, angry little man," the bottle thief says, rubbing his head. "Extra dollar for leaving a mark."

I cross my arms and brace my tongue. "Pole —" My tongue unfurls and I shake my flyer in his face instead.

"Who's Pole? Name's Nico," the bottle

thief says. He settles back into his smelly bags like they are his throne. "Yeah, I've seen it. It's got some depressing fairy tale, cool drawings, right? Found it in a shopping cart."

I know he stole it from a stolen shopping cart, and so he is lying and that makes my cheeks warm with anger. You stole it, I snap, but it comes out scrambled and runny.

"Speak up and talk proper, little man," Nico says. I flush but then I think of Lan limping along in the night, gathering bottles only to have them seized, and I force myself to stand taller and cross my arms so that I feel like Lucy, and that helps. I imagine the fierce tone she would use. "Took. Book. Took can cart."

He pales and struggles to sit upright. "How'd you know about that?"

He grimaces like I have hit him and looks at the ground by my feet. His breath whistles past clenched teeth. I uncross my arms and wait for him to gather himself, and when he does I hand him the flyer.

He studies it and takes a swig of beer and drags a hand across his mouth. "You need to chill out. Your book's lost? Get over it. I'll tell ya something, everything you have's going to be taken away at some point."

As he talks, I skim my eyes over his pile of

155

bags. He took the Book, so where is it now? I take a breath and say, clearly, "Where is it?"

"Some guy has it." He finishes the beer and crushes the can against his kneecap.

What guy? Why? What did he look like? Where did he go? I focus my mind and flex my jaw and Nico bounds, sprightly, across the gaps of my silence.

"I don't need you thinking I'm some thievin' deadbeat. I was a hard worker, man — worked my way up from shit-scrubber to assistant stage manager. Those bottles I took — I *needed* the money. More than canner lady. Get it?" His face is tense, his voice forceful.

I stare at him and his eyes bore into mine, bent on making me understand, and I can't understand and my head moves left, right, left.

"No?" The tension drains from his face. "You gotta understand — you gotta know I got nothing. No home to go to and nobody to love me and — and —"

He breaks off and scuttles back, away from me, and he wraps his arms around himself and starts to rock, and I reach out and suddenly Milton is there, nudging his arm, and his rocking pauses long enough for Milton to lie down and put his head on Nico's knee.

Nico's arms loosen in surprise. Milton crawls forward and settles in his lap and blinks coolly into the distance. Nico untangles his arms and strokes Milton's back and the weight is like an anchor, the warm mass a blanket of security. Once Milton senses that Nico is restored to an even keel, he gets up and plods back to me and sits against my leg. He looks up at me and I stare at him and he tilts his head — *What?* — and then Nico says, "Wait — don't leave me, you gotta listen — here, sit here, cardboard's new."

He looks morose and gaunt now, starved for conversation, and besides, I need to get a closer look at the pile of bags. I sigh and take a seat, tightening my nostrils and breathing through my mouth and surreptitiously patting around for the Book. Milton sniffs the ground and makes three circles and curls up into a big ball at my side.

"I used to think — man, I was doing all right for myself. I was really doing it, taking care of my little brother and my deadbeat parents, making a life for us — got a job, a girlfriend, a roof. Then I lose my brother. Already lost Grampy. Get back one day from the theater and see my parents found the sock, took off with my savings. Girlfriend takes off. Lose my job. Well, shit. Lose the roof. Lose everything. How many times can a guy get knocked down?"

The words pour out of him like they have been welling up, trapped, with nowhere to go. Has he been here all this time with his eyes bloodshot and darting, sleepless, restless, waiting for someone — anyone — to stop and listen to his story?

It can be hard to see the important parts of your own story. It helps when someone listens and can see those parts for you, and in Nico's story I see that he hasn't actually lost everything. Whatever it is that keeps him getting up and coming here — that is *some*thing, and as long as he has it, then he hasn't reached the end, where everything is lost.

Hope, Milton says plainly, standing and stretching his back legs.

The ground rumbles, a subway train pulling into the station, and Nico perks up, holding his sign aloft. Some of the exiting people read his sign and their mouths twitch, but most don't see him. I write, FREEDOM IN CONVENIENT BLINDNESS, and a group of teenagers throw an apple core at him.

"Quarters, you Neanderthals. This is not a — *coin,* it's a fruit," Nico admonishes, lobbing the apple core at their retreating backs. He puts the sign down and says, "You still think I was wrong. You don't get it. Gave her the cart back, didn't I?"

I raise my eyebrows and my head is shaking again because the cart was empty when Lan got it back, and I do not know what forces drive him and maybe they rise up towering and immovable like the landlord, but he did not have to empty the cart and steal her bottles and that is why he is still a thief.

"You gotta see I had no choice," Nico protests, pulling himself onto his elbows in agitation. "Been to every store from here to Chinatown and no job in the world will take me smelling like this, ya know." He raises an arm and I am surprised by my agility as I bend as far away from his armpit as possible.

He tucks his arm back down, resting his hands on his knees and letting them hang. He watches me intently and waits for me to free him from what he did, and finally I shrug to say that I understand even if I do not agree.

"You got it," he bursts. "It was really too bad. It's been on my mind, but now ya know. Wasn't how it looked." He exhales for a long moment. "Although shoulda known there was no point trying. Got laughed out

159

of every shitty hotel. Thirty bucks can't even get a guy a quick hop in the shower. Just a date with my old buddy Jim."

His sleeve has ridden up and I can see the parched white knob of his wrist bone. He hangs his head between his knees like looking into a well and seeing the bottom all dried out, and now he really looks like a man who has lost everything.

"What I wouldn't give to be behind that stage again," he sighs. Memories foam at the edge of his irises. "The lights — the music — the acts, the revelry, the spectacle . . . ."

His stomach gurgles and he shushes it like a fussy baby, patting and crooning and reassuring. It reminds me that I haven't eaten, either, and I take the brittle out of my pocket and break it in two and offer him one of the halves. He takes it and below us another subway arrives, and he balances the slab of brittle on his lap and swings his sign up like a sword and looses his battle cry.

"Hit me," he bellows. "Your quarters, your dimes, your nickels. *Ow* — not in the eye, moron."

He shakes a few coins out of the folds of his jacket and rolls forward to collect the coins on the sidewalk and he stacks them by size, quarters to dimes, and slides them into his pocket. This done, he cocks his head and bites into the brittle with his molars.

"I'll say — little man — wow —" He crunches away, crumbs sprinkling his chin, each crunch escalating in vigor.

"This stuff is magical, magic on my tongue. Magic in my arms and legs," and he thumps his chest instead. "Where's it from?"

I point at the flyer.

"This your shop? Right on, right on, my man, that's some real magical crunchy shit."

I do not respond and I am thinking about the brittle Lucy makes now and how it isn't the same and soon there might be no brittle at all. I crouch over, caving a little around the hollow in my chest, unable to ask my next question.

"Hey, hey, what'd I say? You still salty about that book? Aw, man, like I said, some other guy's had it for a few days now. Traded it for his hamburger — that's what he wanted and I felt bad for him. So sue me, I got nothing."

That's something, and I open my mouth to ask him why the man wanted the Book and what he looked like but the ground trembles and Nico pushes his sign into my lap as a new crop of riders is expelled from the bowels of the subway system with a steamy sigh of body musk and eye-watering florals.

He flutters his hands at me, Go on, go on, like a proud parent before the talent show, and I roll my eyes and give the sign a dejected flop that proves surprisingly effective. When the sidewalk clears, I have collected a small mountain of coins and a dollar bill, and a Kaiser roll and a smashed snack cake and a half cup of raspberry smoothie.

"You're the secret!" Nico says, looking only a little offended. "You gotta stay for a while. Look pitiful."

Nico must have noticed more than what he has told me, other clues that might show me where to look next. Carefully, I ask him what else he remembers, and he says, "What *what*?" and I focus and tighten my diaphragm and increase the flow of my breath so that I can ask, louder, "What else do you remember?"

He sticks his hand out. "Deal," he says. "Stay here and hold my sign and I'll tell ya."

I shake his hand. "What did he look like?"

"No pinkies. Like he'd gone and chopped them both off! Guy couldn't even hold on to his food bag with one hand, for cryin' out loud — he had it crushed up between both hands."

My eyes widen and I lean forward so I don't miss anything he is saying, and he pauses dramatically and I can see how pleased he is to have an audience. He nudges my elbow and I flop the sign about, prompting a fresh drizzle of coins and a can of chips, and a blue sweater with buttons and a miniature box of wheat cereal and the last pair of dress socks in a drugstore pack of three.

"You are a little man of few words," Nico observes. "But you look like you could have lots to say. Why so quiet? Stop staring at me and listening and taking notes, it's freaky."

I frown and hide my notebook. I have spent too long here, where the Book is not, and I plan how to work around Nico's hunger for conversation and extract the rest of the information I need about the man with no pinkies.

"Come on, I didn't mean it like that, don't get all butt-hurt. Here, let's try this — chill out, it's not going to hurt. So, see, as assistant stage manager — *former* assistant — I got to call out cues, Stand by!, Go!, that kind of thing. When someone's daydreaming or being slow to remember their lines or get to their marks, I help them out by mooing. Really, it's motivating. A good proper

163

moo, like so —" Nico leans back and tucks his chin in and takes a deep breath and hurls himself forward into a "MOOOOOOOO!"

I nearly jump out of my skin, and Milton springs to his feet and barks and all down the street startled faces swivel around. Nico waves at his audience and turns to me and says, "Your turn," and I think, Not in a million years. Not ever again.

When I messed up my words, noises like that came out instead and Beaver made fun of me or teachers were impatient or the little boy in the shopping cart dropped an artichoke and said, "What's he *doing*?" I did not have a voice — it was a cow mooing and a duck quacking and a seal barking, and it was an embarrassment.

I examine Milton's fur where it bristles around the neck. Nico wrenches himself back and emits another deafening moo and I nearly pull out a handful of golden fur as Milton torpedoes into Nico's side and sniffs his arms and legs and face frantically. Nico raises an eyebrow at me and gears up for another round, sucking air through his nose, and before an innocent passerby bursts an eardrum or Milton drives himself insane, before I know it, my mouth has formed an O and a staccato puff of air and sound.

"That was the wimpiest sound. How is that going to inspire anybody? Observe, again, like so —" He rears back, nostrils flared, and thrusts his neck forward, and out comes another sidewalk-shaking, bark-inducing moo.

"Together now," he says, leaning back again, and when he says it like that it makes me think that this is different since we are both making the noise and besides, his will be loud enough to cover up mine, and I mimic him and as we're leaning he catches my eye and I am struck by an urge to laugh at his strained purple face, but then he is taking a pull of air so I widen my nostrils and breathe deep and —

"MOOOOOOOOOOO!"

I catch my breath. We were so loud that ghostly moos ricochet off the buildings and that is when I realize that the only moo echoing down the street is mine.

Nico makes a fist and bumps it against mine. "All you, my little man."

I gape at Milton and my eyes feel like they are growing out of my head. Is that what I sound like? That voice came from me and it was mine and it must have been there the whole time, and I have never heard my voice so powerful.

Suddenly exhilarated, I rock back and

165

inhale and "MOOOOOOOOOOOOOOO!" until every drop of breath has dried up and my throat is raw and buzzing.

A different moo comes from farther up the street, a distant reply. I squint and see two men with highlighter vests and helmets, and they are broad and round. One of them has a foot hiked up on a crate and his hands cupped in a tunnel around his mouth, and even though I hadn't said a single word, had not done anything but moo into the wind, it hits me and I am astounded — electrified — they *heard* me.

It could not be more basic. They heard someone and they understood and they responded. A conversation without words, just the noise of an unbridled feeling, and did that mean I had a voice, too, one I did not need to be embarrassed of? Could I be bold enough to be heard, even when my words came out wrong? A pounding grows strong in my ears and I inhale again — soaring and wheeling and inhaling the dizzying scent of escape.

A gaggle of kids with matching purple T-shirts topple out of the subway, corralled by adults in bigger versions of the purple T-shirts, and I moo at them. They hear me; they shriek and dissolve into giggles and soon I am giggling with them, and I do not

166

think the novelty of this feeling will ever grow old, an unseen connection strong and fragile as the bindings of a book you could read again and again. So this is what the view is like from inside the pages, inside the story, and could there be any better angle to observe from?

"Moo," they sing. "Moo, moo, moo."

I rock back again and Nico grabs my arm and says, "Easy there. Don't want a passed-out little man, not good for business."

The hammering purr of an engine drowns out my response, and I look to see an aluminum food cart pulling up at the curb. I don't mind; now that I know that the Moo is there I can always find it again. The bags sink lower as Nico settles in and I prod him in the side to remind him that he still has questions to answer.

Too loud, he mouths, and I shake my head emphatically and he crosses his arms behind his head and starts to doze, and a burst of movement captures my attention, a dart of red — a man in a red sweatshirt hopping out of the food cart.

He surveys the street and his eyes take on a restless, feverish quality, and they wouldn't miss a man with no pinkies if he walked past. I roll to my feet, to see what the food cart man knows.

13

"No tickets today, no asshole neighbors. No tickets today, no asshole neighbors," the food cart man repeats, and it could be a command or a prayer or a mantra. He pulls on a mustard-yellow apron and notices me approaching. "Bad luck spell," he explains. He goes around the back of the cart and slides the window open.

"Open for business," he says, setting his forearms on the counter. A neon strip of light frames the window and flashes in hyperactive bursts. "What can I get you? Lamb and rice? Chicken gyro?"

I tuck my chin down and shake my head. He leans farther out the window to see if anyone else is coming and I sidestep to stay in his line of sight. I hold the flyer out and his lips frame the words, Lost Leather Book.

"I haven't seen it. This is a new spot for me, so I don't know much about what goes on in the neighborhood. You three are from

168

around here —" He points a finger at me and makes a circle to include Milton and Nico slumbering behind me, and there is a tattoo on the inside of his wrist, a cylinder of meat roasting on a spit. "What can you tell me? Is this a good spot to sell good food?"

I look around us and he follows my gaze. "You're right, there are a lot of bars. That says to me, this could be a party crowd, relaxed residents. That's what I'm looking for. Or else they get to complaining — you know, the noise, the smell. You know what, I have a good feeling about this spot," he decides. He reaches out the window to place a speaker on the counter. The music is frothy pop for parties and shouting along, and he twists the volume knob and the meat tattoo rotates on its spit.

I return to the cardboard carpet and nudge Nico and ask him where the man with no pinkies was going but all he does is mumble. I regard him for a minute, and then I turn sideways and rest my head on Milton's back and he lifts an ear to listen. Nico hasn't lost a particular treasured thing and he isn't looking for anything, so what can my rules and I do when what's lost isn't a thing that belongs to him . . . but *him*?

Nico lost so much along the way that I

don't think it felt like much when he became lost too. I picture the wrist bone jutting out of his sleeve and maybe what he needs is a little hope where he's run dry, and for that, I can do the finding.

I have an idea for how to help him before I go. I peel the lid off the smoothie and pour it out on the sidewalk in front of Milton, who drools and bats the raspberry hill between his paws and slurps it up. As he laps at the smoothie, I take the pen out of my notebook and write on the back of the sign, BATH, and it takes a long time and my hand aches and the letters are huge but at least they can be recognized.

I prop the sign up next to Milton's red raspberry paws and the food cart man notices and says, "I have a towel for you."

He disappears into the cart and a striped dish towel flies out the window and drapes on Milton's head. I slide the towel off Milton and fold it into a square, and the food cart man reappears beside his cart holding a steaming tin. I think about saying, Thank you for the towel, and I pause to gather the words in my head and he waves them off and shovels rice into his mouth without taking his eyes off the street.

I take out my notebook and watch him for a moment — IN WAIT FOR PASSING

GOLDFISH.

He notices me looking and says, "You look hungry," and I shake my head and look away. His chewing slows and I shake my head again and he plunks the tin down on the ground in front of me. "I can't eat it all," he insists.

I spear a piece of browned meat with the plastic fork and he says, "Secret spice blend. High-quality meat." I take one bite and my mouth floods and I realize I am hungry after all and take another bite.

"Have some white sauce," he advises, and I drag a forkful of chicken through the white sauce.

"What do you think? The hot, delicious taste of money," he says. I hand the tin back to him and he scrapes together the last of the rice and meat and his wrist picks up a smear of white sauce.

"Don't go around telling people about this — I can't build a street meat empire by giving away my combos for free," he says around a mouthful of food. "But I'll work around the clock to make it happen. Once business is booming, I'm going to the Bahamas. It would be my first vacation in years. I'm going to be a rich man." He licks the white sauce off his meat tattoo.

Years is a long time to work without resting. Every June, Lucy and I take the Metro North from Grand Central to a town sixty miles north of the city. We stay at a bed-and-breakfast surrounded by woods, and the owner makes quiche for breakfast and during the midday lull he draws intricate to-scale pictures of pyramids and coliseums for history books and documentaries. In the mornings before breakfast, I follow the trail down to the Hudson River and if it is early enough, I see herds of short-tail deer, and I roll up my cuffs and stand ankle-deep in the water and out there in the early-morning calm, my silence is, for once, the thing that connects me.

The food cart man spots a woman making her way up the street and retreats back inside. He flips a pile of meat and the fat sizzles, and he cranks up the dance music and the light strip whirls with lollipop colors.

The woman digs a travel-sized bottle of shampoo out of her gym tote and hands it to me, and I stand it on top of the towel. The lights and sounds of the cart do their job, catching her attention and reeling her in, and she orders a bottle of iced tea. After the towel and shampoo, I am given a plastic serving of flea treatment that is nice to have but not necessary for either Milton or Nico, and the lady who gives it to me mentions that there is a self-serve dog wash eight minutes away that she takes Sir Kippleton to sometimes for $1.25 per minute. The lady and Sir Kippleton have the same curly poof of brown hair. She makes a kissing sound and coaxes Sir Kippleton away from Milton.

I elbow Nico and this time he swallows a snore and sputters awake.

"Wall," I announce over his sputtering. I imagine gargling water to remind myself and repeat, "Walk."

"Look here, this is my spot. Why I gotta leave my spot? It's my spot," Nico protests. I cross my arms and stare at him and let the silence seep in.

"Fine! Fine, you bossy little man. My ass is sore from all this sitting around anyway."

Pouting, he gathers his things and shakes out his sleeping bag and I goggle at the crumbs and wrappers and smashed leaves and twigs that rain down — every piece glowing, a shower of silver light, and he doesn't notice the page of yellowed paper that falls out too.

He busies himself tying his bags to a knapsack but I am transfixed by the fallen page, and the nest of debris around it shimmers with raindrop-lights.

I pick up the page and there is a howl of wintry wind, hard and swift as a punch to the lungs, and the edges of the page flap madly like hummingbird wings, sending me spinning back into Lucy's story, and I see her waking that night in January, blinking sleepily at the falling snow, touching a hand to the dark fogged glass.

The wind dies down and I smooth my fist across the fourth page of the Book, circular motions like clearing the glass and peering through to the emerging illustration — the girl lifting her arms like wings and the wind descending around her and the cloak of ice melting as it comes down, a lake of water like moonlight.

Nico yanks on the strings of his hoodie and the hood puckers around his face. "This better be good, else you're fired."

Eight minutes later, we stop in front of a gas station with Nico on the left and me in the middle and Milton on his haunches. We watch a neon sign flicker above a building jutting out of the larger car wash. Dog Wash it says, and a flicker later, Do Wash.

The inside smells like damp fur and fishy lemons, and we hear water running in one of the stalls at the far end and a voice saying, "Atta boy, good boy, don't shake, don't shake —"

Milton presses himself into the wall and tries to melt into it and when he doesn't, he issues a command — *No!* I reassure him with a scratch behind the ears.

I present Nico with the travel shampoo and striped dish towel and the $10.55 we have collected, and I hang the blue sweater and socks over one of the stall doors. He stares and comprehension dawns and a small miracle occurs: he has no words.

"I'm telling ya, it's the little silent ones," he finally says to himself with a broken grin and a rueful shake of the head. He folds himself into the stall and the coins go *plunk plunk* and the shower hose hisses and spits and Nico warbles. Milton howls along mournfully, man and dog slogging forward with their funeral dirge, and the voice at the far end snaps, "Good grief."

Steam rises, and it billows out of the stall and envelops me in clouds and the sound of running water, and it's almost like I am back at the shop, standing at the kitchen sink and watching water run over my hands as the dough I've kneaded for phyllo cups rests on the counter. Dough coats my fingers, and I soap up my hands and the dough sloughs off in pasty rolls and clean skin materializes, rosy and energized as a fresh start, and I know how much that fresh start can mean.

Most lost things I find are useful, or valuable, or old. It takes time to attach memories and create shared history, which is why it was an unusual day when a customer came back to the shop to see if he had left his brand-new dress shirt there. He had been unemployed for most of a decade, having made a string of unlucky bets in a declining industry. He was due to start a job at a call center the next day, and to prepare for it, he had bought a shirt.

The lost shirt wasn't in the shop and we moved the search to his apartment and the shirt wasn't in any of the closets or trash cans, either. I met with his wife and the cleaner and the tailor and at that point I suggested he wear one of the other shirts in his newly organized closet, but he wouldn't do it. This was a new chapter, and he wanted to start it as a new person, and he could only do that with his new shirt, which I ended up finding in the briefcase he had packed ahead of time with all of his first-day items, so that he would be ready to go.

Nico can't start fresh with so many weeks of dirt and oil and sweat accumulated and hardened around him like second and third and fourth skins. When it is stripped off and scrubbed away and he feels clean at long last, like something new . . . maybe it will give him the push he needs to find himself.

The water clicks off and the steam-clouds disperse and I look for Nico. His head and shoulders appear above the stall and water sluices down his back and heat rises from his skin. His shoulders bunch like he's bracing for a ghost weight, and he cracks his neck, rolls one shoulder and the other. Abruptly, he straightens and sets his shoulders free.

"Ya know what, little man?"

He towels off, turning pink from the scrape of the towel. "I think —" He changes his mind. "I'll try —" He gives a quick shake of his head and turns to face me. "I got this," he says, and he's clean and dry and I see the beads of hope clinging to his skin like water, irregular, glistening, weightless, and I almost break into applause. He wouldn't like that, though, so I take out my notebook and lean nonchalantly against the wall to write, A DIP IN THE INFINITE WELL, and he throws the sweater over his shoulders.

"Always did my best thinking in the shower," he says, balancing on one foot and pulling on a sock. "So I'm crouched there with the water streaming and I practically

177

fall over, I'm hit by this idea. I gotta do it. You've inspired me, little man."

He flings the stall door wide open and he's still wearing his smudged black jeans but he has the sweater buttoned up and his feet are fresh in their new dress socks.

"You've inspired me," he repeats as we emerge from the dog wash and raise our arms against the runny light of day. "No, really, listen to this. Picture this — Silence Is Golden. You listening? I'm serious, I'm gonna march right in and take my job back, and that's gonna be our next production. We'll have the pounding music, the bass, the flashing lights, and out of nowhere, *boom!*" He explodes his fists and wriggles his fingers and drags out the silence. "They're plunged into total silence, blinded by pure light. It'll be shocking and unsettling and fucking transcendent."

We walk and Nico elaborates on his plan and even his voice has changed, animated, fuller, and now that there is no reason for me to stay, my thoughts turn to my own search. Two pages out of seven and five more that make all the difference, with the possibilities scattered endlessly like stars and the way gone cold if Nico has nothing else to tell me. I shiver and wonder.

We pass Nico's spot and he shrugs off his

178

knapsack and stands over it. The line for the food cart has doubled to four and the food cart man is holding court, slapping balls of rice rapid-fire into a row of tin containers. He leans out to take the next order and sees me.

"What did I tell you?" he says.

Nico nudges his knapsack with his foot and hugs himself. "There's one more thing I thought of in the shower. About that guy with the hamburger. Mr. Needs Pinkies. He was heading home, said your book reminded him of it. Didn't make no sense to me because he was headed to the City Hall subway station, which I never heard of, but hey, what do I know?"

He moos in farewell and I moo back and descend with Milton once more into the subway station.

14

I don't know anything about City Hall station and when I run my fingertip over the subway map, tracing its network of capillaries in primary colors, I find a Brooklyn Bridge–City Hall but City Hall is nowhere to be found, a no-place, a lost place. I consult with the attendant who sits in a glass box across from the turnstiles. Her face is smooth as black coffee and as I approach she leans into a silver microphone. Where is City Hall station? I tell myself. The din of an incoming train engulfs the station and she yells, "What?" into the microphone.

Leaning back and sucking in a breath through my nose, I bellow the words I prepared, "Where is City Hall station?"

"City Hall station," she yells back, except the train has stopped moving and her voice rings in the sudden quiet. She winces and readjusts her volume. "You're here for the tour? You'd better get going, they've been gathered on the platform for a while now. They'll be in the first car."

I approach a turnstile and swipe my Metro-Card — too quickly, in my hurry to catch the train, and the machine beeps twice as I slam into the solid turnstile bar. Frantically, I lean back and swipe the card through another time and the machine beeps twice and I grit my teeth and force myself to swipe a third time, unbearably slowly. The machine burps and lets me pass, and Milton and I make a run for it.

The train dings and the doors begin to slide shut, and the front of the train is too far away, on the other end of the platform, but if I can just get in I can get off at another stop and move to the first car. I wave my arms at the conductor hanging out her window and she points at the still-open doors of her car. I push my legs harder and the doors are just out of reach, they close — they open, and the conductor is saying, "And we're down to the final seconds of the quarter . . . will he make it?" — and I dive forward, I'm slipping in, and Milton bounds in after me and the door closes on his tail.

"Goooooooooal," the conductor belts, her opera voice vast and rich and earthy. She reverts to her normal tone, dusky with a bite. "For the little boy and his dog. Ladies and gentlemen, let's give them a hand."

Milton wags his tail at me and is confused when it doesn't respond, and he thrashes harder.

"Whatever you have hangin' out, pull it in!" the conductor barks, and the door opens a sliver and releases Milton's tail with a final ding of disapproval. Flushed from the dash and the smattering of hand-clapping, I wrap an arm around a pole and drop into an open seat across from the conductor's box. Milton crawls under the bench and rests his head on the floor, pushing his nose through the fence of legs.

I sit and let my shoulders sway with the train as it rattles and picks up speed. There is a small square window in the door of the conductor's box and I can see the bill of the cap she wears backward. It moves to the side.

"That was Broadway-Lafayette," she says over the intercom. "The next stop on this Brooklyn Bridge–bound 6 as in 'Six-pack abdominals' and 'Six feet under,' is Spring Street, where you can spend your money, hunt for celebrities, and feel the art ebbing away. If that sounds appealing, the next stop is for you."

182

People exchange looks with their neighbors and smiles break out across the car like rays of sunlight lancing through the clouds. She is just another voice to them, nameless and faceless, and such is the power of that voice that it has stirred their emotions and found a small place in their memories. I do not know if she grew up catching fireflies in the grass like Lucy or if she skirts high places like me, or the shapes of the people and places and habits that comprise her day and the stories that become her life. But her voice has arms and legs, like it can do things and go places all on its own, and with it she has shared with me something of who she is, and she has made me want to listen. With a pang, I acknowledge that I would be the perfect foil to her — the fearless voice.

The bill dips and stills as she gazes into the space between stations, and I wonder what she looks like, the set of her face as she watches the train burrow deeper into its snug tunnel, a metal worm chomping through damp concrete and earth, blinded by little yellow-white suns wired at ten-foot intervals. Perhaps her expression is meditative as she ruminates over the occasional undershirt or gym sock. Maybe she wonders who consumed the cookies and orange

183

sodas and pistachios and left their shells in heaps next to sections of rail where no one is supposed to be, and then she pulls into the platform and watches the way people come, and then go, and then wait.

I shoot to my feet, unfolding my flyer and steadying myself against the pole, and Milton shakes himself off and braces himself against my other side, in case the pole lets me down. Among all those people, maybe the conductor has seen the man with no pinkies; maybe she saw him tottering for the train with the Book hugged between his hands and she waited an extra beat before shutting the door so that he could slip in.

I inch forward and the train shudders and I balance myself, letting the floor roll under my soles like riding a wave. I knock on the door and she raises a finger and the bill bobs to the left as she announces the next stop.

The doors ding and close — "Toot tooooot," she sings in lusty victory — and when the train moves, I knock again and press the flyer into the window, and I think I can see the smudge of her head through the paper, turning and growing larger as she approaches, and after a moment it turns and shrinks. I remove the flyer from the window and the bill leans to the left.

"We interrupt this train broadcast to bring you this important message. A book has been lost. If you have seen, or know anything about, a *lost leather book,* please come forward. *Pronto.*"

I scan the train for signs and people shuffle a little, glance to the side, to see if the Book has crept among their feet.

"If you know something, don't sit on it like some lazy punk-ass 4 train," the conductor warns. "To encourage compliance, I'll treat you to a little aria called 'Habanera.' You may have heard of it."

The bill wags and the intercom crackles. I find myself on the edge of my seat and I can feel the waiting around me, a collective held breath, and then the conductor begins to sing. Her voice swells with spirited emotion and the bill jabs and feints like a conductor's baton as her passion rises, and my heart beats faster and the train erupts in applause and everyone is beaming. Milton does not even howl and his muzzle trembles.

When the applause tapers off, she jumps back on the intercom and says in her normal voice, "You can return the favor by looking out for this book." The bill turns to the side and I imagine her throwing a wink my way.

"Thank you, ladies and gentlemen. I'm Sally Fields, someday-superstar. Next time

185

you're in Sydney or London with your ticket to *Carmen,* look for my name in lights. You'll say to yourself, Sally Fields? And then you'll know — that's the day I finally got mine. Here we go, this is Canal Street. All you cheap people, get off here. See you at the Palais Garnieeeeer. Next stop is Brooklyn Bridge–City Hall."

The intercom squeals and blinks out, and Milton and I step onto the platform and reenter at the front of the train. There are twenty or so people clumped together in the middle of the car and a man standing in the aisle with a black logoed vest and caterpillar mustache and jolly cheeks, and he has paused in the middle of some kind of speech and everyone is looking at him, waiting for him to resume, and I drop into a seat and slide toward the fringes of the group before anyone can take a rare interest in my presence.

"Now, the station we're about to see has been closed for over half a century — it was incompatible with the new, longer train designs, and you'll see why when we pull in," he says, continuing his introductions without seeing Milton and me slip in.

I keep my expression neutral, leaning over like I belong to the neighboring family carrying matching green whistles, and it is a good thing that people tend to look past me and the tour leader is saying, "You're among the lucky few. It's only accessible a handful of times each year through this tour. If you look inside the pamphlet I handed out on the platform . . ."

Milton meanders away to look for hidden things, sniffing and thwacking knees as he works his way down the aisle. I lean against the back of the seat and close my eyes, and the tour leader starts going through the rules, no littering or leaving anything behind, and photography for personal use is permitted but camera stands are not. The space of the car seems flabby without the conductor's voice stretching it, and it is evident to me that she yearns for a new and bigger stage. Her longing is so different from mine that there should be nothing for me to identify with but I can see how the core is the same, the underlying urge to look, even if it is for different things. I feel a fleeting moment of solidarity as we brush past each other, the voice and I, like lone ships searching in the night.

Milton returns to me and his face scrunches when he buries it in my lap. He peers up at me and the whites show along the bottoms of his eyes. I look back at him and wonder. There are others out there, and how many are they, searching for things that were not owned or advertised in Lost flyers or even known and named? Does that mean that as isolated as I feel, alone on the waters, I only need to cast a light and look around to see that we are all a part of the same ocean, the same story?

Milton sits back and puffs his chest out — *We're on the right track* — panting and squinting like a wind is blowing at him, and I can feel it too. I have two pages in my pocket, and I am getting closer to finding the rest of the Book.

The train accelerates and shudders and the fluorescent lights flicker, stabilizing when the train slows and enters the station.

Finally the voice returns — "Last stop. Ladies and gentlemen, get steppin', get steppin'. I need to get a soda," and the conductor signs off with a final click.

The doors pull apart and because it is the end of the line, I rustle and prepare to de-board along with everyone else. Throats are cleared, spines straightened, legs braced, bulky cameras cradled at the ready.

"Not quite yet," the tour leader says. He hitches up his too-big pants with its hanging key rings and walkie-talkie and regards the group and his gaze falls on me and he dimples.

"For now, picture the year 1904. America is hurtling forward into the new century — to the tune of Joplin's 'Maple Leaf Rag,' merry and bright as an ice-cream truck, and the groaning of hundreds of thousands of immigrants — borne on the steel wheels of industrialization and names like Rockefeller and Carnegie and J.P. Morgan. It is October 27. As the day dawns, as the world grows toward the sky, dwellers in the city of dreams and the city of despair and most of all the city of possibility, go underground for the first time."

The tour leader's voice crackles warm as a fireplace and our car fills with a distant clamor and I catch a whiff of shoeshine and sepia-toned anticipation and the shrill keening of a whistle. The train lurches into motion again, its lights hollowing out the black tunnel, slowing to a crawl to take a sharp turn.

"In the next four decades, Model Ts will appear in middle-class driveways and legs will emerge bare and bold and pale beneath shortened skirts, whiskey will be shaken and stirred in hushed quarters and the Second World War will consume the earth and City Hall station will lie still and silent as a tomb, misplaced by time. But on this day in 1904, we are untouched by what is to come, for

189

New York's first subway has opened and its crown jewel is City Hall station, where the future swells large with promise, glorious."

The tour leader's voice diffuses like a misty breath as the tunnel yawns open and our train surfaces from the gloom amid the haunting siren song of wheels on rails. The doors release and open, and he bows with an outswept arm.

"It's just past eleven. You have an hour, and I'll be here if you have any questions," he says, and the group claps politely and files out, and I clap a little harder.

We step out and the air feels like old metal against my skin and Milton noses the platform and sneezes. I face forward and the station uncoils ahead of us like a snake, a tunnel of white and emerald-green tiles, cool and gleaming and decaying in places. The top of the snake's back is studded with three amethyst glass windows open to the sky outside. Everything is curved — the tracks and the platform wrapped around them, and the arches holding up the ceiling and lining the water-stained brick walls, and the entrances to passages and stairwells and the rusty lead flowers blooming in the skylights; and all the colors of the platform, white and green and blue, are drawn out poison-bright by the light of day falling through the glass and the lit chandeliers descending from the arched ceilings like wrought-iron spiders.

The others fan out around me and behind me, milling about at various intervals with their cameras blinking and clicking, speaking in whispers. One hand trailing along the wall, I wander forward with my head tilted up, mesmerized by the unexpected opulence of the colors and the shapes, the sense of faded grandeur old and fine and palpable as the dust coating the archways and chandeliers, and I nearly bump into a cluster of tourists that have squatted for photos.

I redirect my path and when I take my hand away from the wall the pads of my fingers are dark with steel powder, each smudge containing at its center a bright whorl, an island galaxy.

I follow the tunnel as it veers up into a mezzanine area, elegant with its arching walls and vaulted ceiling, a tiled dome topped by a skylight eye. A shaft of light pours in and I can see dust motes turning in the rosy softness, and beyond it a ladder leaning against a crumbling part of the wall with a floppy pile of sandbags and a crusted bucket underneath.

I step and turn and step and turn under the dome like waltzing in the ballroom of an aging queen, and it makes me feel a little sad to breathe in what once was, and to see that even something so solid and strong, a place of pride and great affection, could be left behind and forgotten, made to hobble through the unforgiving passages of time alone, no longer useful and no longer wanted.

FILTERED THROUGH THE LENS OF DAYS GONE BY, I take a moment to write as I try to puzzle out why the man with no pinkies would pass through here on his way home.

I put my notebook away. It does not make sense; with its time come and gone, the station is closed and cut off, not connected to anywhere or even open to the public. I note the disquieting sense that something important is missing, a hollow space underneath the quaint chipped tiles spelling CITY HALL, the thoughtful wooden benches and handrails, the informative arrows pointing the way to exits, the stairways with their first and last steps striped with yellow caution paint.

All of it is meant for people, for crowds, their liveliness and purposes and ambitions meant to fill and animate the empty spaces — the elderly resting on the benches and the children swinging from the handrails and the commuters hurrying up and down, up and down. Instead, now, the empty spaces gape, with only a curious group of tourists to flit across them and the faded light of yesterday slipping through the cracks.

Footsteps approach, the others arriving to explore the mezzanine, and Milton and I dodge them on our way out. I know that the man with no pinkies was going home and I know that he came here, and now I need to figure out where his home is. I repeat the first rule in my head — look in the obvious places — and could his home be *here,* in the station itself, and if so, where would he choose to build his house?

I think of the forts I used to build in my bedroom, in the corner with the window and the built-in wall lamp. Since there was no one else, just me, I entertained myself by attaching sheets with clothespins and pitching the sheets over the curtain rod and the lamp and chairs dragged from the kitchen. I weighted down the ends with stacks of books and plugged gaps in the sheet-walls with pillows and turned a mesh laundry hamper with zippered lids into an entrance tunnel. I brought snacks with me, and water, and a flashlight, and with no one else, just me, I played and napped and day-dreamed.

I stopped when my forts started making me feel suffocated and abandoned rather than safe; I worried I would be forgotten there, with my limbs all crammed together, but perhaps the man with no pinkies was still in his. A secret nook in the lost station — a fort where he could hide, a place he could keep the Book.

I think of the places it would make sense for a fort to be. Like mine, his would be somewhere out of the way, a small far corner and not a main area, and so I pay careful attention to recesses in the tiled walls, shadowed alcoves and secondary passages.

One passage loops back to the platform and I start over, climbing another set of stairs and poking my head into a second passage, and this one slopes up and ends in a graffiti-covered wall and balled up at the foot of the wall is a mixed clump of plastic bags and softening newspapers and a thin blanket, mottled purple-gray like a sheet of dryer lint.

Milton snuffles down the passage, and at the end he stops and turns to me with the same confused look he wore when Lucy found him surrounded by stuffing torn out of the Easter bunny she intended for a countertop display. His tail thumps against

194

the brick, swings back and bounces off the trash-stuffing.

I slide my gaze down the wall, a canvas of blackened bricks, starting with the bubbled names at the top, JACKIE + JOHNNY, and underneath that a green octopus stretched out like a neuron and a skull with monkey ears, and midway down a thicket of thorny letters.

The crack in the wall is threadlike, barely noticeable, but I can see the mercury-bright insides dribbling out and my heart leaps and I hurry up the passage to join Milton. I pinch my brows and study the bricks beneath the graffiti paint until I catch another glimpse of the sign, the liquid silver-blue light bleeding out of a hairline fracture in the wall. The Book has come this way. The trail runs down the wall and appears to point straight to the ball of trash but that can't be where it leads.

I kick the trash into a corner and see what was previously hidden, an uneven hole in the base of the wall where someone knocked out what looks like an air vent. I bend at the waist and peer inside like I am four or five again, checking under the bed for monsters, and I see a coffin of space beyond the vent, a two-foot gap between a dirt floor and a cobblestone ceiling, and then, beyond that, darkness.

I stretch out on my stomach and my heart beats against the concrete floor of the passage. I make sharp points with my elbows and knees and pull myself forward to poke my head into the hole, and it smells like gray sand and iron and in these close quarters the darkness feels compressed, settling against the back of my neck like a blanket, warm, with a gentle weight.

I pull my head back out and straighten, sitting on my knees and breathing deeply, the air now light and loose in comparison. I look to my left, which leads back to the platform, and I look up and to my right, blink and shift to catch another glimpse of the silver-blue glimmer, and I lean over and look straight into the darkness of the tunnel. I think again about building forts, and the mesh hamper I tipped over and unzipped. A tunnel leading into my fort — an entrance, a point of departure.

Even if I missed the clue pointing the way, where else would the Book be but in there?

I kneel in front of Milton and make a gesture, Stay, because I know him, and I know that his first instinct will be to come with me, ears swiveling and nose twitching, alert to potential dangers. One rainy afternoon when I returned from school, I hurried across the street to reach the shelter of the shop as he watched from the window, and a horn blared and tires screamed and suddenly, before anyone else had time to react, he was there, quaking as he braced himself against my shins, and I blinked and saw the full flag of his tail turned limp and scraggly from the downpour and the minibus swerving harmlessly away.

Milton may shy away from fort entrances and tunnel slides at the playground and kennels at the veterinary clinic and gopher holes when they collapse and threaten to swallow him, but I know that he will go where I go even though enclosed places are to him what high places are to me. I resolve to go forward alone, to spare him that terror, and I repeat the gesture, Stay, and he cocks his head, not understanding why, and I turn away before I can lose my nerve.

I sprawl out and push forward, scrabbling over the dirt like a sand turtle, and as the light starts to slip away I clamp my jaw shut and breathe dry and tight through my nose and try not to think about the cobblestone ceiling pressed low over me.

After a few feet, I crane my head back to remind Milton not to follow, and sure enough, he has inched his way into the mouth of the hole, dragging himself slowly through the sticky syrup of his fear.

Stay, I think, holding up a palm, and his eyes beam back an anxious gold. He slides another paw forward, gingerly, like he is afraid the crawl space will implode, bits of rock and mortar pattering down around him like hail.

I repeat the command, more firmly, and he whines and wriggles out and plants himself in front of the tunnel to keep watch. *I'll be here.* I can see the proud feathering of his chest, his tail stiff, frozen to the ground as he holds himself straight and still.

I crawl forward until I can no longer see Milton when I look back for reassurance, or even my own forearms braced underneath me. In the absence of light, my head seems to inflate like a balloon and drift away, and the sound of my breathing is too loud and muted at the same time, the woolly darkness soaking up my breaths as quickly as my lungs can press them out.

I twist onto one hip and fumble for the two Book pages in my pocket to remind myself of what I am looking for, and I reach past the lump in my throat, feel the shape of the steel in my chest and the Moo that lives there now too, and I move forward, one arm in front of the other, one knee in front of the other, eyes stretched open, blind and unblinking.

My arms and legs tremble from the strain of holding up my weight and propelling myself forward. My head grazes rock and maybe I am imagining it but it feels like the space is tightening around me, the ceiling pressing closer.

I continue on, another ten feet — twenty — there is no stopping and I crawl forward in the darkness and microscopic hairs rise and prickle in my ears and nostrils and soon the prickling is everywhere, under my fingernails and behind my eyes, as my senses stretch and fine-tune. I guess that I am about forty feet in when they pick up an almost imperceptible shift in the air, a watery colorless quality spreading through the inky dark like just before dawn, when night and day touch and start to overlap.

I crawl forward and the darkness recedes until I can see the blot of movement when I pick up my left arm and put it back down, and the dizzy swelling feeling subsides, my head deflating back to a normal size, and then I see where the dirt floor drops away, a fuzzy cone of yellow light sent up by some light source below.

I inch closer and a damp chill emanates from the bright hole, a slight breeze, the exchange of air from different places. I lean over the edge and promptly withdraw from the blast of light, blinking rapidly as my eyes well up, and I wait a moment before leaning forward again and squinting over the edge.

This time I can make out a crude shaft, round and narrow like a straw jammed into the dirt and rock, with a rusted metal ladder leaning against one side. The light is coming from somewhere in the shaft and it is too bright to see the bottom, which is for the best.

I flip over and swing my legs over the edge, searching with one toe. I find a rung and hook my feet around the sides of the ladder and test my weight. The ladder squeaks in protest but it does not move, does not snap down the middle, and so I suck in a breath and start to climb down into the shaft.

I am careful not to look for the ground until my foot hits solid dirt. When it does, I breathe a sigh of relief and take a few steps away from the ladder and look around.

My first thought is, I am in the space between stations. But I am not observing the scene from behind a rattling train window anymore; the tunnel stretches forward as far as I can see, a packed-dirt floor strewn with tea-colored puddles and trampled yellow tape and bunched foil wrappers, unfinished stone walls caked with dirt and framed by wooden beams and lined with exposed wires and pipes and dingy lightbulbs that are too weak to illuminate the tunnel — just emitting dense spheres of light that cast everything in shades of gray.

As I set off, I see that the tunnel is not actually the space between stations. It is smaller and there are no rails installed down the middle, no thundering trains and shrill whistles, only a distant dripping, a tense stillness like I am being watched, and I shiver as a compulsion to hide sweeps through me.

I lengthen my stride, staying close to the wall, near the lightbulbs. I wonder where this is, where I am. The tunnel might run under City Hall station and the 6 train track, or above it, and I picture layers upon layers of earth piled overhead, an asphalt lid sealed over the top with people and cars shuttling up and down the street, going about their day.

I look at the wall speculatively. Perhaps the tunnel runs alongside City Hall station, and I stop and lean one ear closer, imagining the platform on the other side, a tourist leaning in to tap a shiny green tile, unaware of this tunnel's existence, of me on the other side with my head pressed to the wall.

The thought sends a rush of loneliness through me like nostalgia except rain-gray, and I shutter my mind, focus it on the search for the Book. I walk steadily, keeping my eyes open and sweeping them systematically back and forth.

I pass by a closet-sized hollow in the wall, and in the dim light I see that it is bare, maybe a place for resting or storing supplies, although that would require someone who needed to do those things. I shiver and gaze into the shadows, searching for glints of eye and tooth and nail, and I tell myself that it does not mean anything. It was probably carved into the wall when the tunnel was built, a shelter to duck into as cattle streamed past, bound for the slaughterhouse, or maybe it was dump trucks, belching and rumbling toward the landfill, but now this place is just an abandoned tunnel — one where the man with no pinkies has constructed his fort and hidden the Book.

I glance around in case he has left the Book here but the shallow room is mostly dark and empty and Book-less. There is a squeak from the corner and tiny fingers with tiny nails scratching against the ground, and that sends me scuttling back into the light's orbit.

As I continue my forward progress, I pass another hollowed-out section of tunnel, another room, and this one is a little larger and not totally bare: there are piles of clothing inside, separated by type, tops and bottoms and sweaters and socks. I start to rummage through a pile of shorts, wondering if this is some forgotten lost-and-found room, although, strangely, the shorts I push aside are all child-sized, and stiff and puckered like they were shrunk in the dryer.

My hand strikes the hard surface of the floor and I move on to the T-shirt pile, fishing around for the Book. I shake out a gray-white shirt with a basketball-playing potato on the chest. It bears the marks of its favored status, a rust ring on the front shoulder and a tear along the collar, and the fabric around the stomach has been stretched into near-translucence. I toss the shirt to the side, wondering how it got here and where the owner is, and he must be panicked as he searches to no avail for his favorite T-shirt.

The Book is not buried in any of the clothing piles, and I exit the room and continue down the tunnel and I realize that I am walking too fast and will myself to slow down, so that I miss nothing.

I pass another room, and this one is littered with clocks that are lying on their sides and cameras with cracked lenses and phones with wheel dials and game consoles with dust-choked slots. Another lost-and-found?

But that is two rooms of unusable items collected and categorized and separated like a museum, and I look around the room for signs of the Book and all I see is a graveyard of machines. Once trusted helpers, dutifully oiling and packaging and freezing time, now here and broken and useless. I crash through the room, tossing things over my shoulder as I search, and when I finish I dust off my hands but the smell of forgetting — mothballs and mold — lingers.

My distress mounts and I jog toward the next room and the ground crunches under my feet when I enter. It is full of broken cups, chipped water glasses and coffee mugs with missing handles, shattered wine stems and cracked teacups and smashed champagne flutes.

I stomp twice around the room and return to the tunnel, shaking off rogue shards of glass and wondering what this tunnel is — some place for unwanted things? I feel like a burglar, sneaking into a place I do not belong, and then I think of the lunches I spent sitting on the sidelines and the spitballs arcing overhead.

Maybe I *did* belong here, and what would happen if I couldn't find my way back? Lost things can be found but the things that belonged here cannot — they are unwanted, meaning no one is attached to them and no one will come looking for them. Milton would come for me, I remind myself. Lucy would find me.

Still, dread rains through me and I break into a run, running as hard as I can to escape the pouring dread of museum-rooms full of sad defective things. I cannot become lost. I have to find the Book so there is no chance of that happening, and it is more important than ever for me to save the shop and keep hold of the last place and people that want me.

The tunnel starts to slope down and I zoom past the next room and have to drag myself back up. It contains a pantry loaded with products in loud, colorful containers that I don't remember seeing in any grocery store. I comb hastily through the shelves, knocking over cereal boxes and candy packs in my hurry, scanning for ripples of air around the box of Carnation breakfast bars or puddles of light under the radioactive bottle of Squeezit. I see a white-wrappered Caravelle bar sitting on the middle shelf and it tugs my hands to a stop.

The picture shows a bar of crispy puffed rice coated in chocolate, pulled apart by unseen hands to show the flat luster of the caramel as it stretches. I imagine Lan and her husband huddled around a card table with a chocolate bar on a plate, and they pull the bar apart and wrestle over the caramel strings and the crispy rice and chocolate melts in their mouths and they smell like fresh laundry.

I take the bar and put it into my front pocket for safekeeping until I see Lan again, and I press on, still running, but I am running out of steam. The tunnel slopes down for a little longer before leveling out, and I try another room and this one is larger, a cavern dimly lit by its own dingy lightbulbs, and a mountain of stacked cardboard boxes rises up in the middle, discarded toys piled in smaller hills around it.

There are innumerable places here for the man with no pinkies to hide the Book, and who knows how long this tunnel stretches and how many more rooms I have yet to pass and search, and despair licks at me and I smother it as best as I can. I look under the arms of teddy bears with stuffing bleeding out of their seams, and around eyeless rocking horses and behind armless plastic dolls and atop badminton rackets with snapped wires, and there are so many places left to search . . .

Pop! Goes the weasel.

A box by my knee explodes and I swerve away, upsetting a heap of toys, and the toys topple over in an avalanche of sunny plastics and sputtering lights and distorted jingles. A rubber cow grazes my shin and I tread on a gap-toothed keyboard, setting off guitar riffs and drum solos, and a rainbow bear introduces itself over and over through a cacophony of barnyard squawking. I cover my ears, cringing, willing the avalanche to peter out. A donut ring wobbles toward the cardboard mountain and tips over, and the silence that follows is deafening too.

I lower my hands and the air rumbles like darkness gathering and I hold still, waiting. A faint sound carries over from behind the mountain of boxes, some sort of movement, a weak chirping like a nest of baby birds. This near-silence does not feel like a trustworthy one but the Book could be over there, right on the other side of the mountain.

Slowly, smoothly, I slide around the boxes, out of the dusty light and into the long shadow of the stacks, and the floor beyond is dotted with even darker unmoving lumps — mounds of toys — and the darker square of a small door along the wall. I start toward it and register, abruptly, the dark flicker of movement under the doorway, and a delighted exclamation splits the quiet wide open — "Why, it is a child."

A rising and a quickening — the room awakens, and a man steps toward the light, toward me, with a dozen rats draped on his arms and shoulders, clinging to his cape like dark lint and curling along the brim of his bowler hat with their pink hands and pulsating bodies and eyes like plump beetles.

The rats strain in my direction, taut and trembling and screeching like violin strings, and the rat-man shifts and I notice that he is holding a bucket, and he thumbs his nose and starts to say something else and a rat scrabbles onto the top of his hat to keep from slipping off. Another rat the size of a kitten loses its grip and somersaults through the air, and it lands on its feet and bounds toward me and the panic touches down all at once like a bolt of lightning, and I run.

Before I know it, my legs are shooting out from under me and a plastic rattle spins away and the ground rushes up and my knees plow into it. Behind me the squeaking intensifies into a blanket of shrill noise, thick as the screaming of cicadas on a muggy evening.

I push my cheek away from the floor, trying to find my legs, and I know the rats will arrive any moment now, digging their nails into my back, gnawing at the roots of my hair, but instead two hands seize me by the armpits and I open my eyes, see five stumpy fingers, and I twist — a woman's face looms over me, a broad square with two eyes pressed like wrinkled raisins into pasty flesh, a rat balanced on her shoulder — and my vision darkens and I thrash like a hooked fish.

I manage to flip over, breaking the rat-woman's grip, and I scuttle back until I am pressed against the boxes, eyes rattling like dice in their sockets as I cast about for an escape, and I think of the side door but I'd have to wade through the rats, and over the great lungfuls of breath crashing against my ears, someone pleads, "Stop — look — we mean no harm —"

My eyes land on the rat-man. He is standing in the same spot as before only he has turned around and all I can see is the back of his hat and the threadbare billow of his cape around his stooped shoulders as he swings his bucket.

"Just hungry," he pants over his shoulder, tossing the bucket in short frantic swoops like bailing water. "Look, they're eating, they're leaving — don't be frightened —"

He tosses the bucket again, launching a spray of vegetable trimmings into the air, and the rats stream off him, away from him, retreating to follow the arc of corncobs and watermelon rinds and cauliflower leaves.

He sets the emptied bucket on the ground and shuffles around to face me, and his boxy pant cuffs sway as he rocks from one side to the other. He looks like he wants to dart away and hide but he stays and looks back at me, and his face is smooth and guileless as a child's.

He stretches his shoulders back and then he gives me a tentative smile and it is open and clear as a flash of blue sky. I am taken aback, disarmed.

He looks down at the ground. "We didn't mean to startle you. Welcome to our home," he mumbles, stuffing his hands into his pockets.

I shift my attention to the woman crouched in front of me, and now, with the rats a comfortable distance away, I can clearly see the shy apology in her squashed face and wrinkled eyes.

I remember the rat-man stepping out and me charging away in a blind panic. I am flooded with sudden shame. It is just a rat-couple who never meant any harm, and I didn't even give them a second to say hello.

"Are you hurt?" the rat-woman asks.

I notice the raw buzz around my knees and roll up my jeans and it is nothing, really; my knees are red where the skin has been shaved off and a few beads of blood-dew are forming but otherwise I am fine, and I shake my head to say no.

"You're bleeding," she says, crouching closer and sweeping her cape to the side, and underneath it she is wearing a flannel shirt and woolly pants and hairy shoes in clashing plaid patterns, like samples from a warehouse of moth-eaten sofas.

She hooks her fingers through a hole in her sleeve and yanks and the sleeve rips. She shakes out the strip of fabric and I see three round scars on her forearm before she reaches into her cape and brings out a flask with a rusted underside and a dented belly.

She unscrews the flask and tips it over and a dark spot spreads across the plaid. She leans over my knee and I gasp at the sting and she works in silence. I look at the ceiling to forget the stinging, and then at the rat-man as he plods over. He stands next to the rat-woman, rolling his weight from heel to toe, and he takes off his hat and holds it against his stomach and I note that he is not missing any pinkies.

"What drives you underground, child?" He winces as if remembering something painful and runs his thumb across the brim of the hat.

"I am finding," I say. I lift my hip to slip the flyer out of my pocket.

The rat-woman pours more alcohol onto the fabric and moves to the other knee.

"I know what you're here for. Out there, I, too, was rejected and shunned. Out there, they tried to hurt her. But here, you will find the peace and love you are looking for, as we did."

I shake my head and show him the flyer, and the rat-woman presses the fabric down and I curl up tight, hissing at the burn.

"I didn't think it possible, either," the rat-man says, worrying at the brim of his hat and watching me with wide, steady eyes. "I fed the rats, befriended them, and they led me to her, sitting in the tunnels with a lump of leftover candle wax and a dish of burnt tagliatelle."

That smile again, a flash of open sky, and he licks his thumb and leans over to rub at a constellation of cucumber seeds dried to the rat-woman's cheek. She pauses, pulling the fabric away from my knee, and they gaze at each other and a story tugs at me and I remember where I have seen that expression before.

There was no candlelight and tagliatelle when Lucy and Walter Lavender Sr. met, but Lucy's eyes softened all the same when she told the story, her voice rising and falling around the rhythmic wick-wick-wick-wick of the mixer as it whisked egg whites for soufflés.

They met on a ship that once patrolled the coasts of North Carolina and had since been docked and restored and converted into a bar and restaurant in New York City. It was a sunny afternoon and half of the ship's patrons were already unsteady on their feet.

Lucy found out earlier that day that she had landed an internship with the pastry chef at a two-Michelin-starred restaurant. She wanted to stay in the kitchen and practice until she could reliably produce soufflés that rose high enough and didn't taste so eggy, but the woman she shared a stovetop with vetoed the plan and dragged her out to celebrate.

So that was why Lucy was there, standing with her elbow propped on the rail, holding a bottle of beer and basking in the salt and light. Next to her a ruddy-faced man danced the foxtrot with himself, slow, slow, quick-

quick — right into Lucy. The bottle of beer plunged straight into the water and she might have followed if Walter Lavender Sr. hadn't been so quick on his feet.

"I've got you — I'm here," he said, holding her upright as she reeled from the near-disaster.

She scraped her hair back and he took a good look at her and laughed at the mutinous look she shot at the oblivious dancing man. He invited her and her friend to join him and some friends from flight school over their bucket of beers, and before Lucy knew it, the stars were out and their knees were touching under the table.

There is a tap on my own knee and I shake my head to erase the stars and the rat-woman says, "There."

I bend my leg experimentally, and the rat-man coughs and touches the edges of his dusty cape.

"It's no trouble," he says. "We've longed for a child of our own and here you are, the answer."

He bows lower as if embarrassed by his admission and the rat-woman rises and wraps her arms around him, beaming into his stooped shoulder, and they could be any couple gazing at the life they built together — farmers looking out over the lands they

214

tilled, parents watching their child take the first unsteady steps.

A viscous sick feeling rises in my throat and I put my head down, busying myself with unrolling my jeans. They think that I have come here to stay and I am like them and I am their answer, and none of these things are true. I already have a mom and, even if he is lost, a dad, and I have an urge to insist I don't belong with them until we all know that it is true.

I swallow instead and push the urge down, because I can see how much they have wished for this. Lucy tells me that I am *her* answer, a blessing, and I know how long she and Walter Lavender Sr. waited for me, talking about the future to pass the time, carving out the details of our would-be lives like an intricate diorama and their disappointment each time it did not work out and their joy when the wait was over and I became real.

I climb to my feet to show them the flyer again, and I explain that I am looking for a book and a man with no pinkies. He mistook the Book for unwanted and spirited it away, and I need to find him and insist he return it because it is not unwanted but rather lost, missed, which looks the same but is fundamentally different.

The rat-woman's beaming face slides into darkness like a solar eclipse and it is hard to watch because I know what it is to yearn for a missing piece and the two of them are something like me, people who do not belong, even though it seems like they do not even want to anymore. They have *chosen* to confine themselves to a world of their own, and that is not like me, since I long for the opposite.

When I finish explaining, the rat-man reaches for the rat-woman like she is going to keel over and she shakes him off. From the folds of her cape, she produces a fire truck that has been leached of color and holds it out to me. I look down at her shortened sleeve, the ends jagged as shark teeth above her wrist, the line of scars that I recognize now as cigarette burns.

"Keep going," she says, running the truck up my arm. "Past the rest of the rooms. Until you reach the end."

She parks the truck on my shoulder and says, "That's where you'll find the Junker."

Through the swell and swim of her irises, she smiles.

She tugs at the rat-man and he turns and shambles ahead to pick up the bucket. He extends his free hand, waits for her to catch it, and together they approach the side door and the sea of rats parts and closes and sweeps them away.

I skirt the base of the cardboard mountain, keeping an eye on the side door, and there is no sign of movement, no kitten-sized rat bounding back into the toy room. Once more, I am alone in the silence, and this time it is deep and still and I figure out what the rat-couple reminds me of — the time I lifted the trash-can lid and saw, in the dark humidity, two gentle brown caps sprouting out of the slimy floor despite lacking nurture, lacking light.

I return to the front of the toy room and my scraped knee throbs with a dull heat. I tilt my head and sight down the length of the tunnel. The rat-couple is content to stay here, thriving on love and solitude, waiting for their one missing thing to come to them. As for me, there is no time to wait and I have to keep moving forward, running, running, running without stopping, without looking back, away from the dread and toward the Book, and as long as I find it I will not become like them, forced to be content with being unwanted.

The thundering in my chest becomes the rush of the wind, and even though I know the rat-couple will keep the rats from following — still I keep running with my lungs aflame, because I know that as long as I keep moving, the tunnel will lead me straight to the Book, and to the place where I belong and there is no becoming lost.

I open my mouth to drink in the air and it tastes like rock and earth, damp and mineral, but in my mind I am already back in the shop and the sigh of the oven is warm and buttery-pure, and I have never tasted anything so delicious.

15

Gradually, I slow to a jog and then a walk, and the lightbulbs in the tunnel grow fewer and farther between, and I pass under eye-watering patches of light and I pass through stretches of darkness and I pass by more rooms but I don't bother to search them anymore now that I know the Junker is at the end of the tunnel.

I walk, placing one foot in front of the other, and I walk in a straight line and the line I walk is so straight that my senses warp.

I have walked to the ends of the earth.

I have gone nowhere at all.

Time melts into a seamless loop, a figure eight. The tunnel stretches before me, unbroken, the stone impenetrable, and my knees ache and I don't know where I am or where I am going or how long it will take to get there, and that confirms my inkling that I might be lost.

The notion that a person could lose a

219

piece of himself without realizing it had seemed fantastic and abstract when I was sitting beside Nico. Wouldn't you feel it the moment after you took a wrong turn — the chill down your spine, the urgency of being lost, the danger?

But maybe it is something like this, where the journey to being lost goes on for ages and there isn't much to alert you of treacherous territory, just miles to go in an endless tunnel of banality. Still, I put one foot in front of the other, because I have started, and so I must finish.

The tunnel goes on, and has it been five minutes or an hour? The tour group will board the train again at the end of the hour but it does not matter if they leave without me; I am not leaving until I find the Book.

My feet start to throb, and then I hardly notice them moving anymore and I have to train my gaze on them to make sure they are working. The next time I look up, I see the chain links of a fence growing out of the tunnel walls in front of me, and beyond the fence is a swing set in shades of black and white and gray, and farther down the tunnel is a hopscotch grid inhabited by painted kangaroos.

I know this place, those cartoon kangaroos: it is the playground of my elementary school. I consider the fence and step through it. The swings are deserted except for a little boy rocking absently with one toe and tracing melancholic patterns on the ground with the other, and I hear a metal squeak and remember how rusty the swing set was and how the squeaking grew louder when the air turned humid before rain.

The little boy regards my approach with eyes round as dinner plates and the ends of his scarf bump lightly against his chest as he rocks. The sweater he is wearing is a medium gray but I know by the three fish on the front and the starfish on the elbow what time and scene we are in. It is the first day of first grade, when I thought I could become friends with Vara Mae.

"Hi," I say to mini-Walter.

"What are you doing?" he says suspiciously.

I sigh and lean against the side of the tunnel. "I'm looking for the Book. It's lost."

Mini-Walter stands up, aghast. The swing bumps the backs of his knees. "You have to find it," he says.

"I know. If I don't, we'll lose the shop. But don't worry. I know how to find lost things."

"Okay." He looks doubtful and does not move, does not blink.

I try again. "Do you remember the wings pin you lost? I found that. Remember the last time you had it? You were sitting at the table by the bookcase. You unpinned it and held it in your hands and polished it with your shirt. You pinned it back, and it became lost."

"Where was it?"

"It was under the bookcase, behind one of the feet."

"That's good." Mini-Walter sits back down. "Did you find him, too?"

"Not yet. I'm still looking, the oil lamp is still in the window."

"Are you close to finding the Book?" His expression says it all, his eyes wide and wondering, worlds of crossing lights and hidden patterns and all of it revolving around the Book, the shop.

As I study mini-Walter's face and the three fish on his chest, I feel a skimming sensation under my skull followed by a cool clarity.

"I think so. But I don't know if finding it will fix everything," I admit. "Being here has made me see some things I've been tricking myself into not seeing."

I'd told myself that I was alone because I was different — I had a disorder, I had no dad. Because of who I was, I would always be lonely, separated. I could not be any other way. But I have met the rat-couple and I am forced to see how I, like them, have *chosen* to give up and be alone, and to be content in a world of my own. This was not how I was meant to be; it was how I decided to be. I am more like the rat-couple than I first thought; in a way I have been wandering these tunnels for a long time, from the moment I made my choice to stop trying six years ago. Are they what I will become if I continue on in my silence? I think about the buried fear that I would become unwanted, the unleashed dread, and I imagine myself cutting pants out of one sofa and shoes out of another, with rats swinging from the overgrown garland of my own hair.

At least they accepted the reality of their choice and did not try to convince themselves otherwise. I wrapped myself in the warmth of the shop and I convinced myself that when I learned about people through their lost things, these temporary, one-sided reprieves meant that I was not actually alone.

I run a hand over the rough stone of the tunnel and barnacles of dirt crumble under my touch and I see, clearly, where I have put myself, the kind of life I have learned to be happy with. That is not something the Book can fix. I swallow and force myself to continue. "But I also know that I can't stop looking for the Book."

Mini-Walter's expression is serious. "I hope you find it," he says.

"Me too. More than anything."

Mini-Walter draws a circle with his toe.

"What are *you* doing?"

"You know," mini-Walter says, and I do. He looks down and fades away a little, wanting to forget about the first day of school, but I think of it now because that was, I understand, when the seed was planted.

It had taken me an hour to decide what to wear, that sea-blue sweater with the starfish on the elbow and the three fish swimming together across the front, each one a different color and shape. When Lucy dropped me off in the first-grade classroom, she pulled the teacher aside to tell her about my talking and I looked around the room at the planets orbiting the rug and the desks pushed together in groups of four and the girl wailing over glue on her dress. I did not know her name but I recognized her immediately.

She rode her bike by the shop sometimes, and it was white and powder blue with manes of blue streamer coming out of the handlebars, and they galloped alongside her in the wind. Her hair was straight and shiny under the classroom lights, strawberry and gold, and at lunchtime I saw her across the playground and decided to introduce myself. I was a little nervous but she seemed familiar to me and I had spent the summer rehearsing the movements for my greeting with Lucy.

But when I walked up to her and went through my sentences with painstaking care — *My. Name. Is. Wal. Ter. Who. Are. You* — she stared blankly and she didn't say, "Hi, Walter. I'm Vara Mae," or "I've seen you at the shop," or "Do you like riding bikes, too?" Instead, she did something I had not thought to prepare for.

She scrunched her nose and didn't say anything.

My throat tightened and I tried again. It came out worse the second time and I tasted the fear and dismay curdling at the back of my tongue. Gagging on the sourness, I forced myself to try a third time and she opened her mouth and blurted, "You talk funny!" with mingled bewilderment and disgust and excitement, and that was the beginning of the commotion.

A circle of children gathered around us as Vara Mae stomped her feet and shrieked,

"Say it again! Tell him to say it again," doubling over with the force of it.

I couldn't escape; I staggered toward gaps in the circle but each time the circle tightened, buffeting me back, trapping me in. I wheeled about, searching for a friendly face, and the children lunged at me, snapping with laughter, and someone taunted, "Talk normal."

And, "He's going to cry."

And, "You're so stupid."

And, "Dumb crybaby."

The words they hurled were hard and small and I flinched and my jaw opened and my throat tightened but I couldn't get it out, not a single word that I could hurl back to defend myself with. I shrank and wilted in the center of the circle, wrapping my arms around myself to hide the three fish on my sweater.

The mob didn't disperse until a teacher marched over with a laborious pigeon-toed gait and Vara Mae promptly burst into tears. I tried to explain to the teacher that I only wanted to talk to her and she wailed over my stammering so that she would not get into trouble, howling louder whenever I spoke.

"Enough," the teacher said, grabbing my shoulders and giving them a little shake.

"That's enough from you."

She turned to Vara Mae and tried to console her, and I tried hysterically to say, I talked to her, I talked to her, and that made Vara Mae cry so hard that a butterfly clip fell out of her hair, and the teacher swiveled around.

"I don't know what you're saying. Stop talking, you're making it worse," she said sharply over the sobbing.

I jerked back, stung. She reached to brush a lock of strawberry hair out of Vara Mae's wet eyes, turning away before she could see the words latching onto my skin and growing veins, faint speckles of black, like a patch of ugly warts.

I never saw Vara Mae again after that year but the memory lingered, and after that, whenever I tried again and failed, I wondered if the teacher was right. That day was the beginning of the fear that drove my choice. I stopped trying because I did not want to open up and bare the tender blue-purple of my insides and that is what real bonds require — not just listening and taking in but also giving back some of yourself in kind. There is a risk to connecting that way and I decided it wasn't worth it, not when I could mimic the feeling of the real thing without the risk.

I thought I found an easier way to connect and a place to belong, but even as I longed for friendship I was secretly unwilling, the entire time, to face the truth of what real friendship required.

My face must have crumpled for a moment, because mini-Walter's voice is alarmed when he stands and says, "You have to go."

He sweeps his arms. "Keep going," he urges, over and over until I do, moving past the swings and over the hopscotch grid.

One . . . two . . . three . . .

I put my head down and count each step, the scene fading, mini-Walter too, as I leave him behind.

Twenty-three . . . twenty-four . . . twenty-five . . .

"I'm not much to see, but you're going to crash into me if you don't look up."

The voice is nasal and polite and morose, and my eyes slide away from my high-tops, up to the saddest man I have ever seen, sitting in a chair in the middle of the tunnel and shifting gingerly like the chair has been molded uncomfortably in just the wrong places. He has a basset-hound face and a lumpy little belly that rests on his lap. He is wearing a long coat of bedraggled black feathers and a stray feather makes him sneeze, setting his drooping eyes and nose and jowls aquiver.

"You don't like my tunnels." His pink eyes are doleful and I shake my head and misery seeps out of him so thick that I almost expect him to deflate at my feet. I look down at his hands, splayed over his knee-caps, and when I count four fingers on each hand, I know that I have reached the end of the tunnel and I have found the Junker — or, rather, the other way around. I avert my gaze before he notices, shifting it back to his face, but he has been studying me the whole time.

"Cleaning out a meat slicer I picked up behind a deli," he says, holding up his right hand. He holds up his left. "Unjamming a saw while cutting out another entrance. It was unavoidable." He heaves a sigh and drops both hands. "This is not a place for things that are missed. So what are you doing here? You're alone and dusty but you're buoyant. Purposeful," he accuses. "Who are you? What do you want?"

"I am looking for this." I take the flyer out of my pocket and unfold it.

"If you're looking for it, it wouldn't be here," the Junker says, but he scoots cheerlessly to the edge of his seat to inspect the sketch of the Book. I wait for the flicker in his pink eyes, and to my horror they retract like window shades into the back of his head and his misshapen body seizes and shivers. I hurl myself forward and he holds out a palm to stop me, and I watch with alarm as his whites jerk from left to right. They lock and unroll and he cracks his neck and stands, and the feather coat induces another teary sneeze.

The sneeze echoes and I look past the Junker, following the echoes, and I see that he is sitting with his back to an empty hall wallpapered in sheet metal and tiger-striped signs, like he is guarding the entrance to a construction site.

The Junker says, "I recognize that book. It belonged to a foul-smelling young man who had no use for it, and so it belongs here now, to me. You probably don't know who I am, do you?" The bags under his eyes sink lower.

I nod to say that I do, which is not what he expected.

"Junker, at your service." For a moment he almost looks pleased, and then his face settles back into its plaintive lines.

I ask him if I can see the Book, prepared to cross my arms like Lucy and fight through his reluctance, and instead he shrugs and says, "It'll probably be a let-

down, but there's no reason why you can't
see it. Follow me."

16

We cross to the other end of the hall and my mind surges and still a thousand thoughts gallop ahead of it, too wild and half-formed to be caught. We stop in front of three doors. They are identical, plain and white with fresh iron doorknobs, and they are firmly closed and it would only take a split second, the slightest shift, for Junker to change his mind. Worry builds inside me and I say without thinking, That Book never belonged to Nico and it doesn't belong here and it's only missing and you have to give it back.

Too long, too rushed; I hear bursts of sound issuing out of my mouth, swapped consonants and dropped syllables and odd groupings.

"Datdoover. Blongtoo. Iico-an?" Junker repeats carefully, frowning and not understanding what I have said, and embarrassment broils under my skin.

"It's just as well. I knew it would happen someday — grip already impaired, then the hearing scrambled. Soon enough it'll be the sight and smell going haywire," he mutters, and cuts himself off with a brisk flap of his coat. "You don't want to hear about that, of course. Choose a door. Your fate is in your hands."

I look among the three doors and none of them stand out as being better or worse than the other two. I point to the door in the middle and my calves tense, threads and wires coiling tight, but Junker only twists the knob and pushes the door open and ushers me through and closes it behind us.

"They lead to the same place," he confesses as we set off down a short tunnel toward a circle of light. "Everyone's building houses these days. With all the extra doors lying around, I thought I might as well install them."

A smell like burnt rubber and rotting eggs wafts into the tunnel as we near the end, and Junker steps out into the light and beckons for me to come with him. I tug my sleeve down and cover my nose and join him on what looks like a fire escape, and I immediately lift my chin and my eyes, so that I do not see through the steel gratings of the platform underneath my feet. A vast space opens up before us, a concrete shell the size of a football stadium, and I forget the smell and inhale sharply.

This looks like a place meant for something more before plans were scrapped, a terminal deemed unwanted once the earth was scooped out and the concrete hardened to create a lost world underneath the populated one.

The light is soft and diffuse as a fog, filtering down through clusters of little glass discs embedded into the ceiling. I picture the people on the other side, treading on the iron covers — and me, too, all those times I avoided cracks and fissures in the sidewalk and maybe I stepped on these very vault lights, rows of bubbled purple lenses set in iron frames, and they didn't look like much from where I was.

But from the bottom looking up, those plain prisms illuminate everything around us — a patchwork of grays and blues and the occasional roof of red or orange, a city in miniature.

"Proceed into my kingdom, if you will," Junker says, turning to climb down the ladder-stairs in the middle of the platform. I follow, breathing through my mouth, and we descend to ground level.

At the bottom, the concrete floor is covered with clumps of dirt and coiled heaps of rubbery cables like beached kelp and planks of splintered wood and corroded metal, and Junker leads the way through a network of corridors — roads — cleared out of the rubble, lined with mismatched hovels made of scrap metal and tarp and faded posters and string.

"You're probably wishing you were somewhere else," Junker says. "These shacks are going to take a tumble any second now."

But we walk on anyway, stepping over bottles and cigarettes, and there are bedsheets and items of clothing hanging everywhere, pants and blouses and undergarments clipped to wires and strewn over roofs and dripping from ledges. I hardly notice the smell anymore because I am straining to hear the babble of indistinct voices, babies crying and pots clattering and dogs barking. The streets should be teeming with life but no matter how hard I look and listen, our surroundings remain abandoned and desolate.

Like its keeper, this kingdom is the saddest I have ever seen.

We take a right onto a street riddled with potholes and Junker stoops and picks up a handheld tape recorder half-submerged in a puddle of dust and exclaims, "This must be new. I don't recognize it. I must've picked it up last time."

He gives it a shake and presses the button with a sideways triangle carved into it. He cradles the recorder in his hands and holds it up to his ear and waits. After a long crackling moment, he pushes the button labeled with a square. The tape is blank and I wonder how the tape recorder got there and what it is doing there too.

When I point at it, shrugging to ask the question, Junker cranes his neck back to look at the vault lights.

"Do you know how many unwanted things are out there, if you look? I find them everywhere, on my excursions aboveground when it gets too quiet around here. That's how I built this city, scoop by scoop and piece by piece."

We continue down the potholed street and Junker fiddles with the tape player, rewinding and pressing the play button. "I quite like these projects, creating something out of — well, worse than nothing, if you think about it. If I didn't do anything with this unwanted stuff, it would just pile up and it would be a weeping mess, and I happen to have nothing but time on my hands."

There is something at once forlorn and noble about it, and I fish out my notebook.

FOR EVERY THING NEEDS ITS PLACE AND REASON, I write.

We take another right. More homes and clotheslines crisscrossing overhead, and lively splashes of yellow and purple run along the side of the road where Junker has planted dandelions and thistles in broken pots.

"Where are we going?" The ramshackle houses peer back at me, docile and eerie, and I wonder which one the Book is in.

"Where else would a book belong but in the library?" he says, and somehow this knocks me off-kilter and I laugh.

Junker's face lifts. "I do very much like stories."

His face lengthens again and he rewinds and plays the tape recorder with increasing agitation. "I don't suppose you know any stories," he says halfheartedly, but the tips of his black feathers tremble ever so slightly and his knuckles whiten against the tape recorder clutched between his two hands.

I shake my head. I wouldn't tell it right, and he would react in the wrong way like I have learned most people do, and he wouldn't understand. I can't look at him, and so I look around. The home next to me has a window made of cellophane. Inside, Junker has set up a table with outdated

237

teacups and plates, and arranged nonmatching pairs of chopsticks beside each plate.

I stop and move closer to the window. The teacups, handles dutifully pointed to three o'clock. Chopsticks carefully laid out on the left. The table, held together with duct tape. Each item unwanted, but once again given a reason for being. Still, in the end, they are only pretending.

Standing in the home Junker has built for himself in his loneliness, scoop by scoop and piece by piece, I wonder if he is another possible future version of myself.

The same sad existence, and yet fundamentally different.

Junker has no other choices and he does not shield himself from his plight. Instead he faces it full and wraps his arms around it and that, at least, is brave and true. He is not me.

A feathery rustle — Junker stands at my elbow and looks at the kitchen scene he replicated and, clenches the tape recorder, and I understand that he wants to give it a purpose, and I also understand the purpose of his stories because mine do the same for me — they take him away from the pain, for a while.

I can't fathom how much greater Junker's pain must be, and for so long, and that

238

means he needs this story more than I need to protect myself.

I step away from the window and open my mouth, and then I close it. It's hard to move forward, away from the old lie that speaking will make things worse, even though I know about my voice, and it can be heard. I can try, even if I fail.

I lift the tape recorder out of Junker's hands and pick my words deliberately. "I know a. Tale."

Pretending that I am gazing into the flame of my oil lamp, I recall the end-over-end swirl, the memory made of water and sun — the deep voice all around me, timeless and boundless as the night sky. I concentrate on this, and the shop alive and the flame unwavering, and I hold down the red button.

"Once upon a time, there was a boy who never imagined he could fly very far."

My voice is small and breakable and not like I imagine Walter Lavender Sr.'s to be, and I almost stop right there, hearing it out in the open like that, but slowly, unevenly, as best as I can, I continue to tell him the story Walter Lavender Sr. told me before he became lost, the one I think I can tell best because I've told it so many times in my head.

We turn right, heading into the center of the city, and I keep my eyes glued to the blinking red light so that I won't accidentally catch a glimpse of Junker's expression, and as long as the light blinks I continue to tell, and somewhere along the way I start to hear his voice in my head again, little by little, layering over mine until my words become his.

I tell Junker about what the boy's life was like when he met the mermaid and what it was like after she helped him find his wings, and I finish, "And one day he did it. Spread his arms and flew over the water," and it does not feel right to end the recording like that. I am inspired to add something new.

"And no one saw him for a while. But that is not the end."

Like any lost thing, he would have left clues that pointed the way. There would be a silver vapor in his wake, a trail of tears frozen into cloud. I learned everything I could about Walter Lavender Sr.; I knew what to look for, and if I saw the signs, I would recognize them. I looked for the trail he left behind and so far I've picked up empty spaces but I know better than to give up, because I've had cases where people stop looking right when they are on the verge of finding the lost thing.

The woman with the pickled fruits business had given up just a moment too soon, and that was why I didn't meet her through a Lost flyer. We met at the farmer's market; I was there with Lucy, who wanted to create a napoleon recipe inspired by the sticky rice and mango she tasted during the month Walter Lavender Sr. was assigned a line to Thailand. At the pickled fruits stall, she placed an order for two dozen jars of pickled mango and the woman apologized for being distracted because she had just lost an assortment of pewter thimbles that belonged to her mother.

When I interviewed the woman about the lost thimbles, she revealed the secrets only a friend would know — how she found adoption papers stashed inside a pair of mules her mother never wore and how she stopped speaking to her mother because of it, and how her mother got into a car accident while they still weren't speaking. Since then, she kept her mother's thimbles close by, and sometimes she wore them on her fingers and had conversations with them about her life and they talked back like little pewter puppets.

She held up her hand and gazed at her bare fingers and I saw their silver tips, permanent thimbles of light — the larger truth she didn't say about how she wore them all the time, the regret, the missing.

The thimbles were not in their box on her dresser, and so I asked her where she kept her sewing supplies. She dismissed the idea, saying that she had already ransacked the pine hutch, and I looked closely at it anyway and noticed what she missed, wrapped around the ring pull of the last drawer — the tail end of a length of lucent yarn, the beginning glowing now too, dangling from the place inside her cuff where she had patched up a rip.

I found the lost thimbles in the back of that drawer. She had indeed searched the pine hutch, but as she turned out one drawer after another, her despair mounted and by the time she started on that last drawer, she assumed the thimbles were gone and gave up before she reached the back.

She wasn't the first one who stopped looking too soon. It's not an uncommon mistake, but it's a big one, and I can't get rid of that itchy, niggling feeling that I am right on the cusp of finding a sign from Walter Lavender Sr., and so I keep looking, directly and indirectly.

The red light of the recorder blinks a little faster and I finish, for real, "It is to be continued."

At last I steal a look at Junker, and he is gazing into the distance with an odd grimace. I release the red button to end the recording and prepare for the slash and the sting. Junker sneezes and slides back into focus. I pass the tape recorder over to him. He puts it into his coat and his feathers tremble and we turn right, moving closer to the center of the city.

"It's just the thing," he says, patting his coat and feeling for the hard plastic corners of the tape recorder, and that's when I realize that he is happy.

I imagine him planting weeds in neat rows and setting tables for meals that will never come and listening to his new story as many times as he likes while he labors away, eternally buried. For all the times that weren't worth it — this time it was, and it has never mattered more that I was here.

We turn right, and this street is lined with trolleys and buses and vans and I think that we must be close by now.

Junker coughs to clear the cobwebs from his throat and says shyly, "Here we are. The library."

He gestures for me to move ahead of him and I glance around again. There are only deserted vehicles on this street, and not a single dilapidated building in sight. I look at

Junker for guidance but he is leaning against a bus with no wheels and glumly stripping off bits of peeling paint like they are hangnails. I wander down the street, peering under bumpers to be sure, and as I pause in the middle of the road, my gaze skips down the line of broken vehicles and plops onto a trolley.

Junker must've recently given it a fresh coat of paint; it is sapphire blue, and it is missing an entire panel along its flank and the inside isn't empty — it's filled like some densely ridged lung, and I draw near and they are bookcases, placed end-to-end and crammed with books, and I see what he did — the library he fashioned out of unwanted vehicles.

I cross the street to a van and pull open the back doors. Despite the van's rusted body, the door hinges are oiled and smooth. Shelves protrude from the sides, piled with books. I swing the doors shut and hop onto what was once a school bus. Instead of pairs of vinyl seats, Junker has installed bookcases, one on each side, and I shake my head in amazement.

I run down the aisle, brushing my fingers against the shelves, looking for the trail, but no signs jump out at me. Where has he shelved the Book?

I dash up the street to where Junker is waiting.

"I told you it would be disappointing," Junker says immediately, and I shake my head vigorously and he says, "Oh! Do you like it?" and I nod just as vigorously.

He ducks but can't suppress the glow radiating from the crown of his head. "I wondered if they might've been trying to build a track for the garbage trains with these tunnels. So I looked for boarded entrances in the rail yards and found one that connected."

He keeps staring down at his hands, and that is when I notice that he is clutching a book. A tentative warmth burgeons in my chest like pea shoots. Still looking at his hands, he thrusts his arms forward, and supported between his palms, two inches from my nose, is the Book. Joy pours into me like melted sunlight, warm and effervescent.

I take a deep breath. "This is my lost Book. It is found."

I hold out a hand and Junker looks strained. Then he pats his coat, four touches to feel out each corner of the tape recorder, and his expression clears and he gives me a firm nod and unclasps his hands. I hug the Book to my chest and squeeze until my hands stop shaking enough to retrieve the two pages I found earlier.

I open the Book and balance it on one hand and the first thing I see is the first page, no longer lost, and I shut my eyes and there is a flash of light against my eyelids, white and cold as snow under the moon. I trace the lines of ink from memory, the spidery labyrinth of streets, the shooting stars arcing across the page.

I flip the page and my stomach drops and I flip back again. The second page is missing. But the third page is there, and I feel my heart quickening like the wheels of the train steaming off the page, into the tunnels, and the wind rushes after it, parting my hair and billowing under my sleeves, and I stand still and captivated as the young man staring at the girl on the other side of the subway platform, her hair whipping across her proud face, her cloak of ice strikingly bright against the mundane scenery of concrete and trash cans and pillars and subway maps.

The fourth page is the one I found in Nico's sleeping bag — the girl falling in love too, and shedding her cloak of ice — and I insert the page into the Book and the next part of the story is the one Lan gave me, the girl abandoned and alone, and I flatten and insert page number five.

I flip —

And that is it. There are no more pages to flip, and that is not how it's supposed to be.

"Most of the story is missing," Junker says hurriedly. "The middle was missing even before I got it. When I was reading it on my way back, the girl sitting next to me started reading along over my shoulder. She said she saw herself in the second page, and then she also said that endings were the most interesting part. The part that stayed. She wanted them enough that she couldn't look away, so I couldn't take those pages here, where they no longer belonged. It was an enchanting story even with the hole, I should have known better than to think —"

Junker's feathers shrivel a little and he looks at me despondently and says, "I thought that maybe you would leave right away, if you knew," and I can feel my heart shriveling too, and the enormous cavern is too small, too tight, so gray.

I close the Book and hug it once more and tuck it away. Three more pages to go. It should feel like a victory but I am defeated. The Book was found and in the next moment lost again, and I am wrung out from the effort of searching and even more from the effort of speaking.

"Don't be upset," Junker says, flapping

his arms and looking aggrieved, and feathers drift and light on my high-tops. "You can find her. I'll tell you what I remember and you can go find her."

His words send a shot of energy flashing through my veins. I am halfway there. Milton will be waiting for me and worrying and so will Lucy, and she might have already launched a search for me. Time resumes ticking down and I have to get going, I have to find the rest of the Book before the landlord seizes the shop or a policeman seizes me.

"How can I find her?" I ask, buoyant once more.

Junker goes rigid and his eyes roll back and gleam glossy-white as peeled eggs. After a second, they roll forward and he brushes a feather away from his nose.

"She had black hair in a bun. She was wearing a backpack. The tag on it said *Ruby Fontaine.* Her T-shirt said Rudolf Steiner School and PE."

"Let's go," I say.

Our return journey mirrors our arrival; we take the same route, this time past the yellow and purple lane first and then the potholed road and clothes hanging to dry and scrap-metal shanties, and as we approach the fire escape Junker slows, turns iron-

248

heavy, fighting with each step to keep from sinking into the ground, and the corners of his mouth are weighted down too.

"You probably don't want to, but you can stay a little longer," he says.

He peers up at the gray window in the ceiling, waiting as if a great hand will reach in and scoop him out, and the wan light filters through like dawn coming and the little city is spilled out underneath it and a fearless energy floods across my skin.

I can't stay any longer, with a Book to find and a shop to save, but even more than that, I do not want to. The rat-couple opened my eyes; instead of choosing to wander these tunnels until I, too, am unwanted, I must acknowledge my fear and batter through it so that my mind is open and my voice, my words, come pouring forth.

Maybe Junker notices the change, because he moves out of the dawn light and assumes the lead again. I take a breath, my mind clear. "I need a shorter way back."

"You want a shortcut, to leave as quickly as possible," he says, which I can't deny, and his face droops. "There's a broom closet in the hall."

We climb up the fire escape and return to the hall, and he sits on his molded chair.

"Climb," he says, pointing at a door to his left.

"Thank —"

"Climb — climb —" he says gruffly, flapping a feathery arm at the door, and so I say instead, "Good-bye."

He hunches over the tape recorder and refuses to look at me. As I slip around him, he depresses a button and stares into the spokes of the tape as it rewinds.

I step into the closet and gaze up at the staircase spiraling into the darkness, and the hall fills with my recorded voice, grainy and resolute, and I shut the door behind me and begin to climb, gripping the railing, grateful that I can't see the ground shrinking below me.

17

My legs are heavy, my knees numbing, by the time I reach the top of the staircase. I fall against the door and it swings open and I stumble out into the tunnel, and the door swings shut and I see the cheerful canisters of processed products littering the ground, the rows of shelves — the pantry and now, I know, a hidden door too.

The tunnel is empty but I don't want to take any chances, and I set off at a brisk pace, alert for signs of rats or the rat-couple. Up the rusty ladder and through the crawl-space, I swim through the darkness until I spot a pair of glowing amber eyes. Milton barks and I swim faster for the opening and he wriggles himself out of the tunnel and I clamber out after him. By the time my vision adjusts, he is already rolled over on his back, squirming and flailing about, and I scratch around a shaggy armpit and his left leg beats the air. From somewhere not too far away, a train whistles.

"Five minutes," hollers the tour guide, and it takes me a moment to place his voice and another to understand that I have landed less than an hour from my point of departure.

Milton and I emerge from our passage and join the tourists buzzing and converging on the platform. The leader waves us onto the train and I twist and watch the station slip back into the shadows amid the amiable hum and chatter.

We get off at Broadway-Lafayette because I know there is a library down the block where I can look up Ruby Fontaine's school.

"No animals," the inspector at the door says, and I stop and do not say anything until he waves me inside, where it smells like warm sleep and the computer has fingerprints on the screen and the clock reads 12:19. Lucy definitely knows by now that I never made it to school and she would not waste any time in reporting me missing, and because of my age and my disorder the responding officer might escalate the case quickly — and what if an alert has already gone out?

I search for my name and my face blossoms across the screen. A shock of fear jolts through me — a block of text, fire-engine letters screaming MISSING — and I scramble to close the window before anyone sees.

I stare at the keyboard, waiting for the fear to drain, my hand twitching with aftershocks. It is critical to evade that search while I conduct mine, and I have to stay invisible and keep my eyes open for idling cruisers and lingering gazes. It bothers me that Lucy might think I ran away, and I hope she knows that I am searching and will be home as soon as I can, and I send her a telepathic update that I am not hurt.

Without wasting any more time, I look up Rudolf Steiner School and write in my notebook, 79 AND MADISON, and then Milton and I catch the next 6 train going uptown and I am disappointed when the voice over the intercom does not belong to Sally Fields, singer extraordinaire. I sit and observe the car, and first it's the rounded noodle-laces of a man's running shoes, and then the pacifier rolling down the aisle, and then the shiny lining of a forgotten beret and a sunny bottle of juice and a tube of lip balm — the yellows jumping out at me, reminding me of Junker's dandelions, and I think of Junker planting them in tidy rows and setting cups to three o'clock.

Standing there with him in the dawn light, I felt conviction for my bold choice to change, and I gather that conviction as the train stops at Seventy-seventh Street and we climb out of the station. It is the beginning of my second chance.

The traffic light turns green and triggers a torrential outpouring of yellow taxis. It's the middle of the day and people cross the streets in tailored neutrals and running shoes with their earphones and backpacks and totes, and a lady with pinned hair and a walker stops by the fruit cart next to us and examines a bunch of bananas.

Even though I know it is too early — it will be two hours before the Steiner bell rings and Ruby Fontaine can leave for the day — I orient myself and head uptown, because I also know that she is somewhere inside the school building and I can't stand to wait for the bell while the minutes thicken and stretch like saltwater taffy.

I picture her leaning over a test sheet, filling in the bubble for D, None of the Above, and glancing at the clock to see how long she has left, and that will be my chance to catch her attention through the window, pull her out of a class for just a minute to tell her why I am there, or there is a possibility it won't come to that and I will roam the hallways and stumble across some sign that points me to her locker, and the Book pages stashed inside, without needing to ask any questions at all.

I duck under a scaffold draped in orange netting, mulling over the possibilities of the case as I peer into shoebox-sized restaurants serving up green curries and baba ghanoush and sushi rolls. I think of other natural places for the Book pages to be, so that I will have a plan by the time I arrive — if not her locker, then her backpack, around her desk — and I pass by a gap between the buildings, an abandoned lot with a flea market that has squeezed itself into the space.

Lucy likes to slow when we pass one of these, to give the tented stands a chance to catch her eye, and out of habit my steps drag a little as I walk past.

Ruby could have left the Book pages at home, I think, and then I notice a brief ripple of light, something rolling underneath a display of vintage nutcrackers, catching the sun, and quick as a hiccup I sharpen my focus but there is nothing more to see, and someone bumps against my elbow and says, "Keep it moving," but it was there and I am sure of it, the shimmer-bright cascade and the rapid fade.

I step forward off the sidewalk and the person stuck behind me rushes past, his relief descending around my shoulders like a peppermint mist, and I get on my hands and knees and pat around under the nutcracker display, feeling asphalt roughened like tree bark, and then my hand closes around a smooth weight.

I pull out a chess piece, a king marked by the simple silhouette of its crown. I turn it over in my palm and again there's the reflective ripple like it is made of melting mirrors instead of ivory plastic, and that means I have picked up the trail but it is not where I expected it to be, and where does it lead and how can that be? Ruby Fontaine is supposed to have the Book pages and she is also supposed to be in school a few blocks away. Is she here, skipping school like me?

I study the nutcrackers, looking for any other lingering clues, and they chitter at me with their teeth clenched halfway shut, and I roll the king between my palms, unsure of veering off the path I have already carved out. I look down at Milton and he thrashes his tail — *What's the holdup?*

We follow the sign, I decide. Milton shakes himself off and trots into the flea market, and we pass a stand displaying photographs of people wearing helmets slicing through chilly elements — snow, air, water — and next to that a tent housing two plastic picnic tables and people playing chess. I squeeze the king and bright light shudders down one side, and I follow the clue to the chess tent.

I scan the first table, two games in progress and bystanders leaning over the boards and rubbing their chins, and they don't seem to be looking for any pieces but there is a woman at the second table setting up a third chessboard, and if I were the kind of person to place bets I would bet a dozen mice and a handful of marzipan dragons on her missing a king.

She picks a piece out of a small heap on the table and rubs it under her collar, and a tattoo of a proud lion tears into the folds of her neck, and next to her is a small boy wearing dark glasses who slouches on the edge of the bench, as far away as possible from the mound of her shoulders. The boy taps a white cane on the ground, staring ahead with his features glazed in disinterest. I approach the table as the woman places the polished piece on the board.

"You got the cojónes to face off with Center Sammie and Roman?" she says without looking up from her task, and I hold out the king. She glances at it and says dismissively, reflexively, "Don't need it," and then she bares her teeth and stops to think about it. She raises a meaty arm and rakes through the pile on the table, four pieces left and one knight has some dirt smeared into its mane, and no king.

"Huh," she says. She holds up a finger and roots around in her pockets.

She digs out a handful of coins and a hardened cake of napkins and receipts and drops them on the table, and from the other pocket she digs out a set of keys and a pair of nail clippers and tosses them on the table too, and finally from her breast pocket a folded piece of paper, unusually thick and tinted with age and ragged on the edges, and this she removes more delicately and weights down with the nail clippers.

"Not on me, either. I didn't notice I dropped it." She stretches forward to take the king and says begrudgingly, *"Gracias, niño."*

She plunks it down next to the nail clippers and I can't leave or turn away because my vision is contracting around the folded piece of paper and it is all I can see, that and the king sitting beside it, unmoving, light strumming across its surface.

"What is that?"

She wiggles the folded paper out from under the nail clippers and unfolds it.

"A reminder of what I'm playing for," she says, laying it flat on the table, and I jump forward and my knee slams into the frame and I grab the edge of the table like it is everything keeping me upright because right there — across the table, next to the radiant king — is a page from the Book.

I whip out the flyer, almost tearing it in my haste to unfold it, and I push it toward Sammie. That page is part of the book, I say, and the air rushes out of me too quickly and I run out of breath for speaking. I slow down and say, "That is lost. I am looking for it."

She looks down at the page and then at the flyer and lastly at me, and her mouth hardens.

"Your mistake," she says. "A friend gave this to me a few days ago."

A rubber band snaps around my lungs. "Who?"

"A girl named Ruby. I taught her to play chess."

So Junker gave the pages to Ruby, and for whatever reason, she gave one to Sammie. I reach for the Book to prove that the page is part of it and when I show Sammie the pages I have already found, she stretches and scratches her tattoo, gives her head a quick shake like a mosquito has landed on her nose.

"I see. But I've already become attached

to it. It's still from my friend, and I still need my reminder." My heart sinks and she sees it, and she gives the boy a sidelong glance and looks back at me and the proud lion dips its mane and its eyes soften in an almost motherly way.

"All right, I'll consider it. But I always say, the things you want, you have to *earn.*" Her eye twitches so quickly I am not sure if it is a wink. "So how are you going to earn it back?"

I think of what else I have in my pocket — a chocolate bar, a MetroCard, a notebook. Nothing she would want, and my throat dries, the warmth leaking out, and I cup the edges of the table tighter, trying to hold on to some of it. "It is my lost —"

"You said that already, *niño.* Unless you have something else, I have a game to play . . ." Sammie trails off and I realize that she is waiting for me to ask her to play, and I am silent and Sammie snorts with distaste and the lion puffs its chest and holds its head higher, its neck a proud, powerful curve.

Sammie shields the page with her arm and looks away to end the conversation, but that would mean the end of the shop and how will Walter Lavender Sr. find his way then, and the rest of us too?

260

I think of the rat-couple waiting for a child to find them; I think of me waiting on the sidelines for an invitation to join. I realize that I have to be the one to extend the invitation, to make the first move. I curl my hands into fists and take a seat across from Sammie. The corners of her mouth turn up and she drums her fingers on top of the clock, da-da-da-*dum,* and the chess board in front of her is flimsy and black and white like a test.

I will not be very good at this game, any game, because I have only ever watched. But I cannot run away like this is another dodgeball game and I am Beaver's moving target. I need to convince Sammie to part with the page she has grown attached to, and the only way to do that is to earn it through her chess game.

I take a steadying breath and offer to play her for the page, but my words do not come out straight and she's frowning, stiffening, and I feel the old fear winding through my mind and freezing over the pathways of my brain.

But I made another choice in the tunnels. Giving up and retreating is no longer an option, and there is nothing to it but to keep trying. There are worse things to be afraid of now, and instead of scattering in panic, I redouble my efforts, narrow my focus, and I announce, "I will play you for it."

Sammie's expression flickers with understanding and then gratitude and then her mouth tugs up into a competitive smirk — and I did it! A phrase coming out of my mouth that I have not practiced, words that are not tied to finding, words meant for trying and joining, hearing and understanding.

My world explodes with possibilities. What will Lucy say? When I return home and I open my mouth and she hears my voice telling her, for the first time, that I love her and missed her — what will she say? What will she do?

"Now you're talking," Sammie says, and I stay seated at her table, still shivering with the excitement and the exertion and a profound relief like popping in a dislocated shoulder. I am really here, about to play her game.

Under the table, Milton turns two circles, preparing to hunker down, and I shuffle my feet away surreptitiously but he redirects, crushing my toes with a long-suffering sigh, and soon enough the creeping numbness will come but in the clear golden planes of his mind he is protecting me from freezing or disappearing. I keep my feet where they are.

Sammie slaps the clock and it resets with a flat click. "They call me Center Sammie because a bullet got lodged in my sternum and I got the scar to show it. A little to the left of center and there would be no Sammie. This is my grandson, Roman."

Roman scowls at the mention of his name. "I don't want to play. I want to go home," he says, and even if he cared to, he can't see how the words sting Sammie's fierce leathery face.

"I want to share with you while I still can, *nieto*. It's the only thing I have to give you," she says.

Roman makes a sour expression but stays quiet, tapping with his cane until it jabs Milton in the side. Looking into the distance, he gropes under the table. Milton stretches his head forward and bumps it against Roman's hand — *Over here* — and Roman grasps his ear and stretches it.

"Roman and I are still getting to know each other," Sammie explains, watching Roman brush Milton's ear. "His parents and I — we weren't close for a long time." She starts to drift away and the game reminds her to come back. "So how do you want to open?"

She starts the clock and wraps a large paw around Roman and pulls him closer. Roman squirms away and feels tentatively around his side of the board with his right hand.

Sammie is quiet and attentive, watching him make his move, and a brash voice rises from another stall — "You look like a windsurfer. How about a kite pump?" — and I glance at the neighboring extreme sports tent.

A short man with army fatigues and a head like a shiny dome is circling around someone who has stopped to browse. He picks up an even shinier helmet and says, "Skydiving gear?" His voice is too loud, like he is worried everyone will miss the important things he has to say. A delicate clatter draws my attention back to the board, where Roman has knocked over a few pieces in the process of pulling himself up to his knees.

"That's easy to fix," Sammie says, reaching to tidy the pieces.

"No!" Roman shouts, and he shoves Sammie's arm out of the way and pats wildly around the table to recover the fallen pieces himself.

He replaces the pieces one by one, taking the extra time to line them up in scrupulously straight rows. He pulls back to begin again but his hand sweeps too low and once more the pieces clatter onto the board like dominoes and that is the wrong game. His lip trembles and his face turns white and red with rage.

"I told you this game is stupid and I hate it! I hate you! I can't wait to go home." Roman picks up a knight and hurls it at the ground and Milton interprets it like he interprets any object galloping along a different path — that it is meant for him — and he bolts out from under the table to fetch it.

I look at Sammie, worried, and her face is as white and red as Roman's under the saddle-brown of her skin but she says, "That's okay. I know — he's just frustrated. I should have patched things up earlier with his parents. He was born, holidays, birthdays — I was too proud to ask to be a part of their lives. I thought, they should come to me. They should *earn* my forgiveness." The lion on her neck constricts and her immense shoulders bunch helplessly.

"So stupid. Stage 4 lung cancer — that doesn't leave a lot of time. But we'll get to know each other. By the time I'm saying my good-byes, he'll have a few good moments to remember his *abuela* by. I guarantee you."

For all her strong words, I look into her

eyes as she watches Roman and I see the telescoping of her pupils like looking at something far away, beyond her grasp, and I know what she's looking for is a bridge, like the ex-agent who'd lost his old identification card.

He was quiet and unassuming and if it weren't for the card, I would not have believed his former role in the CIA. He lived with his daughter's family and as his Alzheimer's progressed, his daughter took on more, helping him shave and eat and bathe and use the toilet. His identification card was outdated and useless, but he kept it under his pillow and it reminded him of his past life and the things he had been capable of doing.

Lost things are bridges. They are connections to some other time or place or person or feeling, and for the ex-agent, the identification card was a bridge to the person he knew himself to be. I ended up finding the identification card in the daughter's wallet; it had fallen off the bed and she picked it up off the floor and pocketed it, mistaking it for one of her own cards.

Sammie has not lost a thing but she is far away from Roman, and she needs a bridge to help her reach him. Milton returns and drops the knight in my lap and watches it intently so it doesn't disappear, and I look away to give Sammie some space for herself and to think. Our clock winds down, forgotten, while the other games proceed at a frantic pace, and at the next table a girl with a severe bowl cut knocks over the white king and her mother captures the moment with a practiced point and click.

I tell Sammie that I will be back, and I walk over to the extreme sports tent.

"Anti-fog kit for your sunglasses? Paragliding boots?" the owner bellows at me and everyone and no one.

I point at a knife.

"Two hundred eighty five," he responds immediately like an auctioneer.

I shake my head and pick up the knife, unfolding it to give myself time to prepare my words and concentrate. I take a breath.

"For ten minutes?" I try, and he says, "Ten . . . ?" and I point at his watch.

"Ten minutes? You can borrow this one." He unfolds his own pocketknife and hands it to me and I sit down at the picnic table and clear the chess pieces, try to pick up the board, and Sammie does not let me pick it up until I say, "One more try?"

She watches me closely and releases the board. "One more try."

I set the point of the knife against a corner

267

square and push the knife through and saw in a circle like removing chocolate turtle cakes from their ramekins, and I imagine running the blade along the inside of the ramekin to loosen the edges, and the dark, decadent surface of the cake, and the knife completes a full revolution and a black round pops free.

I hold the board up and blow away the cardboard-dust and peer through the hole. I grab a pawn and push the base into the hole and the hole is too small. I push the knife through and widen the circle, and when that's done I elevate the chess board by placing it on the chess box, one end on each box-half to create Sammie's bridge. I push the base of the pawn through the hole and it squeezes through and catches around the next ridge, and now the piece is planted firmly in the hole.

Sammie touches the top of the pawn. She pulls it out and trades it for a queen and when that fits too, her smile grows broader than her shoulders. "*Nieto,* look at the surprise our friend has made."

Roman reaches for the board. His mouth puckers like tasting something tart and sweet and he pushes his palm against the queen Sammie wedged into the board and it does not fall over.

He yanks the queen out and plunks it back into the hole and he grips the edges of the two boxes and shakes, and with his hands he sees that the queen is still standing.

His face opens, mouth widening and eyebrows rising around his dark glasses. "It works," he says.

I hand the knife to Sammie and she takes it and presses the point against the next square, and then she puts the knife back down.

"You've earned this, *amigo.*"

She slides the page under the chessboard bridge and I take it, looking down at the illustration — the door opening, light falling across the page and pushing the menacing squall to the edges and corners, and within the idyllic glow of the doorway are a few simple lines to denote the shop's tables and chairs.

Overhead, the clouds part and rays of sun fall across the table in warm patches and I watch the patterns of light dancing across my chest like looking into a swimming pool, and this must've been the feeling of seeing a new door opening. The light leaps down my arms and ripples over my hands and held there, in my palms, is the seventh page of the Book.

"Board ready?" Roman wants to know,

balancing on his knees and tipping into Sammie's side.

Sammie glances down at his unruly brown hair and the slash of her mouth quirks apart at the unfamiliar angle, and I understand why it was hard for her to part with the page before — it reminded her to keep trying until Roman opens the door and gives her a chance to come in, and now she does not need it anymore. I take out my notebook, thinking of the strength draining from her massive shoulders. It must have hurt when she tried and Roman pushed her away and each time the space between them grew.

Even without the page, though, she would have gone on trying all the same, and what did she know that kept her from giving up? I poke my head under the table to look at Milton and he scrapes his tongue up my face like he does when I lie on the floor and pretend to sleep, and that reminds me of the simple reason — AT THE END, A DREAM WORTH WAKING FOR — and that is how I felt after sharing Walter Lavender Sr.'s story with Junker, and the moments that matter are the ones I need to remember.

"The board will be ready soon, *nieto*," she says.

She saws out round after round and the air darkens as a cloud blocks out the sun. I have been bold and I have been a part of the game and I have found another page because of it, and now it is time for me to continue my search.

Before I leave the tent, I ask Sammie what she knows about Ruby Fontaine.

"These days, not much. It's been a long time since we played chess — besides bumping into her this week, it was months since I last saw her. Sorry," she says, and I mean it when I shake my head to tell her that I am not, and I stand and Milton stands and stretches his back, arching and exhaling and holding the pose like a yoga instructor.

With the page in my pocket, I leave the flea market, heading west now, striding purposefully toward Rudolf Steiner. The possible places sing in my eardrums, pound against my chest — Ruby, school, home; locker, desk, backpack — and still I can't help peering into windows, looking through the breaks in traffic, waiting for the moment to come, watching for the sign.

18

Down Seventy-eighth, past Park and Madison, strings of lights have been wound around tree branches, red bows affixed to streetlamps, pinecone-studded wreaths and fluffed snow arranged in display windows. Milton and I trot down narrow streets lined with brownstones and trees and wrought-iron fences, past smart awnings and mild doormen and spiral-shaped bushes.

The school is housed in a four-story limestone building, easily identifiable by the white flag hanging over the second row of windows. As I make my way up the block toward the mansion, a woman in a gray blouse comes out of the arched doorway and down the steps and her hair is the same shade of gray, cut above her shoulders. She pops a cigarette in her mouth and sits on a red bench.

A teacher? An administrator? Immediately my steps drag and my mind races and

Milton bumps into me. What will this woman assume if she sees me outside the school at this hour, accompanied only by Milton?

Even if she concludes that I am not an escaped student of the school and therefore none of her business, I will become her business if she sees me snooping around the building or attempting to enter, and that will be the end of it.

The woman cups her hands around her mouth and there is a flare of light and she inhales and exhales smoke that is gray too. She rests her hand on her knee and smoke curls over her head and she gazes like a watchful dragon in the other direction. She inhales again and turns and I can tell by the way her head tilts that she has spotted me.

I drop my eyes and keep them trained on my high-tops as I walk toward her, trying to look like I am doing exactly what I should be doing, and I can feel her watching me when I pass and the air between us pinches but she is not saying or doing anything and I am coming up to the doorway now, and maybe I have misjudged and she is just a visitor and does not think anything of me. I steal a look at her and she looks like she is trying to solve a sudoku, and when she sees my brief pause in front of the steps she

273

pushes Milton's nose away from her gray tights and stands.

"Walter Lavender?" she says uncertainly, watching me for confirmation.

Smoke burns through my nose and the alarm in my head blares. Do not answer, I instruct myself. That is not you.

I put my chin down and rush forward, telling Milton, Come. I speed-walk to the end of the block, hurrying away from Ruby Fontaine and the Book but also away from the gray woman, and Milton lopes after me and I take a peek over my shoulder. The woman is not running after me but she has taken a few steps forward and stopped, held back by her indecision.

I speed-walk on, pushing a silent message back to her, It is nothing, it is nothing, and hoping she does not throw her restraint to the wind and give chase. After the woman finishes her smoke break — after she flattens the cigarette under her gray shoe and climbs the steps and disappears into the building — only then can I return and venture inside.

The cramped, car-lined street opens into the wide boulevard of Fifth Avenue and the east wall of Central Park. I cross the street, weaving around tourists and cars. On the other curb, I chance another glance over my

274

shoulder and jump at the gray blur, but it is just a double-decker bus and I try to laugh even though my stomach is still coiled in ropes.

That was too close, and on this street corner it is still too easy for us to be found. We need to lose ourselves. Before us is the vast expanse of Central Park, and so we move west and up, slipping through a maze of sinuous paths alongside bikers and joggers and strollers, and over ponds and lakes on stone bridges, and across grassy meadows strewn with leaves and tripods and blankets, and trees everywhere grasping for the sky, gossamer-wild and stark as ink lacework. The city falls away and my jumpiness turns soft and muffled and distant too.

We stumble onto a great lawn and Milton senses the open space and breaks away, racing across the swath of pasture with his ears flapping in the wind until he is a speck against the gray-green grass. The speck lingers for a moment and then it grows larger and resolves into Milton again, frothing and heaving like a racehorse as he slows and pads in a circle around me.

I stick to the border of grass and path, walking past a bundled-up woman lying on her stomach flipping through a magazine and two men with a baby cuddled between them and a group of people playing field hockey, and the grassy ground is better suited for the sport now than in the spring or summer. A blister is forming where my little toe rubs against the hole in my high-top and hunger is scooping a concave hollow in my stomach and I wonder how long I have to walk before going back. A few more minutes, to be sure.

I am cutting across a secluded corner when I catch a smell like fresh wet stone and feel a slight give under my feet like the ground has turned to mud underneath the tough surface.

I investigate, a little embarrassed at first to be walking in on someone's sorrow, but there is no one to be seen, just a large tree with a hulking kite propped next to it, a long bag with a zipper down the middle lying twisted underneath one wing. The ground sinks more as I move closer to the tree and I halt and prod the strange soft earth with my toe, and I guess that the source of the tears is behind the tree.

RAINY DAY REFLECTIONS, I add to my notebook, and then I sidle toward the tree to check on the person behind it.

Lucy liked to tell me, with a shake of her head and a half-smile, that Walter Lavender Sr. always seemed to be at the right place at just the right times, like when she almost went over the ship's rail or when he found the man who needed an electrician crying on the corner. There was also the time he walked by someone's parking meter right as it expired and a uniformed woman pulled up on a scooter and he stopped to drop two quarters into the slot, and the time he stood behind a woman in the checkout line who flushed red when three of her cards were declined and he told the cashier that the bread loaf and eggs were his, actually.

When Lucy told me these things — about his knack for appearing right when he was needed — it never seemed like the time to interrupt and remind her that he wasn't, not always, or not when he crossed his heart and said he would be.

Still, Walter Lavender Sr. was not one to look the other way, and so I knock three times on the trunk and turn around to wait, and Milton watches a dimpled white ball roll past as a field hockey player in red knee-socks sprints over and hooks the ball and slaps it back and sprints away.

No one emerges from behind the tree and so I peek around it and there is a man sitting there, calmly eating a sandwich with his legs stretched out in front of him and his head resting against the trunk. Next to him is the kite, and it is banded in black and red and yellow. Milton's heavy breathing fills the air and the man sits up and twists to the left, his mouth going slack around a mouthful of bread when he sees me.

His face is dry, tired, and behind frameless square glasses his eyes look limp and wrung out too; he is not distressed, or not anymore. I wave apologetically and pull back to leave him alone. Beside me, Milton perks up at the sight of the sandwich and by the time I react, grabbing for his collar, it is too late and he is lunging forward.

He bumps the man's knee with his nose and sits up soldier-straight, watching the man solemnly until he surrenders the rest of his sandwich, stripping off the plastic wrap and turning it over onto the ground.

I reach for Milton, sputtering apologies, and I hear from somewhere behind us the ear-splitting crack of a field hockey stick connecting with the ball, and Milton strains against my pulling and gobbles up a slice of roast beef.

"That is okay," the man says in brusque, flatly accented English. He is thin and angled — elbows and knees and pointed nose — and he wears a turtleneck with a tweed jacket over it.

"Actually, I have packed quite a lot of food. It is a little much for me. Would you like to have some lunch?" *Vood,* he says, tapping the dent in his chin. His brown hair is greasy and parted in the middle and he pushes it out of his face to study me better, and I release Milton and the man nudges aside a can of paint and unzips his cooler.

"Today I have a Spanish-inspired roast beef, with marinated artichoke heart, stuffed olives, red pepper, and provolone on focaccia." He unwraps a sandwich and hands me half and takes a bite of the other half. My stomach growls.

"This is a nice recipe. I will have to repeat it sometime," he says, swallowing. Milton tosses a chunk of focaccia into the air and grapples with the roast beef like it is trying to escape. I give the man an emphatic nod around a mouthful of sandwich.

"It is — how do you say — a new leaf." He adjusts his glasses and leaves an olive oil slick on the lens. "Every day for seven years, I have been eating sandwiches with turkey and Swiss cheese in a ratio of two to one. That is what I like. My wife hated making that boring sandwich all the time. Since she — *ach* —"

He makes a gruff, sad noise like loosening the regret stuck to the back of his throat.

"Last year, she *left* — I have been trying some different things in my life. Such as, for example, new lunch sandwiches. Yesterday was ham and mango with Dijon and parsley on a wheat roll. That one was not so delicious. I think I will not make it again. Tomorrow I have scheduled roasted turkey and cream cheese on a cranberry-walnut loaf. Ah —" He removes his glasses and polishes it with a cloth. "I forget that we are still strangers. I am Karl."

I find the words for introducing myself and before I can think too much I throw myself into them, saying, "My name is Walter."

"Pleased to meet you," Karl says.

Encouraged, I add, "This is Milton."

"Pleased to meet you as well," Karl says.

"I am looking for this." I hunch over to show him the flyer.

"I see a lot of books, but I have not seen that one," he says between chews.

"A girl. Ruby Fontaine?"

"I apologize to be so totally unhelpful," he says, shaking his head. "I will look out for your book and your Ruby Fontaine when I am in the air." He points a thumb at his kite.

I take a bite from where I am standing and he takes a bite from where he is sitting and I chew and consider the kite. It looks like a bird on the verge of flight, poised on a metal triangle with its nose pointed up and its canvas skin stretched in an inverted V over metal wing bones.

I finish the sandwich half and brush the crumbs from my hands. The gray woman should be gone by now, leaving the coast clear to sneak into the school.

Time to go try again, I think, looking down at Milton, who has flopped onto his side for a nap, and then at Karl, to say thank you and good-bye, but Karl has forgotten that his mouth is full and is staring with a hard-focused pain into his sandwich like he has bitten into a fly.

He lowers the sandwich and notices me looking.

"It is strange," he says, swallowing with difficulty, "to miss something you never had."

His words run me through, a piercing blaze like headlights in the dark, and I am exposed. How could he know this about me, and does that mean he has seen right through me and what else does he know?

I want to dart away but my body stays pinned to the spot, and he continues, "These days, I have the thought — you would say, out of the blue — for example,

281

would my son or daughter like this sandwich we are having, if she had been born?"

He is talking about himself, I realize. It could just as easily be me only he doesn't know that, and that is good and safe and relieving.

And yet — I cannot be content with that. I journeyed through the tunnels and now that I have made it back, I know that it is not enough to learn something essential only about him; that kind of connection is unequal, lopsided.

The pressure behind my forehead is hard to ignore, like someone tapping incessantly against a door, wanting to be let out. This longing for what never was — it is one part of who I am that I guard closely. But I want the chance to forge a connection that endures beyond losing and finding, and I think I want him to know this essential thing about me and I think it would help him too — that his missing is something we share.

I uproot a blade of grass and shred it, searching for the right words, and when I find them they flow through me, strong and unafraid. "I do not think it is strange. When it happens to me."

"What is this something you miss, that you never had?" Karl hangs his sandwich over Milton's nose like smelling salts and watches as Milton revives and snaps at it, and I pull up another blade of grass and it is like straw, flammable, and so is my throat.

"My dad. What he would teach me. All I do not know."

Karl makes a noise of assent and says, "I think if I had become a papa, I would learn quite quickly that there are even *more* things I do not know."

I wonder about this and he continues, "Of course, I have also thought of what I would teach him or her. You should like physics but not too much, you should at least understand condensed matter physics but you do not need to be a particle physicist. You should know about love and . . ." He makes a flourish with his hand. "Well, I would not say it like that. I would say it in a better way, such as —" He deepens his voice so that it reverberates in his chest and tells his sandwich, "Nothing lasts forever but my love for you will. Then I will teach, Do not waste money or time. Do be proud of who you are."

And I hear the truth in what he is saying, about the way a father loves. The whole time I have been worrying about measuring up and always falling short, and maybe all Walter Lavender Sr. really wanted was for me to be proud of myself.

Milton whips his tail across the grass so that it thumps against the Book in my pocket — *You should be* — and I am awash in something bright and deep like peace, thinking about the search I have embarked on and the people I have met and the voice I am finding. Milton goes back to sleep and I think about waking him, wondering if it is the right time to go back and search the school —

I am startled by a chorus of shouts and a wooden slap, and Karl flinches and hunkers down like the ball is going to hit him. It comes nowhere close but it does send him scrambling into action, unzipping his cooler and rooting through it.

"Excuse me. Did you want another sandwich?"

I unwrap the plastic and he gets up and stretches his back and moves to stand under the kite-bird, kicking aside the long zippered bag, and I join him and we look up at the canvas wings.

"She is a super hang glider, no? The smallest details have to be perfect for her to fly, especially around the wings. It is hard to believe, but for weeks this building has consumed me more than my physics research ever has."

He steps out from under the wings and

points at the letters stenciled along the inner edge of the right wing where it is banded in yellow — CARRIE — and he says, "Today I completed the naming. Carrie, for my wife." The letters themselves are a little lumpy but the alignment is precisely parallel with the aluminum rib.

I run my hand along the metal triangle and Karl points at the bottom leg of the triangle. "That is the control bar. With the control bar, I will maneuver the hang glider by shifting my weight left and right. Leaning forward to speed up, leaning back to bleed speed."

I gape at Karl when I realize he means to fly with the hang glider, and he says, "Forecasted conditions tonight are ideal for launch, with wind speed around thirty kilometers per hour, although I will have to wait and see to make sure."

I tap the bar and it makes a weak *ting* and he is unconcerned about that as he informs me that it is made of aluminum tubing and stainless steel cable. He points at the straps and metal rings hanging from the top point of the triangle and says, "This is where I will be suspended, flying like Superman." He runs a hand along the wing. "The sail — made of woven polyester fabric, polyethylene terephthalate. The sail and the frame, it is constructed to be light yet strong."

I put both hands on the control bar and try to lift the hang glider and it rises a little off the ground. It feels like a fifty-pound sack of flour — not heavy enough to be strong, not light enough to fly. I imagine being suspended in the harness, facedown to the earth so far below, and my stomach swoops and the strength drains out of my hands, oozes through my palms and turns them clammy, and I scrape them down the sides of my jeans.

"This is the cool part." Karl points at an instrument attached to a side leg of the triangle. "An airspeed indicator, to measure and record how fast the hang glider is going. It took some time to order it and to wait for the delivery, but — ah, it is worth it." He takes out his polishing cloth and caresses the indicator, wiping micro-specks of dust from the surface.

"Think of the data I will collect," he says, and the expression on his face relaxes into something easier, more natural, and it is obvious why he is a physics professor. "The fact is, with the flying, I am not so sure I will do it right. This is the aspect I can be sure — I will do it right."

I lean forward to examine the airspeed indicator and it looks like a thermometer set inside a test tube, and there is a crack like wood splitting behind me and someone bellowing, "Look out!" and the field hockey ball hurtling toward me like a comet. Before I know it I am springing back, my arms shielding my head, and the ball bounces off the hang glider instead and lands on the ground with a compact thump.

"Sorry," a man yells as he races to beat Milton to the ball. I lower my arms and my hands are shaking with adrenaline and I hide them behind my back.

"*Ach* —" Karl's voice climbs high as a yowling cat and he dives and it hits me that the ball might have damaged the hang glider because I moved out of the way instead of trying to knock it off its path. I rush forward but there is no fixing what happened, and he finishes collecting the pieces of his airspeed indicator and a shard of glass cuts him and draws blood and I feel the stab, the bloom of guilt.

He tries to meld the largest pieces together and they fall apart when he lets go. He tries again and stares down at his hands. "It is broken," he says, dumbfounded.

"Sorry, sorry," I babble as he juggles combinations of pieces and tries repeatedly to fuse them together, and I have ruined the one thing that he could be sure about and look forward to. I think about the hang glider he labored over, named for the wife who left, and his missing for the son or daughter he never had, and my guilt spreads like a stain and I rub my hands frantically.

His movements slow and then stop, and he opens his hands to let the pieces drop into his cooler. He zips them in with the sandwiches and stands with his head bowed in mourning over the cooler, which sits leaden and gray as a tombstone on the grass.

"It is true that I do not have to have it," he says distantly, like it is someone else reassuring him. "That is that."

"Sorry, sorry," I am still saying, and he shakes his head and says in a stronger voice, "There is no need for sorry. As long as the weather holds up, I will fly without it. We will at last have the chance to see what Carrie and I are made of."

So he has been waiting for this for a long time, and my guilt sinks deeper and the damp of it prickles and itches. I wonder what it means, his preoccupation and anticipation and the regret lodged in his throat, and why did his wife leave last year when they were in love?

It is a question that I know well. I tell myself that Walter Lavender Sr. did not want to leave and become lost, but with each passing year of the same waiting and looking, I find that there are more times when I am angry and blame him, or ashamed and blame myself — although, after what Karl said, I am more certain that Walter Lavender Sr. is not trying to stay lost on purpose. It doesn't seem like Karl's wife would want to leave, either, and I have to know if she is also lost and needs finding and so I ask, "Where is she?"

On the wing of the hang glider, her name glistens black as midnight silk.

"She's dead," he says, and the smell of wet stone rises into a stench and my guilt over the broken indicator shrinks against the vast ocean of his, and his is a grief that could swallow me whole like it is nothing.

He sags against the tree. "Because I forgot about her," he says, and then the grief and the guilt wash over him and pull him under too.

I sit on the other side of the tree and shift to make room for Milton, who has roused himself to follow me. He believes that he will fit under the tent of my legs if he wriggles enough, and I lift my legs and let my feet dangle so that he can continue to believe it.

It doesn't matter that I can find lost things. There is no looking for Carrie when my search for the Book is over, or ever.

The unsettled churning in the pit of my stomach intensifies and even though I know Carrie is really gone, I wish that I could go back and catch the ball, and why didn't I think to deflect it before it was too late?

Karl has fallen silent and I look around the tree and he is poring over a page covered in formulas with the same hard anguished expression as before. I take a closer look at the page, at the diagrams of hang gliders and wind arrows and the labyrinth of boxes. They look like the jumble of stalls in the flea market and I feel a swing of excitement between my ribs.

"I know where. You can find a new one," I say into the tree.

"I would have to order it. I do not need it," he says without moving, and I explain about the flea market and the extreme sports tent, and there is a chance that among the boots for paragliding and the helmets for skydiving and the kite pumps for windsurfing, the owner will have an airspeed indicator for hang gliding.

There is a rustling and Karl appears in front of me and says, "Where?" and I slide my feet off Milton's back and offer to show him. I can spare the time even if it means starting my search for Ruby Fontaine fifteen or thirty minutes later. The indicator is broken, and I can't go back to change that but I can ensure that Karl doesn't miss the tent.

"Lead the way," Karl says, handing me the can of paint and slinging the cooler across his back.

I ask him if he will leave the hang glider here and he says, "The first time I did not lock my bicycle, I saw someone ride it away through the window. No, there is a lab close by that I use to store *Carrie*."

He dismantles parts of the hang glider and folds the wings like an accordion and puts them all in the zippered bag, and he takes one end and hoists it over his shoulder and I take the other and place it on my head like carrying a canoe, and the three of us march single file through the trees to Karl's lab.

Karl swipes us into the basement of a building crusted in vines and rusted air-conditioning units, and I step into the dim hall, where the air is still and contained and smelling thickly of morning breath, and it makes me long for the shop before the Book became lost — fresh air and light swirling over the displays and tables and shelves and chandeliers.

"Not many people use this place any-more," Karl says, leading us down the hall and unlocking a door. He balances the hang glider bag on his shoulder and turns the knob and pushes the door open with his knee. "It is a perfect place for me to work on *Carrie* without disruption."

He must have forgotten to turn the lights off on his way out because they are already on, and I tread over a Welcome mat and there are three pairs of shoes lined up along it, a pair of slippers and a pair of boots and Milton stuffs his nose into a river shoe that is too small to be Karl's, and also the webbed toes are hot pink.

"She was always the adventurous one," Karl says, nodding at the shoes. "All these interests, hiking and Patagonia and human rights and Marilyn Monroe and so forth. I am just the professor with his nose in the proofs.

"This way," he says, and we walk down an aisle of long counters littered with books and pizza boxes and stamped with sticky rings. I step over soda cans and at the end of the counter there is a sink, and next to it, two toothbrushes slotted into a repurposed ice-cream pint.

We set the bag down on the floor. Karl straightens and rolls his shoulder and gestures down the aisle, and as I walk past him, I notice a cake on the opposite counter. It is small and crammed with candles, and I move closer and see that it's a plain vanilla cake with a rosette of gray mold growing on the side, which does not make sense because the candles are unlit, the cake untouched.

"She would be thirty-six," Karl says, stopping beside me. "I know that she is not here to see, but it is that — it is that when she turned thirty-five, I did not notice."

I count the candles, thirty-six of them, and I take in the pile of blankets under the counter and the Marilyn Monroe pop art mug on top of it — as if his wife might suddenly stumble through the door and recognize the things that are hers and know that this room is theirs. I can guess at how much time Karl spends here, under the buzzing of the wan fluorescent lights, just him and *Carrie* and the depths of his grief, and I have only waded into the shallows.

Slowly, I ask, "What happened to you and Carrie?"

He does not understand me and I try again with easier words, kneeling and putting a hand over the folded hang glider.

"Why?"

"The hang glider? I have been building it since it came to me in a dream." He tugs

293

on his turtleneck and looks sideways at me as if giving me permission to laugh and I do not. He kneels next to me.

"It is the night of the faculty reception at the Cloisters," he says in a low voice, lifting the hang glider out of the bag. "One month before that, we woke up on sheets that were heavy with red. They were clotted with blood. Bright red.

"She got up and made a turkey and Swiss sandwich. I went to work, stayed late, to the normal time. Like other things, we did not speak about this one, either. But on the night of the reception, she looked beautiful and happy and had taken extra time for curling her hair and red lipstick. I thought she had recovered from the miscarriage and I was relieved."

There was a woman who lost the tube of 99 Pirate she wore the morning of her wedding. From my interviews with her, I know the way a swipe of color can evoke particular emotions and mind-sets. I picture Karl's wife painting her lips red with a sure hand and it makes me uneasy.

"In my dream, though, the next parts are different," Karl says, unfolding the wings across his lap. "I notice and I tell her she looks like Marilyn Monroe. She is drinking, we both are, and late in the night she needs some air. There are prominent professors I want to stay and talk with, but I go outside to find her anyway.

"It is a balmy night, and it sounds like trees and fast cars. I call her name, no answer. I follow the path. It climbs higher, tracing the Hudson toward the Heather Garden. At last, I see her on the overpass. She is standing on the stone wall with the cars whistling far underneath and the river at her fingertips. Somehow, she slips.

"It looks easy, graceful. It could have been an accident. I am running toward her and somehow I am running on a cliff above the overpass, running so fast my feet don't touch the ground. There is a weight on my back, and I look overhead to see that wings have sprouted out of my shoulder blades. I run straight off the edge of the boulder, to save her."

Karl finishes reassembling the hang glider and flicks away a leaf stuck to the freshly dried paint. "Tonight I am ready to launch from that same cliff, as I have dreamed. Tonight," he repeats, thumping the spine of the hang glider. "Together with Carrie, I will soar high above the city lights."

He braces himself against the frame and stares past the sail. Standing in the sickly white-green light, in the strange quiet of pizza crusts and long counters and mold roses and unworn shoes, I see something else in his angles, so sharp they could tear through the last of his tattered faith. He wants to make this gesture for both of them, but it is all he can do to stay afloat.

Carrie is not the one who is lost, not anymore. I can see the way Karl moves without moving and all the ways, big and small, in which he is trying to navigate the grief and the guilt, and this, the hang glider, the biggest one of all.

Milton returns to me, satisfied that he has sniffed out the mysteries of the room, and sits in front of me to watch for his next task. I think to him, It happens more often than you would think, people losing themselves. He tilts his head up at me, chewing meditatively on whatever he has found. *Humans are weird sometimes.*

It is similar to my cases but it is not the same. I cannot find a person who is lost, but Nico has taught me that I can sometimes help them find themselves again. The Book tugs at me and the clock on the wall points to 1:40. The afternoon bell is at 2:30 and if I time my arrival for right before the bell rings, I can meet Ruby Fontaine under the arched doorway when she is on her way out of the school. That might be a more effective plan than creeping through the hallways, looking over my shoulder for the gray woman.

I look at Karl and see the hollows in his cheeks where he is starting to collapse and sink, the grief rushing in to overtake him.

I cannot leave him to wander alone with his doubt growing heavier, the holes in his faith getting wider. We have crossed paths on our lonely searches, and if it's forgiveness he is really looking for, I can find some reassurance for him to hold fast to on his way there, to keep him from drowning.

I focus on the muscles of my mouth and tell him, "My dad is. Is a pilot."

"Really? That is quite interesting," Karl says, moving away from the hang glider.

"Yes. He loves to fly. It was like Mark Twain said. The air up there. Pure. Fine. Brace-ing."

"And you? You have flown? Do you agree?"

He could not know how crushing that is. "I do not — do not fly. So — do not know. But for you. It will be like that."

"Pure and fine and bracing." Karl gulps and drinks in the mountain-spring air that seems to trickle through the vents.

"Before takeoff. He did a Safety Dance."

"It is good that he follows safety precautions," Karl says approvingly.

"Yes. He did — but this Safety Dance is a real dance. It goes with the song. Men Without Hats."

Karl looks baffled and intrigued. "I suppose that when men do not have hats, they become chilly, particularly up there, in the clouds. Dancing is good for getting the blood flowing."

Strangely, that is what Lucy also said when she taught me to Safety Dance. It was one of those summer days that stretched long and hot and lazy, and people moved only when prodded and then in slow motion, and air conditioners spluttered and dripped onto unsuspecting heads. Evening came and with it relief, and after closing the shop Lucy and I ventured outside with the rest of the city and Union Square felt like a party. Vendors sold canvas prints and postcards of the skyline and T-shirts with slogans, and a clown teetered by on stilts and a woman took off her shirt to get a henna tattoo on her back. People draped themselves on rails and steps, minding their business, and the street was still warm from baking in the sun.

Lucy handed me a salted pretzel wrapped in a napkin and we joined a crowd that had gathered to watch a break dancing crew. The break-dancers spun on their heads and froze in intricate contortions while "Safety Dance" blared in the background.

"Hold on to your pretzel — it's time to get the blood going," Lucy said, and then, "Follow me."

She skipped and swung her arms and encouraged me to do the same, and as I dodged and swayed and skipped, I could imagine that he was there too, dodging everyone pressed in close and loud and sticky, swaying and skipping next to Lucy, teaching me to do his dance.

That moment seems worlds away now, here with the monotonous drone of the lights and the bland standardized surfaces, hard enough to deflect thoughts.

"I can teach you. If you want," I tell Karl, shrugging to pretend like I don't care either way.

Karl pushes a few soda cans away with the inside of his foot. "If it is a trick of your pilot father, I would like to do it in advance of my launch as well. As you say — take it away."

We wind our way through the aisles, clearing the floor as we go to create a serpentine runway. I play the song in my head and tap my foot and nod my head, and Karl arranges his body like mine and turns out a foot in the same angle and imitates my tapping. The echoes make me realize how foolish this is without the music but that can't be helped now, not with Karl standing next to me bopping his chin and popping his hip and waiting for the next move in the sequence.

I launch myself down the runway, skipping, first my left foot and then my right, and Karl takes his cue and soon he is skipping in the aisle behind me. I make a left into the next aisle and begin swinging my arms above my head, first my left arm and then my right. Karl mimics the arm swing but his timing is off and his arms are stiff and he is still watching me closely so I fight to keep a straight face, and he is so engrossed in copying me that he skips into the jutting handle of a sink as he rounds the counter.

"You should warn me, this Safety Dance can be quite dangerous," he says, massaging his side, and we grin at each other and start another loop up and down the aisles.

I loosen my arms and let them swing, and we skip in opposite directions and the same direction, our paths merging and diverging, and we keep weaving through the room until he shakes off the doubt and catches the rhythm and his limbs are stiff and gangly, unpredictable and confident.

"You are ready," I say, resting against a counter and watching him Safety Dance across the runway, skimming over his grief. He makes a right and Safety Dances to a stop in front of me.

"Super," he declares, and he wipes his forehead with his polishing cloth.

On our way out the door, he picks up the pink river shoe that Milton dropped. He loosens the strap so that the shoe is ready for stepping into, and he lines it up on the mat next to the other shoe and brushes past the light switch without turning it off.

When we reach the flea market, I look over at the chess tent but in place of Sammie and Roman there is a pink-faced man in a shaggy blue costume holding a Cookie Monster head in his lap. The owner of the extreme sports tent pitches himself over a row of tables like a skipping stone as Karl approaches.

"Another thrill-seeker," he booms. "How about a camera mount?"

Karl makes his request and the owner leaps into action and yanks out a bin, and the whitewater roil in my stomach recedes. Karl issues a garbled exclamation and presses a fist against his mouth and the face of his black rubber watch flashes at me. The display features two square screens with the day of the week and the time to the second. *FRI,* it says, and *2:01:10,* and the school bell is going to ring soon and it is time for me to move on and find Ruby Fontaine.

I thank Karl for lunch and he says, "Good luck," and claps my shoulder.

"Keep the greasy side down," I say, because Lucy says that is how pilots tell each other to stay safe and it is good advice for anyone.

As I leave, I can't help turning back for a last look, just in time to see Karl break into his gawky Safety Dance, and back and forth he skips while behind him the owner searches through bins, twisting his head like a shiny doorknob.

I smile a little to think of Walter Lavender Sr. dancing around his plane, and as I walk away the distance between me and Karl grows but I can still picture the gaunt lines of his face filling out enough to remind him of being young and brazen in his faith. I am on my own again in my search for the Book and I have not found anything yet in my search for Walter Lavender Sr. But teaching Karl the Safety Dance has shored up my faith too, reminding me how to fend off my own grief for what is missing, and I can hold fast to the knowledge that Walter Lavender

Sr. always meant to come back for me, and that whether I succeed or not, he still wants to be found.

19

The bell rings and the door swings open, catching me standing under the archway, examining the carvings in the stone. Propelled by fleeing students, I ricochet to the safety of the sidelines, and from there I rise to the balls of my feet and scan the scene. A bun, Junker said, and a backpack tag with her name on it. I look for a bun, and already I pick out three girls and a boy with a bun. I take a breath.

"RUBY!" I thunder, and there are a few glances my way but no responses. Kids walk by with their thumbs hooked around backpack straps and I sweep past rows of faces, trying to keep up.

"Ruby!" I call again. What if I miss her and what if I have already missed her, and I shout her name again and my heart grows heavier as the crowd thins.

The last few stragglers slog out. A girl kick-kicks by me with a Hacky Sack and I say, "Ruby?" and the Hacky Sack thwaps against her toe. It's not her, and I lean against the black-iron fence and my back sinks into the fanged points. Milton sits and waits for me to finish thinking. How can I find her now? Can I find out something about her inside the school? It's my best option, and I reach for Milton and the door opens before my hand touches it.

A girl marches out, trailed by three friends. She steps to the side, away from the arched entranceway and next to my stretch of fence, and the others flock around her. The tag on her backpack swings and the freckled girl on her right tugs on her elbow and says, "Ruby, my mom's over there. See you at my birthday party on Sunday?"

And that's her — I've found Ruby Fontaine and all is not lost yet, and a raft of hope inflates under me.

"I'm not sure," Ruby says. Her hair is sleek and piled on top of her head in a big bun and she bounces impatiently on pink-slippered feet and strains her neck forward like that will take her closer to where she wants to be instead.

The freckled girl reddens and Ruby adds brightly, "I'm trying my hardest. I'll beg Grandmother to take me. If not, I'll see you at the boat races tonight — bye, Jane, bye,

Heather, bye, Gabby." She shakes her friends off and swivels toward me and narrows her eyes into sharp slits, glittering green against the caramel of her skin.

"How did you get there? There was no one behind me." She advances, looking like she could spit fire as she glides on her pink slippers, and I shrink back and the tips of the iron fence dig into my fleece.

Her eyes pop open. "You skipped school! You did, didn't you?" she says gleefully. "You're not in my class. Are you twelve, too? You must be with Blaise. Or Kenner? Who are you, anyway?"

Milton senses my hesitation and whacks me with his tail, barks, and then he steps forward first, sniffing her hand in introduction. She busies herself petting him and admiring his coat, and that takes some pressure off me.

"That is Milton," I say, grateful for the bridge he has built for me. "I am Walter." The next part is easy, one of my familiar phrases for finding, and I show her the Book and say, "Have you seen it?"

She snatches it out of my hands and rifles through it and stills.

"I've seen this before. Oh my God, don't you just love the artwork? Look at how the artist emphasizes the contrast, the use of light and shadow — you didn't steal it, did you?" she says with a gust of accusatory passion.

I shake my head and take a breath. Maybe it will take me too long to explain but that can't keep me from trying, and I tell her that the Book belongs to the shop and it became lost and some of my words do not come out straight but I keep going, telling her that I have been following the trail and I am still missing some pages, and her pointed glare softens.

"I only have one of the pages the little birdman gave me. It was my favorite one. I'd give it back, but it's in my room and right now I'm going to the Met. There's a new exhibition about death I want to see."

She hitches her backpack higher. "See you later," she tosses over her shoulder, quickening her stride.

I hurry to catch up with her. "I can come."

"Pass," she says. She tries to leave me behind again and I match her pace and she walks faster like we are in a competition.

"It is important," I say, swinging my arms to keep up. She stops short and I speed-walk past. "Very important," I emphasize, backpedaling.

She folds her arms and pins me with a threatening stare. "Fine. But don't be lame." She resumes walking. "It's about the fashions of death," she says without looking to see if I am following. "The dresses and accessories women wore during the stages of mourning. The way those styles have evolved over the century."

"Morbid," I say, shivering, at the same time she sighs, "Glamorous."

The Met is a short four blocks away. Neither of us speaks. At the foot of the stairs, Ruby suddenly takes off and I look about wildly to see what she is running away from or toward.

"Race you," she yells.

I look at the kinked blanket of steps and time seems to flow away from me and I wonder how long this will take. Does she understand how important the Book is? Milton looks at me and does a little side hop with his front legs — *Better get to it.*

I bound up the steps, picking my way around people lounging or reading books or watching the scene. The museum looms above, a stone palace with arched windows and towering columns, topped with elaborate sculptures.

We skid into the hall and Ruby is prowling in circles, waiting impatiently, and trees are sprinkled with lights and groups of people travel and wait and plan in different languages that echo from the vaulted ceiling and distant walls and marbled floor.

"That was easy," she says, adjusting the straps of her backpack.

I stick out my tongue and she snickers. We bypass the admissions stand in front of the Egypt wing and Ruby flashes a card at the guard and tells me, "Grandfather is a patron," which is a good thing because the admissions line seems to have broken. The guard makes a stern swiping gesture at Milton and Milton promptly sits on his polished shoes.

"Seeing Eye dog," Ruby says, and hauls us away.

"Grandfather used to take me here all the time," she says as we walk through an exhibit of Egyptian vases and reliefs. "We would spend the afternoon exploring the Cubiculum and the Chinese Garden Court, talking about ancient Egypt and van Gogh. Did you know he painted *Starry Night* in a lunatic asylum, after he cut off his ear? At the end of the afternoon, we would sit on the roof with hot chocolates. Once in a while he would order a martini, which according to E. B. White is the elixir of quietude but I'll tell you something — pinkie-swear you won't tell, Walter —"

She hooks her pinkie through mine and

plants a kiss on her thumb. "Okay, I snuck a taste once when he went to the bathroom." She pauses and whispers, "It burned like *hell*." Her eyes water and I make a choking sound because it does not seem appropriate to laugh in the museum.

"Shhhh," she says anyway. "We're here."

The entrance is down the stairs, white and black and spare and exquisite. We enter a softly lit showroom where people are gliding in unison in the same direction — counterclockwise — around a center platform, buoyed by a current of choral music, and I feel like I am interrupting a solemn proceeding. Ruby ignores the flow of the processional and shrugs out of her backpack and settles in front of a trio of mannequins wearing dresses in shades of black and somber cream and bruise-purple, with nipped waists and skirts like bells. Their cold elegant hands pluck at the air and curl under shawls.

A woman breezes by and her roomy white jumpsuit billows like a parachute and Milton trots after her, leading with his nose. I settle down beside Ruby and pull out my notebook, and I am distracted by a nearby rustle and I see that Ruby is flipping through her own notebook. It looks something like mine. Penciled lines rise from the page, the bell sleeves of a dress, a hint of curve to suggest a neck, and she smudges a line with her finger.

My mouth drops open and I stare, shake my head clear and write, INSTANCES OF RECOGNITION IN ACCIDENTAL PLACES — and a cough makes me pause, and Ruby raises her open notebook and clinks the spine against mine.

"Cheers, mate," she says, to capture the strangeness of it.

"The house is pretty weird," Ruby warns as we walk down the steps with Milton lashing out a path in front of us.

I think about the shop and about myself and say, "I do not mind."

Ruby makes her cat's eyes at me. "What does it matter if you mind or not?"

She hoists herself onto a ledge built along the side of a church and stretches her arms out, pointing her toes as she walks. "And, duh. You've got an art journal, too. We're like, practically the same kind of person. I'm just saying you need to be prepared. You have to be careful not to touch any-thing, not even on accident. My little sister, Debbie? She's eight, and she's an angel. She was supposed to die when she was born and she lived. Except — my Mama and Daddy were supposed to live and they died when I was six and Debbie was in the hospital, but they were angels, too."

That is not something I thought she would say. I thought she was the opposite of me; her world did not want for anything. I saw that she had friends or at least people who wanted to be her friend and invited her to their birthday parties, and I assumed she had two parents, and she did. But she doesn't anymore, and although there is no unfinished feeling to it and she does not need to look, they are not here all the same and that is not the perfect contentment I imagined for her, and I say, "I am sorry."

She makes a bow with her foot. "The robber shot Daddy when he protected me and Mama, and when he shot Mama anyways she wrapped me up so that he forgot about me." She wobbles and her toes strain and flex around the ledge through the pink leather. I hold out my arm but she stretches her arms wider and steadies herself, and she reaches toward the sky and points her toe again and swings her leg around in a bold arc.

"We live with Grandfather and Grandmother, that's where we're going. They used to ride on boats and I would stay with them when Mama and Daddy were taking care of Debbie. Now they have to take care of Debbie most of the time, which is a lot of work. Debbie has severe intellectual and physical disabilities, OCD, lymphedema . . ."

I have not heard some of those words before. Ruby says, "You'll see," and pirouettes off the ledge and lands gently on the ground like a spinning maple tree seed. She bounces on her toes as she waits for me.

"This book that you lost and you're looking for. What's so great about it?"

I show her the flyer. "It is part of the shop," I say.

"There's more to your story," Ruby insists, and so I try to imagine the way Lucy tells it and I tell Ruby about the making and gifting of the Book and the shop awakening.

"It was part of the magic," I say, thinking of people finding the shop and coming in for the first or fifteenth time with fresh eyes, open to small wonders and the awe of discovery. That is, until they stopped. I think of Lucy's fingers leached of color, trembling over the letter, and I imagine the shop closing, my oil lamp winking out, and the roar of a plane passing over.

"There's a *real* place like that?" The greens of her eyes swell but for me it is a sobering reminder of how there isn't for

313

now and maybe forever. After she gives me the one page she kept, I will still have one more page to find. I am getting close, but my search is far from over.

I nod and she stops under an awning that extends all the way to the curb and says, "This is it," and a doorman pushes open the golden grates of the double doors.

"Good afternoon, Miss Fontaine and guests."

Milton drags his bottom along the red carpet inside the entrance and the doorman scowls and pulls at the turkey skin under his throat. Milton does not notice and he flicks his paws and his hips sway as he ambles ahead into the lobby, a quiet hall with shiny wood floors and paintings in gilded frames and chairs with curved arms and legs like thrones, and rising up in the middle is a marble platform overflowing with flowers both real and sculpted.

At the end of the lobby there is an elevator bank. We step into the wood and warmth of the elevator and ride up, and Ruby unlocks the door to 1442 and Milton pushes past our legs and keels over at our feet like a round-bellied ship. I step over him and look around the apartment, and I don't know what to make of it.

I have seen enough homes to know how

314

different and hard to predict they can be. There are always places to sit and sleep and hold things like books and plates, and it is also true that in more cases than not, the homes I visit are in some state of disarray, because that's when things are more likely to slip through and become lost. But besides that, I have no expectations.

Sometimes, people live in their homes and the homes soak up some of who they are, like the big-game hunter who lined the hall with framed animal heads like portraits of deceased family members. Other times, people's homes are a contradiction, like the palm reader who had a taste for minimalism and white although she wore swathes of mystical jingling fabrics and a bindi that looked like the eye on a peacock tail.

Ruby's home is full of open space and windows that look like walls and plump damask sofas and my feet sink into the carpet. The flat surfaces are decorated with vases and asymmetric bowls and the kitchen space to our right is made of glass and steel. Then there are the other details, and they are the ones that render me speechless.

"Forty-five degrees," Ruby says from behind me. "Don't mess with the angles or else Debbie will have an uncontrollable fit when they get back."

315

I guess that she is talking about the wall of silver cabinets. There are maybe twenty cabinets in total, and every door is cracked open to the same angle, lined up in perfect gleaming rows like soldiers. All the drawers are pulled halfway open, exposing their insides, knives and cutlery and tubes of wrap and scissors. Cookie tins and mailing boxes are scattered throughout the kitchen and living room, standing or lying on the floor or leaning against furniture legs.

"Stay," I whisper in Milton's ear, and he sighs and slumps onto the floor behind the door. I suck in my stomach and take cautious steps like the floor might detonate, and Ruby flounces past me.

"What is it like?" I indicate around us, careful not to disturb the cabinets or the drawers or the minefield of square containers.

Ruby cracks up and intones, "Welcome to the Twilight Zone." Her bun stops bobbing and she taps her cheekbone. "Here's my first memory of Debbie," she says. "Mama and Daddy bringing her home. She'd been at the hospital for ages and still had some tubes coming out of her, but I could see her fist poking out of the blankets. She was just the smallest thing but I could tell she wanted me to hold her hand. Sister telepa-

316

thy. I just wanted to tell her I would take good care of her but Daddy said, No touching yet, and Mama took her into the other room with Grandfather and Grandmother. They shut the door and I had to wait outside, wishing I could go in and get Teddy."

She thrusts out her chin. "Anyway, I kept my promise. I know how to take care of her now. I help with the feeding tube. You have to take the button off right or acid bubbles out of the hole the doctors cut in her stomach."

My belly button stings and I forget and walk into a side table and the cookie tin propped against it tips over, and I look down to see a rotund snowman with a carrot nose. I right the fallen tin and check to make sure that it's positioned the same way, and I continue making my way across the floor.

"I'll learn how to make things better for her. I'll be an artist and a doctor. It might take a long time to go to medical school and do a residency and pass the board, though, so right now I'm mastering the art of patience like Grandfather suggests. . . . Get that switch, will you?"

She points to my left. A spotlight above the coffee table turns on. "That light needs to be on. How'd you lose that book anyway?" she asks, abruptly changing the subject. "That's *dumb.*"

I clench my teeth. "Taken," I correct, feeling cross.

"Touchy subject," Ruby says.

"The shop died. If I do not find the pages. It will close." I can't bring myself to elaborate on the next part, after the shop is closed forever, and what will we do and where will people find their everyday magic and where will Walter Lavender Sr. find his way back to, if the shop he knows Lucy planned to open is no longer there?

"I didn't know," Ruby says. "That's serious." She touches the tasseled side of a hanging tapestry, looking hard at the birds of paradise. "If it was stolen it was the thief's fault. I hate thieves." The word sizzles behind her teeth and she spits it out.

In the hallway, she checks the door on the linen closet. "This door has to be closed. Come on, my room's over here. We'll get your page."

She tosses herself onto the bed and I breathe easier and allow the weight to seep back into my feet.

"Is it hard?" I cross the room and perch at the foot of the bed, sitting on my hands.

She retrieves her art journal and looks

through it, fidgets with the pages. "Like I said, she's an angel. She's pure. She finds joy in the stuff I don't even see. Rain drumming on the window. Holding hands. The veins on an orchid. Smiling when someone else smiles. She reminds me that I wish I could do that — she notices what matters and not the other stuff. She just can't eat the same way."

"You notice things," I say, pointing at her journal and a sketch of a mourning costume, the oversized brim of the bonnet undulating and beckoning, shrouded in mystery. She snaps the journal shut.

"Just death." She jumps out of the bed. "Now, what you came here for . . ." She skips to her dressing table, white and curved with an oval mirror like a fairy tale. On it is a gold box shaped like a heart and a model sailboat with a tall triangle sail trimmed in lights. She picks up the boat and turns on a switch and the sail lights up and the gold box shaped like a heart lights up at the same time, even though the gold box is not trimmed in lights.

"It turned out pretty well, didn't it? Grandfather and I built it for the Light the Night Boat Race — that's the fund-raising event tonight at Conservatory Water, raises awareness for children with mental disorders."

She swaps the boat for the gold box and the slow weight of expectation drags me down like wet sand. She plunks herself onto the bed and opens the lid and unfolds a sheet of paper with ragged edges.

"I don't want to let this go," she says, studying the picture and chewing her lip. She looks away and pushes the sheet of paper at me and says, "But it's yours."

I take it and I know that it is a page from the Book without having to turn it over and look — it throws a spray of sparkling light against the wall like a gift pendant unwrapped and held up to the sun, and I tilt it to the right and to the left as I inspect it and of course Ruby would choose to keep the second page of the Book: the girl free as the wind and searching for adventure, thundering in from above on storm clouds that entwine with her cloak to form the sky, the snow, the sleet.

I flatten the page against the wall and iron out the wrinkles with the bottom of my fist and fit it back where it belongs inside the Book, and now the only missing page is the sixth one. I close the Book and the sparkling light goes out. Ruby stares into her lap and her hands are inert as dried butterflies.

"Thank you," I say solemnly, to fit the mood.

As I wait for her to bounce back and tell me where the sixth page is, I map out the possibilities and there are three of them — lost, given away, and sold, which I don't think is likely, and then Ruby says, "Okaaaaay — so — don't freak out, but I have good news and bad news."

She gives me a stricken look and I think that must be it — she must have lost the last page — and she draws in a large breath and says in a rush, "I gave the other two pages away and the *good* news is I know where to look for one of them today and the *bad* news is we have to wait until Sunday for the other one — it's with this old chess master I used to play at the Chess and Checkers House, Center Sammie — I ran into her after the little birdman gave me the pages, and I didn't know they were yours and it seemed like the right thing to do at the time — she got choked up just looking at the page and Grandfather and I hadn't stopped by the Chess and Checkers House in a lot of Sundays — but anyway, it's not really bad news because we'll just wait and on *Sunday,* we'll go and get —"

I tap her arm and she stops talking, her face alight with determined energy, and it is hard to picture her playing chess, her leg jiggling under the table, the chess board shaking. I show her the seventh page, Sammie's page, already reunited with the Book.

"Oh," Ruby says, losing steam. "Great. Just the good news, then."

The front door slams shut and she raises her head and says, "They're home early. It was probably one of the better visits."

Plastic bags rustle and keys drop onto the counter and then comes a *stomp . . . stomp. . . .* Ruby's oval mirror vibrates. *Stomp!* The ponderous stomping pauses somewhere in the hall and I look at Ruby.

"That's Debbie," she supplies. "She likes to know where her feet are. Hey, Deb." She slips off the bed and says, "Walter, in case you were going to, don't even think about crossing your ankles."

I imagine my legs as railroad tracks and glue them to the side of the bed as Ruby opens the door and kneels with her arms open. A tangle of limbs pummels the air and a body barrels into her, and Debbie lifts her face and it ripples with laughter, naked, elated.

Ruby hums the opening bars of a Van Halen song and Debbie collapses onto the floor and her mouth peels apart and at first it just sounds like keening and then I notice

the breaks, how they repeatedly fall somewhere around Ruby's breaks, and her fists
punching the floor like fleshy drumsticks.
Her eyes roll around and come to a rest on
me, and they are a transparent lens — there
is no filtering, no layer of processing and
judging and concluding. She simply takes
me in and beams at what she sees, and it is
impossible to not smile back.

"This is Walter. I met him at school,"
Ruby says, and Debbie pushes back onto
her feet and stomps away. Ruby's grandmother appears in the doorway and inclines
her head.

"How do you do," she says, combing her
fingers through the fur of her collar. I wave.
"It's a treat to see a friend of Ruby's visit-
ing."

"Grand*mother,*" Ruby says. "It's not my
fault the other kids aren't very interesting. I
see them enough during the day, five days a
week, thirty-six weeks a year."

"I think you like being difficult," Ruby's
grandmother says, and Ruby gives her a
wicked smile. Ruby's grandmother turns to
me and says, "Make yourself comfortable,
Walter — Oh, pardon me, not so fast,
Debbie." She hurries past Ruby's room and
Ruby eases the door shut and rests her
cheek against the wood.

"Where do I look?"

Ruby bats the question away with a flip of her wrist. "I'll look with you. I'm the one who gave them away, I should help you find them. Plus two is faster than one — how long have you been looking?"

"All day. I know it is crazy. To miss all of school. But it is the one crazy thing —"

"You're not serious. You're *twelve* and that's the only crazy thing you've ever done? It isn't even crazy. You are *so* boring," Ruby says, and her head is pulled back by the weight of the drama and her giant bun.

"It . . . is not?"

"It is not acceptable!" Ruby barks. She grabs my hand and yells, "Get up, Milton. We have work to do." Yanking me along, she rushes to the front door and rouses Milton just as her grandfather is attempting to enter.

I expect him to ask her where she is going and who I am like Lucy would but instead he says, "Your shoes. Remember to put on your shoes. As the Egyptians donned sandals of papyrus to protect their feet from the scorching sand, so, too, must we shield ourselves from the Manhattan sludge."

I hesitate, and in case I am supposed to answer the unspoken question, I clear my throat and start to tell him, "I am Wal—"

324

and Ruby shushes me.

"They trust me. Debbie needs most of the attention and I need my freedom." She squeezes us around his wool-encased midsection and flutters her hands at her slippers. "Did you know the ballet shoe was perfected by Bill Nye? His toe shoe delivers an upward force to counterbalance the downward force of gravity to support dancing en pointe."

The elevator dings. Her grandfather rumbles with genial interest, "You don't say. The Science Guy."

20

Ruby steers us into Central Park, and that is where she loses us too.

"How does anyone ever find what they want in here? What I *need* is a way to see where we're at," she grumbles.

"I can help. Where is the page?" I ask her.

"We're not looking for the page right now. We're looking for the Carousel and fixing your grossly well-behaved ways."

I don't know what she means but I do not want to do whatever that is if it doesn't lead me to the last missing page, and I feel a clench of worry and shake my head. No, I start to say, and Nothing could be more important, and Let's go now, but she takes me by the sleeve and pulls me along the path.

"We have to wait for mail time to look for the page. How dumb would it be to sit around and do nothing while we wait?"

I think about it and her logic is not wrong

and when I don't respond she says, "Smart, for a boy," and considers the trees around us with a glint in her eye that makes me queasy.

"You can help by finding a good climbing tree," she says.

I have no desire to climb a tree; as far as I know, the only thing worth considering when leaving the ground is the risk of falling, arms and legs and spines crunching like the twigs under my feet. I inspect a trunk, the bark scabbing off in hard platelets, and I am not sure how to assess the tree for climbing potential. Trees are for shelter and for storing the secrets and trinkets of time, and they are not for climbing to high places.

Ruby halts under a tree with branches that begin above her head.

"A mature beech. Stout branches," she mutters, stepping back to better eyeball the tree. "Lateral. Balanced, evenly spaced."

To me, it looks like it hadn't been able to decide whether to grow up or out and so it sent an army of branches to do both. Ruby takes a running leap at the lowest branch and manages to skim the bark. She sizes up the tree again and puts her hands on her hips and rises to the balls of her feet.

"This one will do the trick. You're tall enough to get up on your own but give me a boost first. Once we're up there, I can see which way we need to go."

The skin under my wrist withers and the veins throb. "Pie. High." I put my hands down and back away and Ruby rolls her eyes and throws up her hands.

"Just give me a boost, then," she says.

Grudgingly, I help her up and she grips the branch and walks up the side of the trunk. She flips onto the first branch and Milton snuffles around the trunk for squirrels and gophers, and I breathe in and the breath whistles through my nose like a plaintive wind. She stands and reaches for the second branch and my legs feel feverish. I decide to stop watching her and collect leaves instead, gathering them into a pile under her just in case.

Milton romps unannounced a few times through the pile, each time stopping and looking back at me, panting, to show how enjoyable it is. Despite his efforts to entice me, I continue building up the pile and then I run out of leaves in the immediate vicinity and there is nothing left to do but to look up. My gaze travels up the tree, jumping from branch to branch, and Ruby is perched like a bird at the top, utterly unafraid, surveying the small world fanned out before her.

It does not make sense. With everything that Ruby has seen and experienced with her parents and sister, I would expect some kind of avoidance response. That was the term the zookeeper used when we found Jerry the penguin in the walk-in freezer where the zoo kept beef shanks and horse heads for the lions. After the zoo posted the Lost flyers, they received calls from people who had seen Jerry paddling for freedom up the Narrows and various other bodies of water, including the swimming pool at the top of The Standard hotel.

Instead of starting with the leads, I visited the zoo's penguin exhibit to see if Jerry left any clues behind. I looked past the penguins doddering around on their rocks and zooming through the water tank, and I saw the blockade in front of the cave entrance, the edges and cracks slathered in a glowing ice like cement.

"We're renovating it," the zookeeper said. "We had to carry Jerry out of there. He's shy." I learned that Jerry became noticeably distressed when there were too many people around him and too much noise; his habit was to stay in the cave, away from the crowds, until closing time, and I couldn't imagine him bobbing amid blustering boats and ferries loaded with passengers. He would be somewhere cool, and dark, and quiet.

We opened the freezer and the zookeeper moved some meat around and there Jerry was, rested and round as a beach ball.

"Why didn't I think of that," he said. "He had a scare a while back with some kids being rowdy, throwing stuff at him. Avoided crowds since."

Remembering that now, I feel a surge of empathy for Jerry; I had done the same thing, after all. Fear and avoidance — but not Ruby, and not only is she unafraid of brushes with death, but in an unforeseeable twist, she is fascinated by them and seeks them out. She is defiant and daring and she has something to prove, and so she taunts, and she moves closer. I open my notebook — DEFIES DEATH BY STARING HIM IN THE EYE.

Ruby looks down, straight through the branches, and my palms begin to sweat as if I am the one with a long way to fall. She kneels and swings herself to the branch below and I put my notebook away. She reaches the lowest branch and hangs under it and then she drops and leaves go flying everywhere. Milton bounds in after her and she pops up in the middle of the flattened pile, throwing an armful of crumbling red and yellow and orange into the air.

"I saw it thataway, slight right. Follow me," she says, pointing, but then a couple in complementary fall outfits saunters into us, embracing and posing for their photographer. Ruby hauls me off to the side and Milton stands in the middle of the path and wags his tail.

"That's it," the photographer says. "Tell me why you love her."

"One look from her fixes up a shitty day," the man says, and his grin collides into his ears and the photographer says, "Good, good, give me more."

The couple makes a kissing bridge over Milton and he pants at the camera, and I take a moment to study the woman who can fix a bad day. There is no breeze but a shudder runs through her and her hair sweeps back and up like dancing in the wind — A HEADY RUSH OF HAPPINESS, I jot — and I put away my notebook and wonder about her remarkable power, because it's a tall order to fix up everything that goes wrong.

Even the Book couldn't fix everything for me, although I convinced myself that it could fix most things about a bad day when it helped me forget. It could wake a shop and become the twinkle in someone's day but it could not transform one-sided bonds into living friendships and keep me from being alone. But it will still save the shop and that is the most important thing, and I think again of the customers whose lives we have become a part of, and I think of Flora and José, who depend on their jobs at the shop, and I think of Walter Lavender Sr. and Milton and Lucy, and I wonder how many people are out looking for me now and I hope I can find the last page before they find me.

The couple separates and we move back onto the path. Milton pads after me and Ruby speeds up, pulling me along so quickly that I feel like I am trapped in a moving vehicle.

"We should be close . . ." she is muttering to herself, and then she flings out an arm and cuts me off. We come to a halt in front of a building shaped like a gazebo, nestled amid the trees. It is made of rust-red brick striped with ivory, and doorways and windows are cut out of each slanted side but right now warehouse doors are pulled down over them. The ticket booth is shuttered.

The Carousel is clearly closed, and who knows what Ruby had up her sleeve but I am relieved I don't have to find out and more than ready to resume the search as planned.

Ruby slides a pin out of her bun and says, "Cover me."

"Why?"

"What you don't know won't kill you," she says sagely, sliding another pin out of her bun, and she skips forward and kneels in front of a padlocked door.

An agitated Moo builds up inside me and I swallow and look to Milton for support and he pokes his nose into Ruby's back — *This looks fun* — and I scowl.

"Stop that," I hiss. She bends a hairpin and inserts it into the lock anyway, and then she takes the other hairpin and pulls it apart. Feeling jumpy, I shove my hands into my pockets and look around, wishing I could whistle, but the people who stray past do not really see us since we are just two kids.

"It's in the wrist. Deft. Delicate enough to feel out each pin," she says, holding the lock with one hand and levering at the keyhole with the second hairpin. When it gets stuck, she rotates her wrist.

"Click," she says with satisfaction, and the hairpin sinks into the lock. She stands, rolling the door up with her, and disappears inside with Milton. I hover near the entrance until her hand shoots out and grabs me and yanks.

She slips away and I focus into the shadows and an inky shape emerges in the center. The lights switch on and I shield my eyes against the stabbing brightness — the sound of gears groaning and wood creaking and then music bubbles out, a lulling organ melody and the rat-a-tat-tat of a drum. In the temporary blindness, my other senses fill in the memory of savory-sweet batter frying and the crisp chew of funnel cake between my front teeth, and the hiss of hot oil and the clink of the ladle when Lucy fishes out the puffed spiral nest.

The light becomes less painful and I lower my hands and blink a few times.

"Isn't it wonderful," Ruby says, sidling up to me and bobbing on her toes, and I watch the Carousel turn on its axis, the horses outfitted in jewel brights, rising and falling, gentle and peaceful. Entranced, I step forward. On closer inspection, their heads are reared back, nostrils flared, mouths twisted in endless terror, and they revolve against a backdrop of clowns strapped to rockets and cherubs shooting down chicken-goblins, and it is a fantastic candied nightmare.

"I counted fifty-seven horses the first time

Grandfather and Grandmother took me here," Ruby is saying, trailing me and Milton as we walk along the perimeter of the speeding Carousel. "The first carousel ran on real horses, walking in circles in a pit under the platform . . ."

Her voice unravels and horses gallop by, faster and faster until they merge into a blur of windy color, and a rush of euphoria sweeps through me and takes me away from myself so that I am no longer just someone with a disorder and without a dad. Ruby accepts these as parts of me, like this is how I am supposed to be. Maybe being Debbie's sister shaped her; maybe that is how she has always been. But she treats me like a regular kid and I realize I have stopped thinking about what I want to hide and what I want to show. With her, I can simply be someone who already belongs.

I break into a run and whoop. Grabbing a standing pole, I cycle my legs harder and take a flying leap and I land in a heap on the spinning platform, and Ruby tumbles into me and we dart around the galloping horses and collapse into a chariot and finally haul ourselves onto a horse each, and the world tilts with color and Ruby's laughter and turns round and round and round, crazy.

We bray and lean off our horses with our arms outstretched, and the most crazy part is that since I met Lan and started this search — the first one that forced me to truly leave behind the certainty and safety of home — I feel like I have been walking toward this moment, the final movement of some opus of existence in which I already experienced love and fear and anger and loneliness, and along the way I found courage and vulnerability and connection and conviction, and all of it adds up to this — a counterpoint, sweet and true and simple as the calliope march cranking out of the Carousel.

I look at Ruby's horse and she is not on it, and I turn to my other side and see her crouching on another horse's back, preparing to leap off, and my breath hitches when she lets go and jumps. The Carousel shudders as she lands on the stationary carriage.

"Did you see that?" she yells immediately, looking around for me, and I catch her eye and celebrate the small victory with her, my sunflower seed friend.

The music plays on and the carousel top spirals, and in no time at all the Carousel is slowing and Ruby says, "That concludes your first lesson in fun."

She waits for the spinning in her eyes to

slow too, and then she jumps off the platform and releases the handle, and the music comes to a stop.

Outside, Ruby snaps the lock shut and my ears ring. We glance behind us and everything looks the same, people striding past, and we exchange grins like sharing a secret.

I have seen secrets pass between other kids, the covert whispers exchanged behind hands like walls, eyes darting and flashing like minnows, nimble and bright, folded notes slipped between loose fingers and birthday invitations tucked inside opaque envelopes. I know how secrets are supposed to look and how they are supposed to sound but I didn't know how they were supposed to feel. I watched the others hand off invitations like batons, and I wasn't on any of their teams.

After Vara Mae, the others were polite but content to let me be unless I spoke first, and when that took too long they didn't linger to squander their limited recess minutes. A few weeks before my sixth birthday, I watched a boy pass out invitations cut like race cars to some of the other kids and as usual he skipped over me because he didn't know that I liked race cars too. I thought about my upcoming birthday and considered throwing a party of my own and inviting the entire class, and that would give the others a reason to gather and stay and then they would see that I wanted to know them and that we had things in common, once we got to talking.

But the more I thought about it, the more nervous I became, and I was uncomfortable being the center of attention and what if no one came for me and I remembered — Stop talking. You're making it worse — and I decided it wasn't worth it. My birthdays were little celebrations with Lucy and Milton and Flora and José, splitting an ever-growing maple mille crêpes round with my name looping across the top.

Now, as Ruby and I exchange grins, I know how secrets are supposed to feel, like cinching a drawstring and the two of us pulled closer together by our shared knowledge, and suppressing an urge to laugh until my sides hurt.

"Hey, kids — you two all right there?"

The gravity inside my body cuts out. I see the dark gleam of a wide belt, pouches and holsters and a radio crackling with code words and static, and I realize it is exactly what cannot happen — the person who caught us is a police officer.

Terrified, I twist my head away to hide my

face and Ruby elbows me in the ribs, hard, and says, "Yes, Officer," smiling with all of her teeth as I gasp for breath, thinking, Don't look this way — the search is not over — I cannot be found.

The policeman looks from me to her and says, "Well, okay then. I saw you two huddled over here and wanted to check to make sure you weren't lost. Run along —" and suddenly Milton gags and a brown lump plops onto the sidewalk and I pray that the policeman did not notice, and then Milton burps out a pool of grassy foam.

It trickles toward the policeman's shoe, impossible to ignore. He takes a second and harder look at Milton and then at me. "Hold on." His eyes flit up to inspect something in the corner of his mind. His hand creeps toward the radio on his belt and I cannot allow this to happen, not now, not when I am one page away, and I seize Ruby's hand and we bolt.

Around a curve, I send Milton into the bushes and I take one tree and Ruby takes another and I hold a finger to my lips and we stand as straight and narrow as we can and even narrower when the policeman strides past. I count and when I reach two hundred Mississippi, I peek around the tree and go light-headed with relief and send

Ruby and Milton the all-clear.

Ruby hoofs it down the path, and Milton is thoughtful in hanging back next to me except he runs at a slant to stay close and ends up pushing me off the path. We catch up with Ruby and a raindrop shatters against my temple and it is cold and startling.

"The last page," I say, breathing heavily, thinking, Before I am out of time.

"Mail time," Ruby says in response.

21

Ruby tugs on my elbow and we continue running, and the patter of the rain weaves in and out of our footsteps.

Fifth Avenue is a knot of umbrellas and traffic, and rubber tires sizzle on wet pavement. Rain courses through my hair and rolls down my nose. Ruby steps off the curb and her bun seems to have absorbed the rain and expanded, and she bounces on her toes and stretches her arm out as far as it will go but most of the taxis are already whisking other people away.

"Finally," Ruby huffs as a taxi pulls over in front of us. We sprint toward it and just as I reach for the door handle, a man lunges forward and wrenches the door open and backs into me and I get a mouthful of wet jacket and cologne and something else salty-sharp. His heels crush my toes and Ruby rams into his hip like a bull and her eyes are flame-bright but he releases my toes

without noticing; he ushers in a jangling woman and swats her bottom and she grabs his shirt and they topple into the backseat.

"Rude! R-U-D-E —" Ruby smacks the window to punctuate each letter but they do not hear her and the window fogs and the light turns green. When the next taxi pulls up in front of us, we rush the door with abandon and Ruby snaps her address. Milton bounds in and I slam the door soundly shut behind him, and we are sealed into a gray cocoon and the only sounds are the rain drumming against the roof and the head-nodding hip-hop coming from the radio.

"Over thirteen thousand taxi medallions issued and they practically evaporate into the storm clouds," Ruby says, slouching into her crossed arms. Her limbs spring apart and she whirls around and it is a good thing Milton has chosen to perch in the middle seat, big and content and unflappable. "It's time! You're about to get all your pages and then yooooou're safe." She scissors her arms like an umpire.

Some of my searches take minutes to solve, the ending presenting itself immediately and unexpectedly, and other cases take longer and the ending is slow and I can see it coming, like the half-dollar submerged in a frozen pond. I looked into the bottom as the days warmed and the ice thinned, anticipating the end. I have one more page to go in my search for the Book and I have that nervous-full feeling in my chest of being on the verge of finding, a silver-blood taste in my lungs like running too hard.

I ask Ruby who she gave the last missing page to.

"Our mailman." She picks her nails and won't look at me. "I gave it to him yesterday because he — he wasn't whistling. I passed him in the mail room and he was ashy and out of breath, sort of hugging the boxes."

The taxi driver slams on her brakes and dumps Milton onto the floor, and I narrowly miss bashing my head into the divide. The driver bangs on her horn and curses with vigor and keeps the horn depressed for good measure as the offending car clears the intersection.

"Look, I haven't known him long but something was wrong with him," Ruby continues when the driver releases the horn, and she stops picking her nails and looks at me. "So even though he said, 'There y'are, Mizz Ruby-angelo,' like usual, he looked like he should be in bed with someone making him chicken soup, and he wouldn't

343

listen to me when I told him that. Grand-mother said to him, You're a real catch, what're you still doing on your own, and he just laughed. I thought the picture could scare him into finding someone to make chicken soup for him. Tough love," she adds helpfully.

I twirl a finger through Milton's fur and gather more information for the finding. "Will he give it back?" I ask.

"He'll make sure you get your page, you'll see when you meet him — he's the nicest man. That's why Grandmother's started saving cheesy biscuits for him. He checks on Debbie already." Ruby bunches her mouth and a wispy whistle escapes. "He whistles to her and she about explodes with excitement, and Grandmother was saying how Marybeth Gallagher slipped and frac-tured her leg three weeks ago and couldn't call for help, and he buzzed her apartment like she told him to whenever she had a package, and when she didn't answer the doorman went up and found her wadded up on the floor, and it's a good thing he comes around each day with a smile and a care."

That is more than I can say for the shop's new mailman, and instead of a face all I can conjure up is the sound of the mailbox closing and the *snick* of the envelope opening and Lucy turning as pale as the letter paper.

"Sounds like a con man," the driver says.

"Who asked you?" Ruby says, but the driver has bumped up the volume and is stomping her foot and flapping her arms and pouting in the mirror.

The light turns green and she lowers the volume and puts both hands on the steering wheel to concentrate on her turn, looking out of the windshield, looking as hard as I am, as anyone is, and I know Lucy is out there too, looking for me, and I silently tell her not to worry; it is mail time and not long to go until I can return home, and I will have the whole Book with me and the shop will wake and people will come. Even when it rained, the shop was packed, people closing their umbrellas and squeezing forward until no one else could fit into the door, and they dug their spoons into the blueberry corn bread trifles I recommended to soak up the wet cold in their bones.

The windshield wipers swish and fat splotches of rain distort and worm their way up toward the roof and the driver curls her lip in disgust. She jerks the wheel toward the curb and Ruby careens into me and I am sucked into the door. She pops up none the worse for wear and says brightly, "We're back."

I push the door open and stick my head into the rain and hastily collapse back into the car to avoid clipping a speeding bicycle. The door opens again and the doorman's face appears under the dome of a dripping umbrella.

"Welcome back," he says, and flinches when Milton leaps out of the cab and lands in a puddle with a messy splash.

"Mail's getting delivered?" Ruby asks.

"Not yet," the doorman says. "You're not the first to ask. Mrs. Gallagher called down, your grandmother, but so far no one knows anything. I'm saying it looks like weather delays."

"Maybe," Ruby says dubiously. She pans over the gray gloom, the cars jammed at the mouth of the street, beads of people sliding up and down the sidewalk. "In that case, we should check farther up."

We borrow the doorman's umbrella and totter out onto the sidewalk, crammed under our portable roof with an indecisive Milton tangling his four legs with our four legs. A dissonant symphony rises up from the clumped cars, horns blasting and muffled shouting and rain. People clomp around us in boots with their heads down, intent on ignoring their leaky surroundings, and I look around to find the target of the honking, a mail truck not really parked in a curbside space, its backside still sitting in the lane. A middle-aged man, compact and dressed in a blue uniform, is facing the side of the truck and holding himself up against it with his cap falling into his face.

"That must be him," Ruby says. Someone passes in front of me and my view is obscured and then I see the mailman drop a sheaf of letters and his pocket watch slips loose and time stops. Raindrops suspend overhead like crystal chandeliers and that is without a doubt Mister Philipp's face, and that is Mister Philipp's brass watch chain.

I notice then that he is shaking like an earthquake is going to split him in two and who knows how long he has been here like this, with his gray slacks turning to wet cement. As one, Ruby and I rush to the truck.

He quakes and presses his forehead against the truck and one hand clutches the front of his work vest and the other shudders toward the ruined letters. The brim of his cap tilts up and his eyes find mine, brown and crinkled, and there is no lift of recognition. I can see the ice-shine of his face and the moisture trickling out from behind his glasses as he convulses and gasps for breath like a dying fish.

"Out of the rain," I yell at Ruby, and my words are twisting and melting under the stress and I am sure she won't understand the stream of gibberish but she has, and I jam my shoulder into Mister Philipp's armpit and wrap his arm around me. He stirs and tries to find his feet and we stagger and maneuver him into the driver's seat.

I whip around, scanning the sidewalk and the street, and the world pulses and sharpens around me and I hear myself shouting for help that does not come, and then I feel the pressure of Ruby's hand around my arm.

"Come on, we have to get the doorman," she says, and again, louder. I start after her and Mister Philipp slumps over and I see him boneless and dark purple around the edges, and his hands clamped shut like not letting go, and I cannot leave.

I shake my head and tell Ruby to go ahead and she races away for help and I jump into the truck on the passenger's side and kneel in the middle next to Mister Philipp. Milton soaks in the rain and licks Mister Philipp's cold hanging hand. A sound leaks out of his mouth and I tilt my ear closer.

"David," he says. His left foot slips out into the rain and I crawl over to pull it back

348

in. The bottom of his shoe is coming away and I think that his socks must be wet, his toes marinated and wrinkled as dark prunes. I reach over to slide his door shut. My teeth begin to chatter and I think, Hurry, Ruby, and then I feel like an impostor for staying and thinking that it will somehow help.

What can I do for Mister Philipp? I am not an EMT like the woman who lost a string of milky pearls at the beginning of the summer, and I don't know the Heimlich like the teenage lifeguard who saved a boy's life when he choked on a macadamia nut at the shop. Either of them would be better than me; I don't have anything to give Mister Philipp. I crouch empty-handed in the mail truck, crowding his space, fighting him for air.

"That you, Davey," Mister Philipp mumbles again like talking through a mouthful of sand, and his eyes look through me, reflecting shapes that are not there.

"I — I — it is me. Walter," I stammer.

"I was young and a fool to run." It hurts to hear his voice and my face contorts with his and his breath thins and he whimpers with the loss.

"Rest. You should rest," I say, tucking my knees under my chin. Rain beats against the truck and profiles pass through the window,

349

and maybe on another kind of day — clear and radiant, like the day Lucy almost sank into the Atlantic and Walter Lavender Sr. was there to catch her — on that kind of day, there could be no tragedy, and Mister Philipp would sit up and sling the mailbag over his shoulder and say, "Not today, son."

He mumbles, "I been trying to show you I'm sorry. Where'd you go?" His eyes jump and dart, frightened, seeing nothing. "You grow to be a good man?"

I squeeze my hands into fists and rest my head against my knees. His hand hangs, limp. His breathing grows more faint and labored and his body sinks into the seat, head drooped into his chest, and he could be sleeping if his color wasn't so strange and his eyes weren't open.

He thrashes feebly, barely moving. "Is it enough? I been alone. Eye for an eye. Tell me how to make it right."

He gurgles a little like drowning, everything he wants to say rising in his lungs, filling behind his eyes, trickling out of his mouth, and my hysteria mounts as I think of him dying on this rainy day in a mail truck next to a kid he used to deliver mail to, and I rock and grip my knees tighter, chanting, If only, if only, if only I knew something about saving lives.

"My life to make it right. I'm paying. You see that, Davey?"

This Davey — is he why Mister Philipp is still alone? A deliberate sacrifice, reparations for leaving him behind, and now Mister Philipp closes his eyes and drifts, and we wait. With the street darkened and emptying and the traffic noises fading, I have the lonely prickled sense that we are the only two left alive, and still we wait.

For some reason, I think of the spot on his back, and I wonder if it itches now. I watch him closely, checking for the flutter under his eyelids, and it could be any of the days I watched for him, waiting for him to deliver the sign I knew would come, somehow, if Walter Lavender Sr. could not.

I can be certain now that he wants to be found, so if there is no sign then he will return, looking for the light like he promised, and maybe there has been some wrong turn, some unavoidable delay, and that is why it has taken a little longer than we thought.

Before Mister Philipp transferred, I knew that if the sign came in the mail, I would receive it. His arrival was a constant, steady and fixed as the line on the horizon. One time, Lucy offered him respite from the wintry mix and he swiped the gray slush from his face and declined because he had a duty to arrive on time. People had things to look for, he said, and they needed these small things to rely on. It was his implicit promise to them that he would show, and that he would be on time, and that he wouldn't drop or break or tear or lose whatever it was that they were waiting for.

That is what he did for me too, and I should have wondered who did it for him. Was there anyone there to tell him, "Not today," so he could take a break from the waiting?

I didn't ask when I could and now maybe I will never find out. I already know that losing something unexpectedly leaves no time for asking, and no chance to say good-bye.

Mister Philipp's eyes are still closed, and the dark purple has bled deeper. "Not enough. I'm paying. Where are you?"

He is still looking for Davey, and I do not know how to save him so that he can go on and finish his search like he intended. All I can do is show him that he is not alone in this moment, and that is not really anything definitive.

Maybe, when it comes to endings, it is enough to find something to lean on, and to be at peace.

"Left you alone. I been alone. Make it right." He opens his eyes and they are round as his face, his glasses. He searches my face, seeing and not seeing. "See how much I mean it. You grown, Davey?"

He falls silent but this time he doesn't close his eyes, and he drifts, and he waits, and he watches. I press my thoughts flat and still and into something calm, as Walter Lavender Sr. would have done when he saw the sea of shimmering blue glass rushing toward the cockpit window, foaming with clouds like diving into the sky. In his last moments, the sun would have been forever-bright in his eyes. He lifts his hand, blinking.

I reach out and take Mister Philipp's hand. It is much larger than mine, and weary.

"I am here," I tell him.

Mister Philipp's fingers flicker and pull me back, and he slumps against my arm. To help him know where I am, I start to whistle but I don't know how, and so I hum instead underneath the rainy patter, a song I have heard Lucy sing at this time of the year when she is pouring out mugs of hot spiced wine and cider.

"Should old . . . acquaintance be . . . forgot . . ."

My arm goes to sleep under his weight. I

353

think of Walter Lavender Sr. and I sing to Mister Philipp. "For auld . . . lang syne . . . we'll take a cup . . . of kindness yet . . ."

As I hum, lights flash in the rearview mirror. The doors on both sides slide open, and Mister Philipp is lifted up and taken away by yelling people, and Ruby and Milton are there, crowding into the frame as I step off the mail truck. My joints and nerves have hardened and when I fall into them, Ruby hugs me tight and Milton's soggy tail beats against my knee.

"Walter, look," Ruby says, spinning me around.

The last page is creased and pressed into Mister Philipp's seat — on time as ever, one more delivery for me.

I can't make myself move. Ruby removes the damp page from the seat and we slip into the gathering crowd of curious onlookers, forgotten in the commotion, and make our way back to Ruby's building. I take the page from her and study it, thinking about Walter Lavender Sr.'s last lesson, and it occurs to me that somewhere along the way today, I learned something else about real kindness — seeing and choosing not to ignore what I saw.

I feel in my bones a grinding and settling,

the world finally realigning in the right places.

22

The Book is found. The shop is safe. I test my limbs, stretch, and this is still happening — this is real. I look at my reflection in the mirror and tell myself, The search is over, and I look at Milton and tell him, The search is done. The nightmare is over and I am waking to a thousand more dazzling days. What will it be first? Vols-au-vent mice, I decide — dozens of them, and people will see them skittering through the displays and that is how they will know, and they will come running.

Ruby and I run the hand dryer in the lobby bathroom four times, taking turns holding the last page under the gush of warm air. Milton overturns the trash can and digs into the heap of paper towels, his jaws like steel traps.

"The race starts at seven," Ruby says over the dryer. "We'll go upstairs to get the boat and Grandfather and I can walk you to the subway before going into Central Park. Unless you want to watch?"

I work a wad of paper-gum out of Milton's mouth and lower the black and pink flap of his lip, and the dryer shuts off. The silence is deafening, a reminder that I have to put the Book back where it belongs as soon as possible, before the shop goes dusty quiet and tables and chairs are swept up and stacked in the corner to be taken away.

"No big deal, I figured as much," Ruby says lightly, hopping off the counter. "Your loss, it'll be a lot of fun."

I lay the Book out on the counter, flipping gently through the pages, and as I turn the third page, one of Junker's, the last thread holding it to the spine gives away. Ruby picks up the fallen page and replaces it, leans over my shoulder with anticipation, and I turn two more pages and smooth out and insert the sixth one.

Together, with bated breath, we look down at it, the final missing page, a little puckered from drying but whole and stirring in its scope: the expansive grid of blocks and avenues, the towers and skyscrapers and building blocks, the people and memories and shadows that inhabit them and flow over into the streets, the ground, the air.

A city, a girl, an army of the lost.

"And this will bring the shop to life?" Ruby says, holding the bathroom door open. "Let's get a snack before you go."

"See for yourself," I say.

"I will. Who knew life could be so — glamorous, too." Ruby links her arm through mine and skips toward a waiting elevator. "Skip better," she says, hauling my elbow higher. "Like Milton." Milton stops frolicking and snapping at his tail when he hears his name, and his tongue lolls from the side of his mouth.

We hear the screaming from the hallway. Ruby starts running and unlocks the door and a fresh scream blasts it open, and the screaming voice is choked with impotent rage and my blood sours, burning through my veins. Ruby's grandfather rushes past, hair disheveled. Ruby grabs his arm.

"Is Debbie okay?"

"Yes — yes, it's just — she's having one of her tantrums — who knows, maybe the wrong door opened, a box slipped down —"

Another scream of anger shears off the rest and his bloodshot eyes drain and dart toward the hallway. "Sorry, honey, I have to get back before Debbie hurts herself."

Ruby stares after him and I can't see what she is thinking, and after a while she lets out a heavy breath, forgetting about the

358

snack and walking straight to her room, and I trail her, powerless and ghost-like. She does not bother to turn on the light and the sail of her model boat forms a dark solid peak against the cool glint of her mirror, and she picks up the boat and the block with an antenna sticking out of it.

"I'd better get going." She shrugs and tucks the controller under her arm and constructs a steel-plated smile. "And you, obviously — you have a shop to wake!"

She's right — the Book is found and there is nothing else keeping me away. Beyond her window lurks the dark unknown, and I reach up and put my hand against the glass and the cold press of it makes me shiver.

I have been waiting all day to return to the shop and Lucy has to give the landlord a decision tomorrow and surely she is sick with worry about where I am. Night has fallen and I should keep a tight hold on the Book and make my way as quickly as possible to the shop's cocoon of warmth and light. But that means leaving Ruby to venture out alone, and that feels wrong because I can map another way, a new possibility: accompanying her to the races, and out there is cold, uncharted space where anything can happen but at least we would be there together.

It does not take me much longer to decide. I say, "Later," and, "I have a race to watch," and I can see the shine of her teeth as she turns to me, brightening and opening like the face of a sunflower.

The rain has stripped away the tough skin of the city and the night glistens underneath, fresh and raw. We arrive at Central Park and become part of the current of people, coats and scarves, boots and sneakers, model sailboats small and large, all battling against the wind, toward the muffled pounding of music. Automatically, I look for gaps to thread into, slowing down, speeding up, and when that doesn't work I let myself be pushed along, step after shuffling step.

It's the same kind of crowd I found myself caught in when my delivery schedule collided with the pre–Yankees game transit rush — masses of people, similarly accessorized, moving forward as one. It felt mindless then, surrounded by so many people who looked the same — except me, with my delivery box and conspicuous lack of baseball stripes. As I shuffle along now, I take a better look around and I see a boy holding a plastic boat and a man blowing his nose and a woman with hair that skims the folding part of her knees. I wonder what they have seen and what they have lost — not just their things, their possessions, but the parts of themselves they are missing and looking for that I can't begin to know from here. Everyone does not look so similar. I do not feel so different.

"Don't get separated," Ruby shouts in my ear, and I tighten my grip on Milton's collar and on the Book and concentrate on avoiding elbows and heels and the prows of boats. The path slopes down and I catch a glimpse of the dark stillness of a pond in the hollow ahead — full of floating lights, and there are hundreds of them, glowing lamp-orange across that dark mirrored surface. I seize a moment and write, ECHOES OF A LOST CITY, SUNKEN UNDER-WATER.

The people around us disperse in different directions, and the movement and music engulfs us in a storm that roils around the clear hush and twinkle of the pond. We push through the crowd to the nearby booths and Ruby checks in and hangs her number on the side of her boat. A gust of wind lifts the number and it flaps against the sail.

"The next wave starts in fifteen," she says. She flips a switch and her boat blazes, sinking her face into a pool of shadow. "Wish me luck!"

I watch Ruby shield her boat and make her way to the far end of the pond, where a balloon arch billows and glows. She bumps into a girl she knows and pauses briefly, and then the crowd swallows them both. Squeezing Milton's collar, I take a deep breath like diving and plunge forward. I find a viewing spot close to the water, behind two boys sitting on the ankle-high granite rim. They are twisted around toward the pond, making tsunamis in the water with their hands so that the boats pulling eagerly through the water spin off course and crash into each other.

"Gotcha," one boy roars. The larger boy swats his hand down.

"Shut up — stop splashing — look at that one." He points at a boat slicing through the water in our direction. It is larger than most of the other boats and instead of two triangles it sports a network of black sails, and red flags emblazoned with skulls flutter from the black masts. The pirate ship reminds me of the toothless gingersnap cannons Lucy made after the Book became lost, and when the Book is back where it belongs, they will once again inhale and spit out ricotta balls riddled with candied bacon.

"Doesn't *look* like a retard made it," the larger boy says. "Check that no one's watch-

362

ing —" He snakes his arm out toward the approaching pirate ship and his fingertips brush the prow and he strains forward a little harder. A gale pushes the boat out of his reach; he curses and slams both of his hands into the granite and at that moment when he untwists I recognize the blunt knob of his nose and take a fast step backward, my fingers slipping out of Milton's collar.

The movement draws Beaver's attention. His lips retract and his teeth sharpen. "Lucky me — if it isn't Walrus, king of the 'tards."

My mouth is parched. I lick my lips and search for an escape but the crowd cheers and presses forward with the launch of the next wave of boats, so I try to look past Beaver and Todd and scan for Ruby's boat instead. I know that if I tune them out long enough, they will lose interest and look for something more satisfying to poke at.

"Over here, Walrus." Beaver snaps his fingers under my nose and the hair on Milton's neck bunches into porcupine quills and he growls.

"Dog talks better than you do," Beaver sneers. He eyes Milton warily. Todd feints at me and I shield the pocket that the Book is in.

"What're you hiding, 'tardie king?" he

363

taunts, and Milton snaps at his hand and misses and he laughs and Milton seizes his foot, so swift and sure that I think it was the plan all along. Todd yips like a Chihuahua and tries to shake him off, and Milton digs in his heels and suddenly Beaver is there, snatching the Book out of my pocket.

"Now, now. He doesn't know — he's dumb as a retard. We have to help ourselves." He opens the book to the first page and holds it up, and the sight of the Book in his hand is paralyzing and I feel the cut of his fingernails against my arm, his foot hooking around my ankle.

A ripple of boats sail past him and my vision clears and I see him silhouetted by the lights in the pond, and his outline is not strong and solid but pocked with holes and bristling with jagged shards. His edges — easily crumpled, nothing to be afraid of. I thought I was a coward when I shrank away from risks, and now he is the only coward I see.

I look straight at him and moo soft as a lullaby and Milton releases Todd's foot.

"What's he saying?" Beaver and Todd look at each other and back at me.

I raise my voice. "*Retards* are not dumb. *I* am not dumb." The words do not flow or come out straight but my voice does not wilt and I take two determined steps forward, my eyes fixed on Beaver's. "But *you* are a sad lump of meat."

Without taking my eyes away, I take a final step forward and stop one breath away from Beaver, and the force and intention of it sends him reeling back. One heel hits the granite ledge and the other is carried by momentum and his body arches and his arms windmill. The loosely fitted pages of the Book flap against the covers, and as the people around us notice and grab for Beaver's wrist, his coat, the wind rises and sends him toppling into the pond with a mighty splash and I count one, two, three, four, five, six pages torn away like rose petals, spiraling into the inky night sky.

Beaver yells but I am turning away from him, pushing through the crowd, and I leap for the first page I see and already it is out of reach, taking flight into the night, and I wheel about for the pages that are still visible, sprinting left and right wherever the wind takes them, chasing in vain until the last page melts out of sight.

"Help! I'm drowning!" Beaver flails in the water, grabbing at the boats around him and snapping masts in half, and the thought smashes into me — the seventh page. Where is the cover and where is the seventh page?

I tear back to the pond, dodging the hands that reach out to haul Beaver to his feet. He stands and the water barely reaches his knees and floating next to him, like a brown lily pad, is the cover of the Book.

I run to the ledge and slide onto my knees and a flustered Beaver grabs at me, trying to climb over the rim, and water slops over the ledge. I lean away and he slips and I reach forward again, my fingertips straining for the cover, and then a tightening around my chest, a backward pressure, and I turn my head and Milton looks up at me through a mouthful of jacket, holding on tight so that I don't fall in too.

With Milton as my anchor, I lean out a little farther and grab the cover just as Beaver finds his footing and sloshes out of the pond. Hastily, I dry the cover and flip it over, and the seventh page is not there, and I put the cover into my pocket and cast both arms into the water and do a frantic sweep and water cascades over the ledge.

"There you are. I thought I was going to have a hard time finding you."

I stop sweeping and Ruby is standing behind Milton, holding her boat. She looks at my arms sunk into the water and Beaver wringing out his clothes.

"Did I miss something?" She is breathless, exhilarated from her race.

"Mind your own business," Beaver snarls, squishing past her, and while she glares at him I turn back to the pond only the water has gone still and so do I, and a bitter ache pools under my tongue.

My peripheral vision shimmers with a new wave of boats, and in front of me the crushed remains of a few old boats float and mix with soggy clumps of paper. I am hypnotized by the largest piece as it sags in the middle and sinks, and the darkly alluring blues and blacks and silvers bleed into the gray of an unalluring blob and the remaining page — the first page of the Book — is now marbled gray, beyond repair.

23

"It could be worse," Ruby says, sliding on her mushroom. We are sitting on a bronze statue of Alice in Wonderland, in an alcove bordering the pond. I knock on the Mad Hatter's hat to disguise what I am feeling, not knowing what else to do with myself.

"Really. The pages got blown away — you can keep searching. I'll help you, of course. And I'll make Grandmother and Grandfather look, and I'll have Jane and Heather and Gabby and everyone I know . . ."

She trails off when I do not respond. There is an unsettlingly slack quality to my skin, like it is a soft baggy shirt that I am wearing. I tug at the loose rough skin of my elbow and there is no thread of tension, no trace of the pull that draws me into and through my searches. It is not that I am afraid or tired: I started and I came a long way and I finished, and if the Book became lost again, I could wring out another drop and keep trying.

But for the first time, I have no heart to search anymore; with the first page melted into the pond and ruined, the Book is lost beyond repair, and that means it is too late. Even if I find the other six pages and put them together, the Book will still be incomplete. Besides, I have used up most of the day and how much farther could I go, really, with my calves quivering and the scalding burn of a blister on my little toe?

The shop is as good as dead. Lucy will have to call the landlord tomorrow and tell him we cannot meet his terms, and then what will become of us?

I lift my face to the moon and its rays are pale and silvery as the wisps of my breath.

Ruby soldiers on. "The pages can't have gone far — the wind was coming in short bursts. I have binoculars. I'll climb a tree tomorrow, get a good high view and scout out the area. Or I'll help you climb the tree —"

She's still thinking of ways to help me because she does not know about the destroyed page and she does not know that tomorrow is already too late. Her knuckles tap-dance on the bronze mushroom because she can't contain herself, and despite the Book being ruined, the fate of the shop sealed, a spot of warmth blooms and fizzles in my chest like a tiny firework.

She rattles off a few more ideas and I interrupt in the middle of one. "Too late. Deadline tomorrow."

Instead of growing small she snaps open like a fan. "It's *not* too late. We'll search all night if we have to."

A few kids run by, cutting toward the pond, and the music pounds and the moon overhead is high and full, and I look at Milton for his opinion. His eyes are dark and fluid and I can see my red high-tops in them, like looking into the surface of a chocolate miroir cake. I picture Lucy pouring the glaze over the cake and swiftly dispatching bubbles of air with a needle, so that when the gelatin cools the glaze will set into a smooth mirror that reflects the best parts of you.

Milton opens his mouth into a grin and lowers himself into a deliberate sit in front of Ruby — *I'm with her* — and with both of them in agreement, I reconsider my assumption that it is too late. I think back to my cases; what could I do when something lost was beyond repair?

There was the case of the missing five-year-old girl whose snowball melted when someone left the freezer door open. Instead of focusing on what was already destroyed and assuming it was too late, she decided to walk from Park Slope to the Catskills — where she made the original snowball — to find a new one. She tried searching in a different way, and maybe I can apply that approach too, for the ruined page, and for the pages that were blown away.

It was not about the particular snowball — it was about the place it came from and the meaning and sentiment attached to that. What if it was the same with the Book — what if I could replace the destroyed original with a new one from the same place?

The original page was a gift, from an artist and a friend. I think of Ruby sketching the curve of a neck and Mister Philipp calling her Ruby-angelo. Ruby is an artist and also a friend — and if she remakes the page and gives it to me, I can make the Book whole.

"Good news. Bad news."

Ruby narrows her eyes in concern and I tell her about the first page falling into the pond, and she gasps and claps both hands over her mouth and I say, "Do not freak out."

Hearing her own words reflected back, she groans and punches my arm.

"You can remake it," I say. "While I find

the others. Will you help?"

Without hesitating, she says, "All right. I'll draw it. But how are you going to find the others?"

I have not figured out that part yet, but I have an idea for the different approach I should take, yet another way of searching that I have not tried before. Searching is something I have viewed as my own, and I did it alone; Lucy has offered to help and I have never accepted.

But now I have a jumble of thoughts that need sorting and an important idea that needs to be thought out and I know Ruby will be interested, and I feel the pressure lifting, cotton balls clearing from my mouth and nose and ears. Ruby is tapping the mushroom and humming and I am not sure if I am imagining it but her humming has been growing louder, and the moment I open my mouth she stops tapping and whips around.

"Yes?"

"I do not know. Can you help me? Come up with a plan. If I tell you about my day?"

"*God.* I thought you'd never ask." She slides her bun to the side and leans against the White Rabbit, and so I start at the beginning and she giggles when I tell her about Nico in the dog wash and bites her

372

nails when I reach the rats and turns pensive when I tell her about Junker and a sorrow so vast that kingdoms could be built in it. I hesitate because it is an insignificant detail, but I show her the Caravelle bar and I am already moving on to the next important part, assuming she will too, when she grabs the bar.

"What's this? Where'd you get it? What are you doing with it?" she demands, interrupting me as I focus on words for talking about Karl, and in my surprise I babble something nonsensical.

"Supercalifragilisticexpialidocious," Ruby says quickly, not to be outdone.

It is like stepping out into the rain and seeing the sun still shining — startling and splendid, something I have not seen before. There was connecting, which was about exchanging the essential things, and friendship was about that too, plus a kind of harmony, shared moments of celebration and tribulation. The rest of the time, though, is filled by the mundane things, the ordinary routine of living and the unimportant thoughts and events that crop up. Now I see that was also friendship — having someone besides Lucy who would be interested in knowing that I am wearing smelly socks from the hamper, that I set a new record for shaping croissants.

Ruby peppers me with questions, When are you giving it to Lan? and What was next to it? and my heart swells as I answer each one. When she surrenders the bar, I stow it away and move on to Karl and his hang gliding plans.

"He wanted to launch tonight. The rain stopped. He could be launching still. As we talk."

"Walter." Ruby stares at me like I have done something unforgivable and I review what I said, half-afraid and half-guilty. "You were going to pass that up? How could you *not* be dying to go up there with him?"

I think it is obviously the dying part and Ruby says, "I would be all. Over. That. And you should be, too, if you want to find the other pages."

Milton and I exchange glances, and then we look at Ruby and tilt our heads — *Why?*

"You said you've been following this trail, right?"

Milton squirms modestly to accept the praise.

"Well, could you do it at night, too?"

My mind begins to churn with fear again, which seems to be my standard response to Ruby's ideas.

"Like I said, all you have to do is get a

good high view. You'll see *everything* from up there."

I have always avoided high places and the mere thought of a good high view sends my nerves and thoughts and pulse skittering, but if I can get high enough to see where the wind has scattered the pages — the blazing signs of all six at once, like looking at a map — then it is a simple matter of rushing to gather them before I run out of time. I can't get any higher than flying over the city, and that is exactly what Karl plans to do tonight. If I can convince him to let me fly with him — that is how I will create my bird's-eye map.

"I have to go," I say, scrambling to my feet.

"I'm coming," Ruby says, waltzing around her mushroom cap. "No, I'm not. I'll be in the lobby drawing the page."

"With Milton," I say, and Ruby claps her hands and squeals.

"Party time," she says, holding her hand up for a high five, and Milton gets it wrong and pokes his nose forward instead and I am sorry to leave him behind too, but I don't think he will take well to a hang glider.

24

With the prospect of the weekend ahead, two entire days wrapped and tied with a bow, the train is crammed with people and spirits are high as we rattle through the underbelly of the city. Three women in sequined dresses are bunched in the corner, preening in the car windows and passing around chewing gum, and a baby girl in a stroller grins gummily up at me and an unkempt man strikes up a conversation in another language with an Asian man carrying a bundle of fishing rods and a bucket of freshly caught fish.

Heads fit under armpits and elbows curve around backpacks and chins jut over shoulders, strangers fitting themselves against each other like jigsaw pieces. It smells like cigarettes and heat and fried foods and shampoo and fish markets. The end door opens and a blast of chill air momentarily clears out the haze.

The train empties as it travels uptown. At Dyckman, I tighten the laces on my high-tops and reach for Milton, remembering with a pang that he is with Ruby.

I follow the conductor's instructions, taking a left out of the station and going uphill until I find a gate and a plaque that says Fort Tryon Park. Behind it, a footpath climbs up and disappears around a bend. I push at the gate but it is locked for the night. Channeling Ruby, I look around first, and then I wiggle a foot between the bars and climb over the gate.

The path wraps around the hill in layers like a tiered cake and I climb up each layer as fast as I can, my ears straining into the night where my eyes do not see anything but shadows. Trees rustle around me and twigs snap and I smell the brittle powder of decayed leaves.

I climb higher with the rush of a highway to my right like a river and beyond that, seemingly under my feet, the actual river, liquid metal in the moonlight and framed by forests of trees dense as broccoli tops. I quicken my steps and imagine my legs long and slight as a deer's and it is second nature to draw the silence around me like a cape and disappear into it.

At the top of the hill, the path bypasses a

medieval-looking castle and then it straight-ens and steepens as I continue climbing, skimming the tops of trees with the glitter-ing highway and river sprawled below. I take one glance over the mossy stone wall and shrink back from the sheer drop. Looking up instead, I see, at the top of a large boulder, two discs of light — planted there by someone to delineate the end of a run-way. I can't see Karl or his hang glider but I know they are up there, preparing to launch, and I am hopeful and fearful that there is a place for me.

I come around the side of an elevated ter-race and the path peaks under a stone arch and that's when I see her — *Carrie,* perched just past the arch like a vigilant bird of prey, straining against the wind, tied down to a sign pole sticking out of a block of cement. DETOUR, the sign says, and I smile to see the airspeed indicator attached to the side of the triangle. Karl must be nearby.

I walk around the hang glider and the path unrolls downhill in a steep straight line, il-luminated by markers that arrow toward the boulder I stood under earlier. On the neigh-boring grassy knoll, a gangly figure skips and swings his arms erratically, flailing like he is trying to keep himself from going under, and I would recognize a Safety Dance anywhere.

I breathe into my stomach and force the air out so that my voice is not blown away by the wind. "Karl!"

At the sound of his name, Karl stiffens mid-spring, alert as a hound scenting the air with one leg hitched in front of him. "Who is it?" He stares into the darkness, waiting for me to appear out of it.

"*Ach* — it is you. Hallo, Walter," he says, perplexed. "I am preparing for the launch. As you see, my launch has been delayed to approximately 9:00 PM, with the turn in the weather and wind situation. I am judging current conditions to be fair, albeit less than ideal. I am now performing the preflight ritual as I have been taught.

"I am pleased you came to support my launch," he says to me. "I did not even ask. That is a kind act."

I scuff my toe on the ground. "I came to. To ask you —" and what do I ask him? It will take too long for me to explain and time is running out; I can feel that insistent pull under my belly button, thin and sharp as a hook. Karl waits with one finger grazing his cleft chin, and I remember a woman who came into the shop this summer, an hour after the morning rush, carrying a cardboard box with pens rolling around the bottom and a desk lamp sticking out of the top.

"I need something light," she said to Lucy, and it was a simple ask, frank, and I could hear the layers in it, and it was the combination that lent her request urgency and eloquence. Lucy asked no questions and made no comment as she reached for the miniature bowls of gooseberry fool that balanced and spun on stilts, and I know that is how I can ask Karl too.

"I am in need of wings," I say, borrowing a little time before each word so that I can gather it and sculpt it into something clear for Karl. I leave it at that and imagine the questions and concerns and excuses clouding his square glasses.

Karl takes them off and polishes them with his cloth, and he replaces them and beams at *Carrie.* "What do you know, I am prepared for a copilot," he says, and I think back to the extra shoes and coffee mugs, the two toothbrushes, one for him and one for Carrie, and then I am jumping, the packed grass a hard cushion under my feet, and I am surprised to feel so thrilled.

"Let us get this show on the road," Karl says, and the reality of what I am going to do sends me crashing and I land the wrong way and my ankle twists, and I gulp and panic coats my throat and it is thick and oily. I do not really want to leave the ground. I do not want to be up there at all, with so far to fall.

Karl Safety Dances to the hang glider but I find it hard to move. I pretend that I am somewhere else, that I am in the shop, but the clean tiled floor and the lush displays have all dried to desert because the Book is not there.

Karl picks up his harness and it looks like padded ski overalls on the top and an unzipped sleeping bag on the bottom. He steps into the leg loops and buckles across his chest and around his waist and when he pulls down the zipper to close the top he looks like a wasp with his legs sticking out and the sleeping bag puffing out behind him like an abdomen.

He turns to detach the hang glider from the sign pole and I see a pack on the back of his harness — a parachute? — and he drags away the cement block and motions me over and my legs move and take me forward and I can't decide if they are being traitorous or loyal.

I stand under the nose, still lingering over the empty dunes of the Book-less shop, vast and bleached and lifeless, watching from a safe distance as Karl buckles me into the harness. My harness also looks like ski overalls with a parachute pack on the back but instead of a sleeping bag on the bottom it has loops that wrap around my knees.

He steps through the metal triangle and hooks his harness into the loops and straps of the hang glider, and he gestures for me to step through the metal triangle next to him, on his left side, and he hooks me in too.

"I am now doing the preflight checks," he announces, tugging on straps and loops, checking zippers and buckles, straightening the lines, and he crouches and kicks his feet into the bottom of his sleeping bag, hovering horizontally over the ground, suspended in the metal triangle.

He puts his hands and knees on the ground and kicks his feet back out.

"Once we are airborne, you will rotate down toward the control bar so you are like Superman. You will put your right arm across my neck and hold on to my harness." He tugs on his right shoulder strap. "That way the two of us will become one weight." He spreads his arms to grab the side legs of the triangle and says, "You grab the control bar," and the wind surges and pops my distance-bubble and sends me tumbling back into my body, and I crouch to grab

the control bar and he says, "We pick it up
—"

And before I can say, Wait, before I can
change my mind and say, Give me a minute
— I am yanked to my feet by the wind pushing against the wings of the hang glider. I
grip the control bar and I am not carrying
any weight at all — *I* am the one being
picked up, and my toes skim the ground
and it feels like the only thing keeping me
from being blown away like the Book pages
is Karl fighting to control the hang glider.

"Walk," he calls, and we start forward and
then he calls, "Yog," and the wind rises and
all at once he is shouting, "Run run run,"
and my toes are groping, searching for
something solid, and I don't even have a
second to close my eyes — the world bouncing crazily — grass, tree — light — cars — I
bite on my tongue and warm salt dissolves
in my mouth, and the world goes silken
smooth.

I squeeze my eyes shut. Karl roars into
the night and it pours out of him like a
cleansing, elation and grief and triumph,
and blood roars in my ears or is that the
wind? I sense the inexorable upward pull of
the harness, the wings of the *Carrie* sturdy
and solid above me, lifted higher by an
invisible hand. My fingers are locked in a

slippery death grip around the bar and I tell myself it is safe now to loosen them. One at a time. Right eye. Left eye. See.

The river is wide and motionless as a picture, a dark swath swiping cleanly through the star-dusted banks of New Jersey on the right and Manhattan on the left, dotted with the moving lights of boats, and we pass over the connecting thread of the George Washington Bridge, a strand of red beads on one side and orange on the other. I reach around Karl and grab hold of his shoulder strap, and he rearranges his arms on the bar and shifts his weight. The air is ice cold and we bank to the left and everything tilts and I am not sick with terror but so alive and weightless that I could explode and dissipate until I am in every breath at once, invincible.

"There's the campus," Karl yells in my ear as we pass over the darkened roofs of Columbia, and I look ahead of us, around us, and from up here things look smaller and bigger at the same time, the opposite from how they seem on the ground: New York a miniature city on a finger of land, bristling with toy buildings that sprout upward — swallowed by land and sea and sky, the rest of the world, without end.

Upper Manhattan scrolls by underneath

us and my ears are hot and cold and swollen with blood and wind and we soar through the night, flying on wings like eagles. I think, This is what he felt. Clear as that day, clear as his voice in my ear — close by, right here. I overlooked it, the very first and most basic rule for finding.

I had forgotten to look in the obvious place. I waited for him to follow the oil lamp to the doorstep and combed through his stories for information and scoured the city for the sign that pointed to him; I was too busy looking for an ending, and then I learned to say good-bye without it, when he had never really left.

The hang glider approaches the enormous unlit rectangle of Central Park and I fill it with the things I see now — my eyes in the display glass reflecting the nuanced depths of his, and my hand reaching out for Mister Philipp's while his larger one reached out to offer a handkerchief stitched with playful planes, and now here I am, two thousand feet in the air, watching and observing with Walter Lavender Sr.'s thirst to see far and wide. My view of the world below, the same one he saw.

He is everywhere I am, a luminous connection that spans the darkest ocean.

I look to the left, and somewhere in the

darkness of Central Park is where I met Karl, and I see the lights twinkling on the other side of the expanse and somewhere over there is where I met Ruby and Sammie and Roman, where I sat beside Mister Philipp. We pass over the ring of Columbus Circle and the sprinkling of light becomes a living thing, dense and lustrous and cut through with running bloodways, Times Square in the center awash in blue light like a strange heart.

The buildings of Midtown rise up in clusters, trying to grab us as we pass, and there are buildings encrusted from top to bottom with windows like crystals and skyscrapers topped with blue caps and green spires and gold pyramids and arched crowns, and the tiers of the Empire State Building are lit in red and orange and as we pass over its blinking antenna I look down and see the crowds of tiny people milling around the illuminated decks.

We pass over the round eye of Madison Square Garden, rimmed in red, and next to it the solid rectangle of the old post office. The topography falls off for a while as if pressed flat by irons of darkness, and rising up at the end — the tip of Manhattan — are the light-capped towers of the Financial District, densely packed along the water, and somewhere there, under the ground, is where I met Junker.

I look at the darkness ahead and to the left, sparingly quilted with strings of light, and I see the orange strand of Delancey leading to the Williamsburg Bridge and somewhere there in the Lower East Side is where I met Nico, and there's Chinatown, where Lan sleeps.

I see the dimly lit elevated strip of the High Line and the surrounding darkness that masks the Meatpacking District party-goers roaming underneath, and then I see the brighter arch of Washington Square Park and somewhere there in the West Village are Lucy and the shop, the place where I started and the place where I will end.

"Central Park," I yell in Karl's ear, because that is where the pages were blown away and that is where I should search.

Karl shifts his weight. The hang glider makes a looping circle and when the nose is pointed back uptown, he leans forward and we pick up speed. As we approach Central Park, he leans back, slowing down, and traces a lazy circle in the air. I look into the black rectangle laid out underneath me and scour the darkness.

We make another circle, drifting lower, and I catch a swivel of light in the bottom quarter, close to Fifth Avenue, and then another, not too far away. A few other points of light catch my eye but on closer inspection they are streetlamps, and they are not what I am looking for.

I open my eyes and search for more signs, and they tell me that most of the Book pages are scattered, as expected, throughout the lower half of the park, not too far from the model boat pond, although one has been pushed all the way down to the southeastern corner.

The hang glider completes another revolution and I take another look, and when I close my eyes the picture is seared against my eyelids, six beacons pointing the way. I signal to Karl with a thumbs-up and he stops looking around at the landscape and fixes his gaze to a spot on the ground.

We circle lower and skim over treetops and the irregular shape of the Lake. Karl kicks his legs out of the harness and pushes his weight down, holding his body perpendicular to the ground, and then I feel the stall of the hang glider and a flash of fear savage as lightning — the ground rising up too fast like we are going to crash, and I brace myself with all my might and clench my teeth.

The impact is jarring but not unbearable.

Karl digs in his heels to bring the glider to a complete stop.

"There you have it! A successful flight and landing back on the Great Lawn," he trumpets, and as he unhooks us from the hang glider and unbuckles my harness, I feel an odd sense of recognition, like reaching the end of a story I haven't read in a while — both of us landed, safe and sound.

"Good night and good news," I manage around it.

It is the best way I can express my gratitude, a small bit of lightheartedness to acknowledge what the flight meant to me, and Karl's face splits into a wide grin.

"Good night, Copilot Lavender," he says. He turns back to the *Carrie* and I can see his mouth moving but I can't hear what he is saying because I am backing away to give him all of this moment, this moment that belongs to him and Carrie.

I face away from them and break into a run, and the night air streams through my hair and whistles past my ears and I see the beacons in the back of my mind, the six pages I have to gather.

25

With the map in my memory as my guide, I know the approximate area of each page, the landmarks they are located in or near, and I know the directions I need to go to form a trail from one page to the next, but I do not know the exact locations, and so I have to run while keeping my eyes open and my head swiveling.

Two of the pages are located close by, between the two middle transverse roads. I run across the darkened Great Lawn, past the dormant ball fields, my footfalls echoing, and I am alert for signs, places that want my eyes to slide by. I find the first page lying on the ball field at the end, its glow dampened by the mud. I wipe it off with my sleeve and it is fine, whole, and I insert it into the Book.

I keep running, down a poorly lit footpath that leads south, past a pond covered in algae that smells of rotting leaves, and on the other side of the water I see the castle illuminated by spotlights. I dart from one spot to the next, rummaging through bushes, the spaces between and under, telling myself that it is like the Easter egg hunts Lucy used to take me to before I outgrew them — but I can't conjure up the fresh warmth of spring and the pleasant buzzing rising from the grass and the voices filling the air and the bright patterns and pastels of the hard-boiled eggs.

The night air is frigid as it whips past, stinging my face, goose bumps rising on my arms and underneath my scalp, and I am alone in a pocket of darkness, the footpath silent as I scramble from bench to tree to bush. The lack of light invades my mind too, and my breathing grows louder, panicked, as images emerge like monsters — pages being destroyed, landing in puddles, torn apart by speeding cars; my body collapsing, hunger gnawing through the walls of my stomach, my feet coated in blisters like pebbly sand; Lucy waiting all the while, growing more scared than I am, pacing, searching, consumed —

Then I hear the rustle of something thicker than a leaf, and I find another page wedged between the slats of a bench, dry and unharmed. I envision my map and the next page is somewhere in the unlit wilderness bordering the Lake. I cross the Seventy-ninth Street transverse and the rumbling of engines, the parade of headlights cutting across the park, are a soothing reminder that civilization is not far away.

I keep running in the direction of the next page and the shadowed footpath curves around trees and hills and leaves crunch under my feet and it smells a little like fireplaces, a smoky undertone to the night air, and I see the lights and buildings of the city like a silent looming mountain range beyond the trees.

As I continue racing downtown, I notice that my footsteps are not echoing so much anymore. The wood is secluded but brimming with nocturnal sounds, owls hooting and insects scratching and small animals rummaging, and the sounds of my running, my breathing, are absorbed into the darkness.

I spot the glow of the third page coming from the bottom of a large rock, sheltered under a jutting corner, and I rescue it and push myself to keep running for the next, which will be somewhere around the lighted boulevard of the Mall. My lungs constrict, tight with pain, and I slow to a walk as I cross a bridge, passing two people sitting on the banister with their legs dangling over the water.

I make the gentle descent to the other side, following the line in my mind to the fourth page, and before I see the fountain I hear the burble of falling water and I can feel the dampness in my nose and then I smell something dry, but without the freshness of fallen leaves. It is musty and sweet and I sprint out to the fountain on the terrace and find a page pressed against the base.

It was a close call. I look at the statue in the middle, an angel casting a purifying hand and water spouting into the surrounding fountain, and if the wind had blown the page a little higher, a little farther, it would have been destroyed.

I try to keep running but my legs are too heavy, my feet like cement blocks, and I walk across the street to the Mall, a noble hallway of elms where people congregate to take walks and eat their lunches and read their newspapers with dimes of sun spilling through the leafy branches. Rows of lamps blaze now, an eerie corridor of deserted majesty, and I struggle down the length of it, gulping down air, clutching my ribs.

How far have I come? Half a mile, a mile — and the rest of the day, miles of street and tunnel and subway, and many more miles of focus for searching and speaking, and the strain of the shop closing, the search closing, too, around me. I drop onto a bench, surprising myself, and my heart hammers against my throat, churning up a sticky glue, and I clear it out, swallow. My high-tops feel too small, my feet swollen. I am not cold anymore but my fingers are stiff and I wonder if it is possible to fall apart like a plastic doll, my limbs hanging down, heavier and heavier, until they pop free from the dead weight.

Three years ago, I had a case with a New York Marathon runner who lost the puka shells he wore to every race. As we went backward, retracing the course, he pointed at a tree and said, "Mile 22. That's where I almost stopped running."

When he struggled into Mile 22, he looked around and saw the runners who had dropped out, cramping and vomiting and bandaging blisters in the shade, and he felt the sheer number of miles in his legs and doubled over and clutched his knees and thought he was done. We found the puka shells tangled at the base of the Mile 22 tree, and that is how I learned about the crippling heaviness of being so close to the end. He had kept limping along, even without his shells, and managed to finish, and that means I can do it too.

I stand, walking and then running under the bright lights of the Mall, and I stop and look both ways to cross a street, waiting for a horse pulling a carriage to clop by. I set off down a footpath and the city sounds drop off immediately and it is graveyard quiet here, close and uncomfortable. There should be a page around here, not far from Fifth Avenue.

I push through sleeping places and under a little bridge and I hear the hushed winging of a bat. A clock tower chimes, the night stirring and bearing me to a different time and place, and a carousel of bronze animals cranks to life, playing their pipes and tambourines and gliding around the clock, trailed by silver wisps. I find the fifth page there, outside the zoo, under the music clock.

That leaves one more page to collect, the one in the southeast corner. Walking along the curb, I follow a street out of the other-world of the park and return to the ordinary one, a bronze monument in front of me and the trees behind it draped in holiday lights and a procession of cars rolling under the flags of the Plaza. A horse is standing on the corner of Central Park South, a muscled boulder rising out of a river of pedestrians, and the sixth page is pinned under one of its hooves.

"Ho ho, our Barb kept it safe for ya," the driver says, nudging the horse's ankle, and the horse does not move at first. With a queenly snort, it shifts its weight to the other side and daintily lifts the hoof.

I insert the page into the Book, a little trampled but intact, and I linger there with the six pages nestled in their rightful places between the Book's covers, feeling uneasy. I borrow a rubber band from the driver and snap it around the Book, and I feel better as I hail a cab back to Ruby.

The doorman opens the door for me and I walk into the lobby hallway, where faint classical music pipes in from secret speakers, and I find Ruby sitting on the floor in the corner, behind an armchair. She is surrounded by scrunched paper, and Milton gazes at her intently with his edges tinged in paint, the tips of his ears and nose and the straggly hairs under his belly, like he is starting to turn into a rainbow.

"Stop staring, Milton. I'll tell Walter on you."

Milton huffs and paws at the carpet.

"Yes, yes, I know, it's done," she insists, smudging a line.

396

They have not noticed me yet. I study the drawing over her shoulder, her portrait of the city on a dark and stormy night. Her version is wild, like the original — with echoes of her own frenetic energy, barely constrained by the paper, and her theatric flair in the details. There's the stormy sky, and there's the city beneath, and there's the water — and that is where the picture changes.

In the original, the sky was enormous and the water was a black mirror along the bottom, a continuation of the dark city. In Ruby's version, the water — the reflection in it — is the centerpiece, and it erupts with a glorious riot of color, fire-reds and bottomless-blues, pinks like salmon and coral and clear greens like glass. It is pure brightness, brimming with verve, and it is like she knows, now, what the glamour and allure of that is too.

I look at the page and I am not looking at a city of the lost; this is also a city of the living.

I tell Ruby it is perfect, and she screams and swings around with her paintbrush raised. I hold up the Book. She recovers from the shock and says, "About time," and then I can't see anything because Milton is desperately licking my face. My sleeves are muddy so I drag the bottom of my fleece across my eyes and when I open them, Ruby has climbed onto her feet and is holding out the picture with a rare bashfulness.

"For you," she says.

And so, her page completes the Book. It also makes the first gift I have been given from someone who is not Lucy, and she clears her throat and I do not have the chance to tell her this.

"Don't thank me yet. You have to see if it works first," she says.

The doorman is too eager to flag down a cab. Milton gets stuck in the door and the doorman hauls him up with uncanny strength and slings him onto the backseat. I roll down the window.

"Let me know how it turns out. Good luck!" Ruby skips alongside the cab as it pulls away and shows me crossed fingers, and the engine splutters and the cab carries Milton and me to the end of a long day indeed.

The taxi stops outside the shop and we squeeze our way out because there is a pole in front of the door and the door can't open all the way before bumping up against it. A damp flyer is taped to the pole, and I can tell before reading it that it is a Lost flyer.

They have a distinct look, different from flyers that advertise garage sales and fund-raisers and performances. HAVE YOU SEEN and MISSING and REWARD, they proclaim, like a crime has been committed, and the colors are alarming, the block capitals ringing with shrill insistence.

I tear off the flyer instinctively and look down at it, and I see my own face looking back at me, the same picture I saw on the library computer, and this time I can take a closer look. I am posing for a school portrait, arranged like a starched shirt with my shoulders angled and my hands folded, and the backdrop is crimson and my face reveals nothing. Next to the picture is a block of text that describes me in letters and numbers. Will not respond verbally to questioning, the description notes, and May be accompanied by 100 lb golden retriever.

The sign on the shop says CLOSED but the lights are on and Lucy is pacing, appearing in the window then the door and back to the window, her eyebrows knitted in a fierce V like they are in the funeral pictures, and a reddish-brown stirring spoon is clenched in her hands and Flora and José sit at a table, keeping vigil. I do not have to knock. As I approach, the door flies open and orange light bathes the doorstep. Lucy envelops me in her arms and sobs into my hair and it smells like pumpkin pies and a melting release in the fibers of my body, the feeling of coming home at last.

"You're here, you're here. You're home," she weeps, and Flora and José surround us with their arms so that we stand together like one tree.

Over their shoulders, the case for the Book stands bare and wrong, and there is nothing as heavy as the empty space of a lost thing except maybe the leaden air of the dead shop. Lucy presses her hands into my cheeks and shoulders and arms and when she has convinced herself that I am really here, she releases me and I walk to the case and pull the rubber band off the Book and lay the Book down on the velvet lining, and I open it to the wintry night and there is a sharp intake of wind at once pained and relieved like a baby's first breath. Lucy presses the door shut under her palms.

"Good dog," she murmurs to Milton, depositing the caramel stirring spoon onto the floor. "And you, young man — where on God's great earth have you been?"

I take a breath.

"I missed you," I say, and from the look on her face, no one could have said the words more perfectly.

26

I wiggle my toes. The sun falls across my eyelids and turns the space under them rust red.

"Mmm." I snuggle deeper into the covers.

Finally rising some minutes later, I put on a sweater and socks and brush my teeth and tighten the laces on my high-tops. I sail down the stairs, which creates something of a ruckus, and I can feel the slap and thump of Milton behind me.

Ping! goes the oven when I enter the shop, and the refrigerators hum and the ground vibrates. I grin at a tray of steamed treacle sponge cooling on the counter, and they sit in motionless golden rounds and dread gathers in my cheeks and my grin wavers. I slink toward the counter and bend close until I can see the sides of the little golden cakes swelling and contracting, breathing with the even, steady rhythm of sleep. I suppress a cheer and creep away so that I do not wake the slumbering sponges.

Lucy is sitting at a table with a steaming mug and a half-eaten tart. "Good morning, darling," she says. "I spoke to the landlord earlier. He's drawing up the new lease. Try this and tell me what you think." She pushes the plate forward. "Espresso mousse, crushed walnut graham cracker crust, cranberry compote on top."

I slice off a piece with the edge of the fork, making sure to get some of everything in one bite. As I chew, the espresso mousse washes the gritty bits of sleep from the surface of my brain and I hear something in my ear — very small, very curious — and I look down at my shoulder and a vol-au-vent mouse waves.

I watch it scamper down my arm and leap from the table to the top of a chair. It runs down the chair and a clean sugared breeze rushes in from nowhere and everywhere — the fireplace, the high ceiling, the jeweled displays, the arched kitchen doorway — pushing the mouse forward, faster, and it races across the shop and everywhere it passes the floor ripples like a lake of liquid stars and the air turns bright and clear as the ringing of a bell, something lighter, even, than happiness.

I beam through a mouthful of mousse and

swallow, and the dream I had last night flickers through my head.

A red-and-white plane — single engine, four seats, a Cessna 172. A shrinking shoreline, an ocean below — a disappearing fin. Walter Lavender Sr. in the pilot's seat, Lucy next to him, me in a backseat — Milton's seat empty because he is squeezing onto my lap.

"I came up with the idea after waking one morning. I knew I'd had the most wonderful dream, but I couldn't, for the life of me, remember what it was," Lucy says, and her new dessert also reminds me of a thought I had, just yesterday.

I take out my notebook and flip through it, searching for the entry.

AT THE END, A DREAM WORTH WAKING FOR, I had written as I watched Sammie and Roman, and I tell Lucy about it now, reading my observation aloud to her.

"What else did you think of?" she says.

I look at the next entry and read, "Rainy day reflections."

"I've been trying to figure out how to keep the gluten-free gingerbread cake from drying out," she says, taking the fork from me and scooping up some mousse. "What if we had a cloud following it, raining simple syrup? It would also be good for gazing at

403

and contemplating." She passes the fork back to me and says, "That is *exactly* what I've been looking for." She taps my notebook, smiling broadly.

Before, when she looked at my notebook, there was a subtle shift in her eyes as she was reminded of the unbridgeable distance that remained between us. Now, with the last gap bridged, she sees something else in my notebook: inspiration, and a new way to grow closer. Junker would be pleased; the disjointed thoughts I hoarded and deemed pointless were finally being taken out and shared and put to good use.

She runs a hand down her apron and stands. "The lava cupcakes should be done cooling. Are we ready to frost them?"

I know she has been waiting for me to wake before piping the frosting because the task calms and restores me at the end of each week. After coming so close to losing the shop, I thought I would never want to voluntarily leave again, but now that I am back and the shop is too, there is something I want to do and it isn't staying in the kitchen and frosting cupcakes. Even though it is my home, and it tells the story of who I am and where I came from and what I love, I made it my refuge and quietly, at some point, it became my prison, only by then I didn't see it that way.

I tell Lucy that I will be back before the shop opens and Milton races ahead and places his paw against the door and concentrates on it, because that is what precedes the door opening. I push the door open and he removes his paw and follows me out, and we take the train to see Ruby.

"Top of the morning to you," Ruby says over a series of muffled thumping sounds when she sees me, and she holds the door with one hand and her hair with the other, and she trades wide yawns with Milton.

"As the Irish say," finishes her grandfather, who is on his hands and knees, looking under a table, and Ruby's grandmother and Debbie are also under the table although they are drumming on the carpet with wooden spoons and don't appear to be looking for anything.

Debbie tries to drum on the underside of the table and hits her grandfather with her spoon, and he makes a bongo noise and she howls with laughter.

Ruby rises onto her toes. "So? Did it work?"

"Come to the shop," I say, and my excitement says it all and she jumps and squeals and looks at her grandfather, and he nods and peeks into a cabinet.

"Wouldn't miss it," Ruby says, still holding her hair. "Just need to find my hair elastic and we'll be ready to go."

"It's not in the kitchen," her grandfather says, pushing his hands into his knee to lever himself to his feet.

"My first rule of finding," I say, tapping my wrist, and Ruby lowers the hand that is holding her hair.

"There you are," she scolds the hair elastic, like it is a misbehaved charge that has snuck away, and she yanks it off her wrist and wraps her hair into its giant bun. Her grandfather reappears in pants that are lavender with turkeys on them in honor of the visit and the season, and we say goodbye to Ruby's grandmother and Debbie and pile out the door to a drumroll send-off.

As we approach the shop, a bell trills and José pulls up on his delivery bike and the sticker on his helmet says, Proud Parent of an Honor Student.

"You should've seen me flying down here after Lucy called," he says, taking off his helmet and wiping his forehead. He places his hand on the doorknob and his mouth stretches until I think I can almost see a glimmer of tooth. "Let's see how it looks, man."

He pulls the door open and we enter, and I see that Lucy has finished piping the frosting and the cupcakes are bubbling away in their display. Ruby's bun stirs as all around us the shop lifts and the flavor of the air brightens with sweet ruffling breezes of lightness and goodness.

José heads into the kitchen after our handshake and I guide Ruby and her grandfather through the shop, pointing out the chip in the floor where I dropped a can of preserved lemon and the lazy Susan I painted with Lucy and the wooden giraffe Lucy picked up in South Africa, and Ruby is astonished to see three mice jumping double Dutch with licorice ropes and her grandfather exclaims over the tray of sleeping treacle.

One of the cakes startles awake and, with a flounce of irritation, squirts him with syrup, and Ruby snorts and collapses into giggles until he picks up a cake and it squirts her too. Lucy comes out of the kitchen and I introduce her to them before we sit, fanned out at the table near the Book in its case.

"Next weekend," I begin, folding and unfolding the corner of a notebook page and thinking about the birthday party I never had, "we could have a. Party for the

Book. Coming back."

It would be a way to get the word out that the Book has been found and the shop saved, and a way to celebrate the people who have helped me on my search, and the last one is mostly for me — a way to bring people into my world, because I am starting to believe that I don't have to be the only one in it.

"You surprise me, Walter Lavender," Ruby roars. She opens her art journal and turns it toward me so I can watch her sketch out extravagant ideas — a five-piece band, a raft of balloons as big as the shop — and I suggest we stick to posting Found flyers. Lucy catches my eye and grasps my hand under the table, squeezing as tightly as she can until our fingers start to slip, and then she lets go.

The week seems to fly by with the weight of the missing Book lifted, and maybe things look a little different after you come close to losing them but the shop seems even brighter than before, like everything is new — even Flora, who has taken to wearing the apron Lucy gave her instead of her old blue gingham. She dropped a spoonful of red wine reduction onto her lap when the croissants inflated at her station on Monday morning, blowing buttery flakes into the air like leaves, and after she switched aprons she learned that yellow gingham wasn't so bad after all.

The day before the party I make a recording of myself telling the rest of the story that I left To Be Continued, and I abandon it in a distant moldy corner of the 6 train so that Junker might scoop it up during one of his junk-gathering expeditions. The next morning, we receive five inches of snow and it blankets the sidewalk in loose powder like confectioners' sugar because it is too cold for sticking. Before the shop opens, Ruby and I put out plastic utensils and paper hats and festive napkins and Lucy and Flora hang streamers and José inflates balloons, and then he locks himself in the bathroom to figure out his bow tie while the rest of us sit and wait at a decorated table.

My excitement grows with the line outside and I press my face into the glass and crane my neck and still I can't see where the line ends with all the people waiting in it, here for the desserts, mostly, but I hope that dotted throughout, waiting to be seen, are the people from my journey, and that they are here for me.

We do not have to wait for long. Lucy gets up to turn over the sign and the door tinkles as she pushes it open and gloved hands reach out to open it the rest of the way. People stomp their feet and fluff hat-matted hair and trill with excitement as the shop fills.

For the first hour, I am kept busy restocking and wiping and greeting and re-arranging. I notice empty cups piling up around a bookcase and go over to harvest them, and I straighten and stretch my back and with a pleasant jolt I see Nico standing nearby, chatting to Lan. The buttons on her coat are shaped like cat heads and most of them are broken in half. Nico glances up and sees me and extends a fist.

"Little man," he says, and I bump my fist into his.

"No backpack," I observe.

"Good for me. Not even room to breathe in this crowd," he says, pretending to melt. He grins and jabs me in the shoulder. "Get this. Directors *loved* Silence Is Golden. Drooled all over it. Anyway, knapsack is on the couch. I'm crashing with a buddy who's also at the theater club while I get some things sorted."

"It is *very* good for you," I say.

"You're gonna be happy to hear — paid Lan back, *plus* interest. Been setting aside the theater's nightly haul for her. I'm talk-

410

ing Dumpsters fulla bottles and cans." He puts his arm around Lan and her hand lashes out and pinches and twists and he yowls.

"My nipples," he wails, clutching his hands to his chest. "Lady, how could you?"

"To steal, still no good," she says crossly.

I tap on her forearm and bend a thumb toward the back, and we weave across the shop and slide behind the counter and into the kitchen, which is also busy but in a more purposeful way.

The Caravelle bar is in a drawer, crushed and sticky on one end from its journey. I push it into Lan's hands and she is confused. I guide her hands to her face so she can see what she is holding and she blinks and shakes her head.

"Where you find? Take much work? Too much work for old lady like me," she says, but she can't help herself; she is tearing off a corner of the wrapper and her hand trembles and she unshells the rest, stows the wrapper in her pocket. She turns the bar over in her hand and considers it.

"I never forget taste. Good taste. You see why if you try," she says.

I take one end of the bar and she keeps hold of the other, and on three we break the bar in half and as we struggle with the bar, stretching and twisting it, she cackles and I join her and tenacious strands of caramel cling to each other, connecting our halves, just like the wrapper promised.

With a final joint cackle, we make our way out to the front of the shop. Nico reappears at Lan's side and directs her to a chair, and I notice that the red velvet fudge samples are running low and Lucy is saying, "Hello, Ida — do come in, you must be frozen stiff —" and so I pick up the gilded tray to replenish it.

I add discarded napkins and crushed plastic cups to the tray as I circulate around the shop, and my eyes snag on someone hanging back by the window as other people come in, and he looks considerably dryer than the last time I saw him but almost as uncomfortable.

I empty the tray behind the counter and swap it for a tray of mocha madeleines. I hold one of the shells up to my ear, angling it until I pick up on a hint of accordion music like Paris in the spring. Balancing the tray on one hand and licking vanilla sugar off the fingers of the other, I approach the window and give it a rap and hitch the tray higher in invitation. Relief smooths the perpetual snarl of Beaver's lip.

The madeleines captivate Beaver and that

is somewhat inexplicable but I shrug and offer him another and he cradles it to his ear.

"You look like a person who can appreciate a good joke."

Beaver jerks the shell away from his ear, looking mutinously at the man who has interrupted him.

"A neutron walks into a bar and asks, How much for a drink? The bartender says, For you — no charge."

"Karl!" I exclaim.

He slaps his knee and his face is flushed from the eggnog and he claps Beaver's back. "I am passing on my passion for physics to the younger generation. Do you make sense of it? A neutron is a subatomic particle that lacks a net electric charge."

Sammie and Roman walk through the door and I leave Beaver to the impromptu lecture. I wend my way across the shop, past new customers and regulars gathering to share this experience I helped create, and the fullness of an ending I have wished for since the beginning.

I slide a panel open and gather two mice, and by the time I locate Sammie and Roman again, they are absorbed in a quiet game of chess and I tuck the pair of mice into my pocket for later, looking around to see where Ruby went, and I see her bun first.

Guess who? she mouths through the window, and my eyes widen and I reach to open the door for them.

Mister Philipp is frail but when he sees me his eyes crinkle and his voice is stout as an oak tree.

"I had to come back and see you," he calls. "The young man who watched over me."

Ruby's freckled friend Jane pops out to ask for her help choosing and I put my hand under Mister Philipp's elbow and match my pace to his and we ease into the shop, past the new customers clustered around the Book and past Lucy telling them her story of how the shop came to be.

Flora bumps into us carrying a dish of plump peach dumplings topped with mint chocolate leaves, and she reddens but Mister Philipp only says, "Aren't those the prettiest leaves I ever saw. Did you make them?"

At the praise, Flora's cheeks glow brighter than the peaches and as they strike up a conversation a shadow falls across the window and blocks the sun, and the landlord is standing there on the other side. I step outside and stand next to him and we look at the Book in its case. I do not know what I am waiting for and turn to go back inside.

"I'm glad it's back," he says without looking away from the Book. I am not sure if it is meant for me but I stay and listen anyway, and he shakes his head.

"The plan wasn't to *take* it."

My thoughts snap around, skidding through the hairpin turn, and he says, "I don't know what it was — I saw it and something came over me. Like it was *whispering* to me, convincing me something better would come if you left. I got rid of it as soon as I came to my senses. I like to make opportunities — love it — but how the hell did I get so damn *greedy*?"

A calm descends, heavy and sudden as a dropped curtain, and through the window the flame of my oil lamp leaps and dances on its wick. It kindles a thought in my mind — a voice whispering to the landlord, and could Walter Lavender Sr. be the whisper?

Within the shop is without a doubt where my world begins, but I let so many things keep me there — my longing for warmth and connection, my desire for certainty, my fear. It cannot be my whole world anymore, and perhaps that was the true lesson Walter Lavender Sr. knew I needed to learn: out there might be dark places to be afraid of and lonely islands to escape from and terrifying heights to fall down, but what also awaits are more places to see and people to know and friends to make and experiences to share, and what could be more worth the pain than to open up and let yourself be a part of a sweeping story?

This is what he knew each time he clambered into the cockpit and buckled in behind the controls; this is the lesson he would have taught me when the time came, but he found a way to do it all the same — the Book's flight from the shop, the trail it left, so that I would search.

I consider the Book and the burnished leather gleams an unremarkable brown, soft and serene, giving nothing away.

"I'm also glad your mother signed the ten-year lease," the landlord says, rubbing his hands together, embers of anticipation settling on his belly. "I really do have a sweet tooth, and money can't buy a double butterscotch pop anywhere else that convinces my girls to share. See you around." He grins wolfishly and walks away, and I find that I don't mind the thought.

The oil lamp flickers when I step inside, and out of habit I go over to check on it. The candle has burned low, and watching the guttering, I am not really sure that the lamp needs to be lit. There is no need to worry about becoming lost when the truth is, what's lost is bound to be found, by the person who stays brave enough to open their eyes and see. The flame twists and turns, and with a single breath I set it free.

ACKNOWLEDGMENTS

The Chinese are fond of their many proverbs, such as *Hit a dog with a meat bun* and *Three monks have no water to drink.* For the occasion of these acknowledgments, I turn to this one: *A thousand-li journey is started by taking the first step.*

To finish, one has to begin somewhere, and this journey, like The Lavenders, has two beginnings. For the first First Step, I owe everything to Mama, who lost her voice reading aloud to me so that I might find my love for stories. You carried me through storms and made a world out of nothing, and I would be happy to be half the person you are.

For the second First Step, I am forever grateful to Kai, who inspired me to write this book. Thank you for taking that First Step with me — not only on this thousand-*li* journey, but also on the grand million-*li* journey we are traveling together, my sun-

419

flower seed friend.

And to Shirley, whose path I will always follow even when it annoys her — thank you for your bold spirit and wit, and for standing by me, no questions asked. As I watch you make your way, you never cease to amaze me.

When I set out to write this book, I didn't dwell too much on the destination. I focused on each phrase, paragraph, and page, and now that I step back to take a look, the view is incredible, because of those who saw this journey through to the end. Thank you to those who helped me in the course of my research, graciously offering up their expertise and opening up about their experiences. Thanks to my agent, the inimitable Jeff Kleinman, who possesses an array of superpowers that includes Unbounded Enthusiasm and Tireless Speed and, most astounding of all, the ability to make dreams come true.

Thank you to my fantastic editor, Tara Singh Carlson, who challenged me to dig deeper and see clearer, whose skill in perceiving beyond the surface, to the heart and detail of things, rivals Walter's. Thank you to Helen Richard, and to everyone else at Putnam who generously put their time, energy, and heart into this book. I'm especially indebted to Carrie Swetonic, Ashley McClay, Emily Ollis, Brennin Cummings, and Alexis Welby, who kept this book from becoming lost, so that it could find its way to you, the reader. I am also deeply grateful to Sally Kim and Ivan Held, whose support has made all of this possible.

Finally, to the Shepherd of all journeys — thank you for watching over mine and illuminating the way.

■ ■ ■ ■

THE LUSTER OF
LOST THINGS

■ ■ ■ ■

★ A Conversation with Sophie Chen Keller ★

★ Discussion Guide ★

A CONVERSATION WITH SOPHIE CHEN KELLER

1. What inspired you to write *The Luster of Lost Things*?

In 2014, while camping on a volcano in Maui, I came across a "Lost" flyer for a camera that contained meaningful family photos. I began wondering whether that camera, with its silicon memory of lost moments, had been returned to its owner. I wondered who responded to flyers like that one. What if there were people out there who made it their mission to look for what others had lost? Why were they doing it? Was there something else people were looking for when they looked for a missing camera? That was when I had my first inkling of who Walter might be.

Aside from that, I knew I wanted my first book to be a celebration of childhood. My memories from then are some of my most vivid: humid summers that went on for ages, imaginary adventures in sandbox castles, PB&Js cut into triangles, bedtime stories that took me to magical places. Those days are lost now, but sometimes, when we start to feel suffocated by darkness, we could use a return to that time when the world was still bright and miraculous, and we could so clearly see the goodness that lived around us and in us.

Walter reminds us to see beyond the surface — the "skin of the world," as he calls it. The tale he tells is simple and uplifting, and at the same time layered with observations on what it means to live and be human. As you're experiencing his journey, I hope you're also savoring the search for the layers underneath, both inside and outside the pages; I hope that what you find will fill you with wonder.

2. The title of the book is very beautiful. How did you come up with it? What does it represent to you?

In one sense, the title refers to Walter's ability to perceive the light emitted by lost things. It also refers to the idea that there is value in being lost — in the quest to find — although we tend to think of losing as a bad thing, and of good things eventually losing their luster.

3. Do you have a dog? Is Milton based on a real golden retriever?

My family had a golden retriever named Thor, after the Norse god of thunder and lightning. (As it turned out, he was terrified of storms.) Like Milton, he was constantly tripping us, whipping us with his tail, and snapping up unsavory things. But at the right moments, he would adopt this look of Zen-like calm and wisdom, like a huggable Buddha. When I practiced the piano, he'd seize on the passionate parts, howling along with the crashing chords. Some dog!

4. What was it like to write Walter's voice? Was it difficult to see the world through his eyes? Is his disorder based on a real disorder?

Walter's voice came pretty naturally. You could say that he found me, while I had to find his disorder in the course of my research; I spoke with parents, speech pathologists, professors, and doctors, who kindly shared with me their knowledge, experiences, hopes, and concerns. Walter's condition is based on a type of motor speech disorder called childhood apraxia of speech, although the particulars of his case would be unusual. Childhood apraxia of speech is often misdiagnosed as autism, cerebral palsy, ADD or ADHD, an intellectual disability, or a developmental language disorder, among others. It's actually a separate diagnosis — a neurological disorder where the brain has trouble coordinating the muscle movements required to produce the intended speech. The mind is a vast, complex, and largely mysterious landscape, and in the case of apraxia, some wires have gotten crossed or short-circuited and signals sent by the brain aren't getting through properly to, say, the lips or the tongue or the face.

5. The novel celebrates the many different kinds of people who live in New York City. Why did you decide to set the story in Manhattan? What draws you to this city?

I moved to New York City at a formative time in life, right after college, and I tend to write about places I understand and connect with on an instinctual level. I haven't been to any other place where it's quite so obvious how different people can be, and how similar, too. You're reminded every day, in the curious combinations of smells and the unfiltered emotions spilling out onto the sidewalk. And you just might discover The Lavenders around the next corner. In my mind, the West Village especially takes on a shade of happy wonder, because that's where my now husband lived — on a certain street named Carmine — when we first met.

6. Do you have a favorite character in the novel, besides Walter?

Lucy. Without her, there wouldn't be an enchanted dessert shop to write about! This is Walter's story, but what we know of Lucy's speaks, I think, straight to the heart.

7. The Lavenders is an unforgettable place. Why did you decide to set the novel in a bakery? Do you have a favorite bakery? Is The Lavenders based on a real bakery?

Mostly because I like eating and watching shows about food; I figured I would also like writing about food. The novel is about connecting and belonging, and food is something we associate with coming together, or with being transported home, wherever and whenever that might be.

I like discovering new places and trying

different desserts, so The Lavenders is an amalgamation of various shops: the whimsical tiles from a chocolate shop in California, the classic brass finishes from a patisserie in France, the sugary sense of brightness from a bakery in downtown Manhattan, the dash of hominess from a *Bäckerei* in Germany, and any kind of edible treat you could imagine from everywhere — and there you are.

8. Walter has an amazing ability to find missing things. Have you ever lost something that Walter could have helped with? Why did you decide to write about lost items?

When I was eight or so, my mom gave me my first real piece of jewelry, a silver ring with a ruby flower, after my rather insistent pleading that I could be trusted — *I promise!* — to take care of it. She bought the ring in the morning; I lost it that afternoon. I was upset enough about breaking my promise that I still remember that lost ring today, although what my mom remembers instead is how happy I was when she gave it to me.

The idea of searching intrigues me. That feeling of incompleteness, of looking for something that we believe will make us whole, preserve our idea of self, bring us peace or joy or purpose or whatever it is, strikes me as poignant and vital to who we are and the lives we lead.

9. What do you do when you're not writing?

I read. I travel. I dwell on things. Sometimes, when there's a piano nearby, I play it.

10. What's next for you?

I'm working on a second novel, and that's about all I'll say. Since I usually figure out things as I go, I have trouble talking about what I'm writing until it's been written.

DISCUSSION GUIDE

1. How does Walter's inability to speak shape his character? In what ways does his speech change throughout the novel?

2. Did you have a favorite character? If so, who?

3. Lan tells Walter to make a "sunflower seed friend" (p. 153). What does she mean? Does his understanding of friendship change over the course of the book? And does he ultimately make a sunflower seed friend? Do you have any sunflower seed friends?

4. Walter's ability to find missing items allows him to glimpse inside the lives of others without feeling vulnerable. Have you ever helped someone find a lost thing? Is there an item you personally remember losing? What did this item say about you? Did

you find it?

5. Walter lights an oil lamp every day in the hope his father will find his way home. At the beginning of the novel, did you think Walter would find his father? What does Walter end up finding?

6. The Lavenders is a beloved bakery, but the rising rents in the neighborhood threaten it. How does the novel portray gentrification? Have you seen this in your own community? What do you think about the landlord's decision to close The Lavenders?

7. How does Walter deal with being picked on at school? How does his attitude toward Beaver and Todd change by the end of the novel? Were you surprised by the way Walter treats them later in the book?

8. Many of the characters Walter encounters in his journey are lonely — the rat-man and rat-woman long for a child, Karl misses his wife, and Junker wanders the streets of his abandoned city, searching for company. How does Walter help the people he meets? What does he learn about loneliness?

9. Ruby gives Walter the "first gift [he has]

been given from someone who is not Lucy" (p. 398). What does Ruby show Walter about the world? How does her friendship change him? Do you recall the first gift you received that came from a friend?

10. Much of this novel is about the power of stories to shape our lives. In what ways does the Book shape Walter? How does he come into his own story? Were there stories you encountered as a child that have shaped you?

11. What is the kindest thing you've done for someone else, or that someone else has done for you? Do you wish you had been kinder on some occasions?

ABOUT THE AUTHOR

Sophie Chen Keller was born in Beijing, China, and was raised in Ohio and California. Her fiction has won several awards and has appeared in publications such as *Glimmer Train* and *Pedestal.* After graduating from Harvard, she moved to New York City, where she currently resides with her husband and a not-so-secret cabinet of sweets.

The employees of Thorndike Press hope you have enjoyed this Large Print book. All our Thorndike, Wheeler, and Kennebec Large Print titles are designed for easy reading, and all our books are made to last. Other Thorndike Press Large Print books are available at your library, through selected bookstores, or directly from us.

For information about titles, please call:
(800) 223-1244

or visit our website at:
gale.com/thorndike

To share your comments, please write:

Publisher
Thorndike Press
10 Water St., Suite 310
Waterville, ME 04901